About *Exile of the King*

"After reading *Quest for a King*, I couldn't wait to continue the riveting sequel in *Exile of the King*. If you love to read well-researched historical books that bring scripture alive, this book does not disappoint! I didn't want to put *Exile of the King* down 'til I'd read the whole book!

Ruth Arthurs, MSW

I loved this second installment in the Age of the Kingdom series. Gary Ivey takes the Biblical narrative of the emerging Kingdom of Israel and makes it come to life with a book that's hard to put down. Can't wait for the next volume of this saga!

Bill Barley, BS, JD, Pastor, Living Stone Church

In *Exile of the King*, Gary Ivey once more shows us the difference between reading the Bible and living the Bible. The author has an uncanny ability to bring the Bible's outsize characters to life by surrounding them with credible characters and interactions that we can recognize from our own lives.

The Bible's tales have always been timeless, but now they are made both timeless and immediate through the unswerving use of vivid detail. David's years in the wilderness, while spanning a few chapters in the Bible, are here given their due as the backbone of an entire novel.

The brotherhood of Jonathan and David, Saul's erratic temper, the sacking of Ziklag by the Amalekites, and the final battle with the Philistines in the Jezreel Valley, are all well-known biblical events that we can now remember as if we had lived through them. The details in *Exile* even extend to the day-to-day details of the characters' lives: the food they prepare, how they dress, and the chores they perform as part of their day. All of this draws the reader in and makes this book extremely hard...if not impossible...to put down.

Brett Goldberg, BA, author of A Psalm in Jenin

Exile of the King

Did you miss the award-winning first book of the Age of the Kingdom series?

Christian Book Awards Gold-medal Winner

American Book Fest Best Book Awards Finalist

A catastrophic battle sets the stage for Israel's first monarchy, but the king's failures endanger the nation's future. No one escapes the palace intrigue, divided loyalties and tribal battles of life 3,000 years ago.

What people say about *Quest for a King*.

"Gary Ivey brings the Bible to life through vivid and intricately crafted characters…. I read it cover to cover in one sitting… it is impossible to put down. I wish I had had this growing up. I would have understood biblical history so much better!"
Brett Goldberg, BA, author, A Psalm in Jenin *and entrepreneur.*

"… a remarkably ambitious saga exploring the lives of a complex array of Biblical and non-Biblical characters… as their lives are swept up and overturned by the move of God and the forces of history."
Terry R. Freeman, BA, MBA, CG, Genealogist, Historian, Author.

"…like an Old Testament *The Chosen*."
Bill Barley, BS, JD, Pastor, Living Stones Church.

Available at garyivey.com or wherever books are sold.

ii

The "Quest" stories have also been honored at film festivals where Gary L. Ivey has submitted his TV pilot script "Lost Glory" from the proposed "Age of the Kingdom" TV series.

2023 Christian Film Festival: Best Script and Best Movie Poster
2023 Branson International Film Festival: Best Script Nominee
2023 International Christian Film Festival: Best Script Nominee
2023 Golden Draft Awards, Official Finalist
2023 Santa Monica Film Awards, Semi-Finalist

Other Novels by Gary L. Ivey

BACKLASH

BACKLASH 2: JUSTICE DENIED

A conspiracy of activists and politicians threatens the livelihoods of hundreds of thousands of people, so Jacqueline James finds herself in the midst of a national controversy. To save her company, her employees and her stockholders, she must launch a daring response called "Operation Backlash."

"It was fabulous!!!! I was so intrigued by the plot... environmental terrorists, murder, politics, moral integrity, a female heroine, hard-core work ethics, and a splash of love made for a great read! (ah...and the evolution/creation thread!)." *L. Z., Facebook post.*

"I found myself cheering Jacqueline on, as she took on Washington and her stockholders throughout the book. The storyline kept me wondering 'what next?' The author meticulously conducted his research, reminding me of a well-developed Grisham-like novel." *D. J., Amazon.com review.*

"Get Ready for a Wild Ride! *Backlash* can be enjoyed on many different levels. As a page-turner, it keeps you on the edge of your seat...but Backlash has a deeper subtext, almost a platonic dialogue being conducted between the lines, that addresses many of the key political concerns of our time." *B. G., Amazon.com review*

www.backlashbook.com

EXILE OF THE KING

Age of the Kingdom Series
Book Two

By Gary L. Ivey

Exile of the King

This book is a work of fiction. Although the story is set against the background of people, events and locations in the Bible, many characters and events in their lives as depicted are fictional and, while plausible in the time and culture, are the product of the author's imagination. Any resemblance to actual events or places or persons, living or dead, is entirely coincidental.

Published by
Studio IV Productions, Kailua Kona, HI 96740

ISBN: 978-0-9993968-4-1

www.garyivey.com

Front cover design by Gary L. Ivey using resources from pexels.com, envatoelements.com and wikimediacommons.org.

.

❦ Acknowledgements ❧

I must say a big "thank you" to several people who gave generously of their time to review the manuscript of *Exile of the King* before publication. Their input was invaluable to help me see typographical errors I missed and steer me away from cultural *faux pas*.

Longtime friend and business associate Brett Goldberg saved me from making a couple of important historical errors. He holds dual U.S. and Israeli citizenship and speaks 11 languages fluently, including Hebrew. He has first-hand knowledge of the geography of the Bible lands and knows well the history of the Jewish people from Antiquity to today. My pastor, Bill Barley of Living Stones Church in Kailua-Kona, Hawaii, has read all four of my novels, three pre-publication and has given invaluable feedback on them all. Ruth Arthurs, a member at Living Stones and in charge of the writers' group for a while, also read *Exile* and noted the "bumps" as she read, which helped me greatly. She was one of my readers who suggested that I add the family trees to this book, making it easier to follow the relationships and keep the many names straight.

As always, my wife, Toni Ivey, listened as I read the manuscript aloud and called my attention to inelegant phrasing and confusing character references. She also followed along in 1 Samuel part of the time because she couldn't believe some of these stories are in the Bible!

❦ Preface ❦

Exile of the King, book two of the "Age of the Kingdom" series, is a work of fiction. The story began in the first book of the series, *Quest for a King*.

Exile continues following the generations of several families against the backdrop of the events found in 1 Samuel in the Bible, which relates the reign of King Saul, the first king of the United Monarchy of Israel 3,000 years ago. Other biblical texts shed light on the story, especially 1 Chronicles, but Genesis through Judges also provide background and context. The Psalms of David figure in as well.

Some of the characters who are front and center in *Exile of the King* are entirely fictional. Others are mentioned, but not named, in the Bible. These I have given names and backstories to flesh out their stories. Still others are the main characters in the biblical narrative, but I have tried to tell their stories from the viewpoints of others.

The narrative of *Exile* follows the dual tracks of King Saul and potential King David (the one in exile) and people who are loyal to each of them. To make following the cast of characters easier, I've included three pages of family trees on the pages just before the first chapter, plus a map of the place names mentioned in the story.

The "Age of the Kingdom" series is in the mode of historical fiction, because I regard the Bible as history, though these accounts of events 1,000 years before Christ were written by author(s) more concerned with how God moved within human history than just dates and places.

I relied on a great many books, articles and online resources in my research, to be true to the current understanding of daily life of the time. Archeology continues to illuminate the past, helping us understand the forces at work socially, culturally and politically.

The conventional wisdom among scholars has been that, as archeology sheds light on the ancient lands and their cultures, the Bible would become increasingly discredited. However, the opposite has proven true.

The default position of scholarship was for many years that David was a mythical character, not a real, historical figure, but when the "Tel Dan Stele" was discovered in 1993 containing a reference to "the House of David," the conventional wisdom had to be revised. The engraved stone contained a record of the victory of a Syrian king over the "House of Israel" and the "House of David," an obvious reference to the northern and southern kingdoms as they existed after the death of Solomon, which lines up perfectly with the biblical record.

This is NOT a children's book, even though some of the stories are among the most beloved Sunday School lessons, full of adventure and romance. One reason for writing this book was to take an unblinking look at the gritty, difficult lives of biblical characters we think we know.

I was serious about being faithful to the biblical text where it is explicit. Some readers may find events portrayed in this book surprising, so I encourage the reader to revisit the ancient record in 1 Samuel for themselves, which contains some of the most detailed stories in the Bible, yet there is much concerning the inner motivations of the characters which the Bible leaves to our imaginations.

I did not shy away from the supernatural elements of the narrative. While skeptics explain away such things in natural terms, if one is a believer in God, as I am, why would one not believe the God who cares about his children would intervene in earthly affairs?

So, I hope the reader enjoys this novel in the spirit it is offered: as an opportunity to see the events of long ago as contemporaries might have experienced them.

Gary L. Ivey

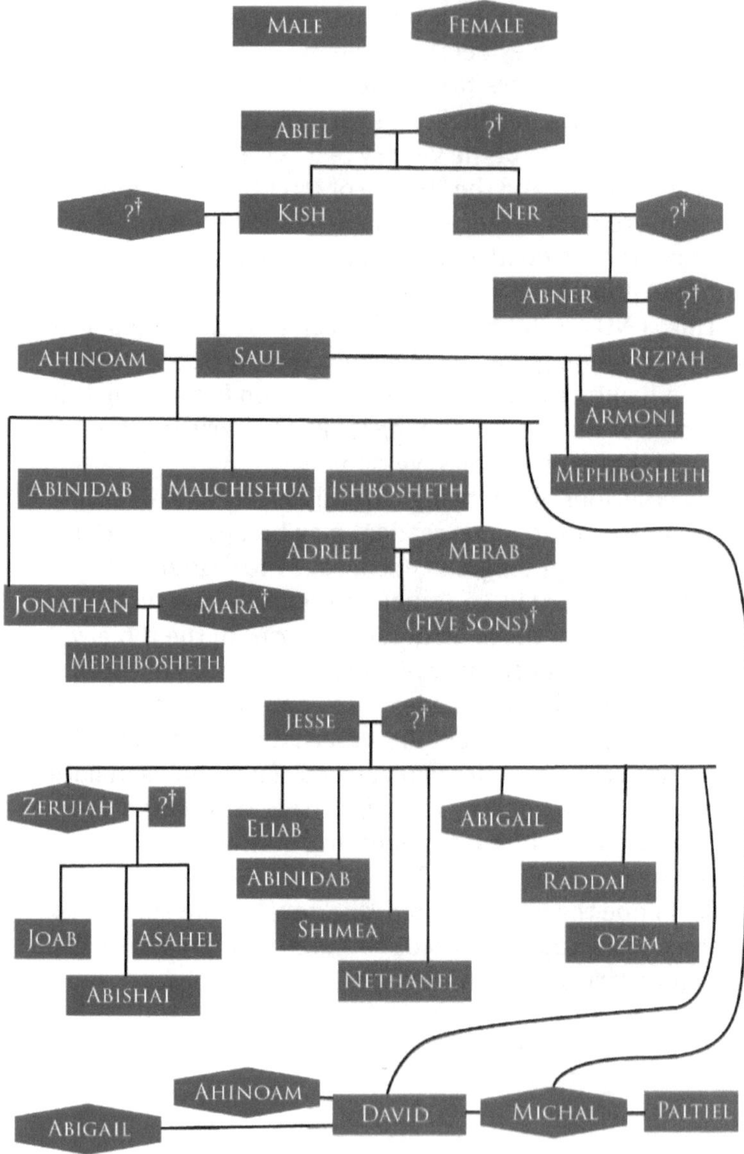
THE FAMILIES OF SAUL & DAVID
*FICTIONAL CHARACTERS   †UNNAMED BIBLICAL CHARACTERS
(NO SYMBOL) NAMED BIBLICAL CHARACTERS
MALE
FEMALE
ABIEL
?†
?†
KISH
NER
?†
ABNER
?†
AHINOAM
SAUL
RIZPAH
ARMONI
MEPHIBOSHETH
ABINIDAB
MALCHISHUA
ISHBOSHETH
ADRIEL
MERAB
JONATHAN
MARA†
(FIVE SONS)†
MEPHIBOSHETH
JESSE
?†
ZERUIAH
?†
ELIAB
ABIGAIL
ABINIDAB
RADDAI
JOAB
ASAHEL
SHIMEA
OZEM
ABISHAI
NETHANEL
AHINOAM
DAVID
MICHAL
PALTIEL
ABIGAIL

Gary L. Ivey

THE FAMILY OF ELDAD OF BENJAMIN

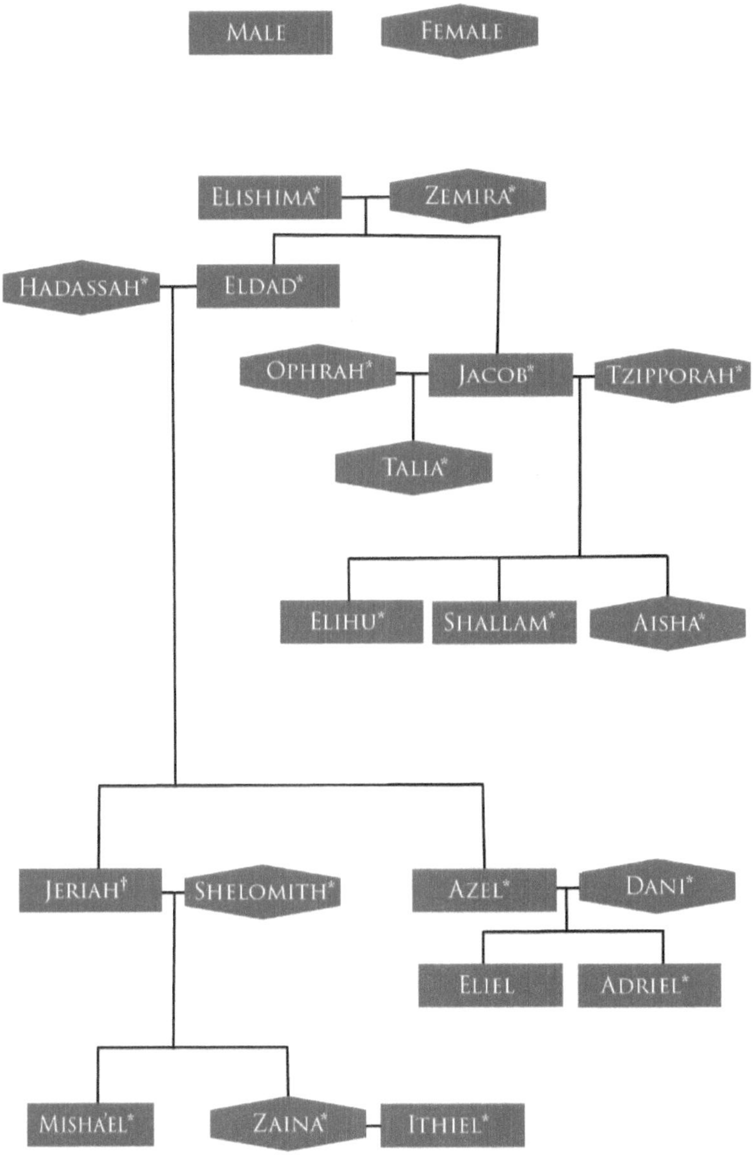

THE FAMILIES OF THE PRIESTS & LEVITES

*FICTIONAL CHARACTERS   †UNNAMED BIBLICAL CHARACTERS
(NO SYMBOL) NAMED BIBLICAL CHARACTERS

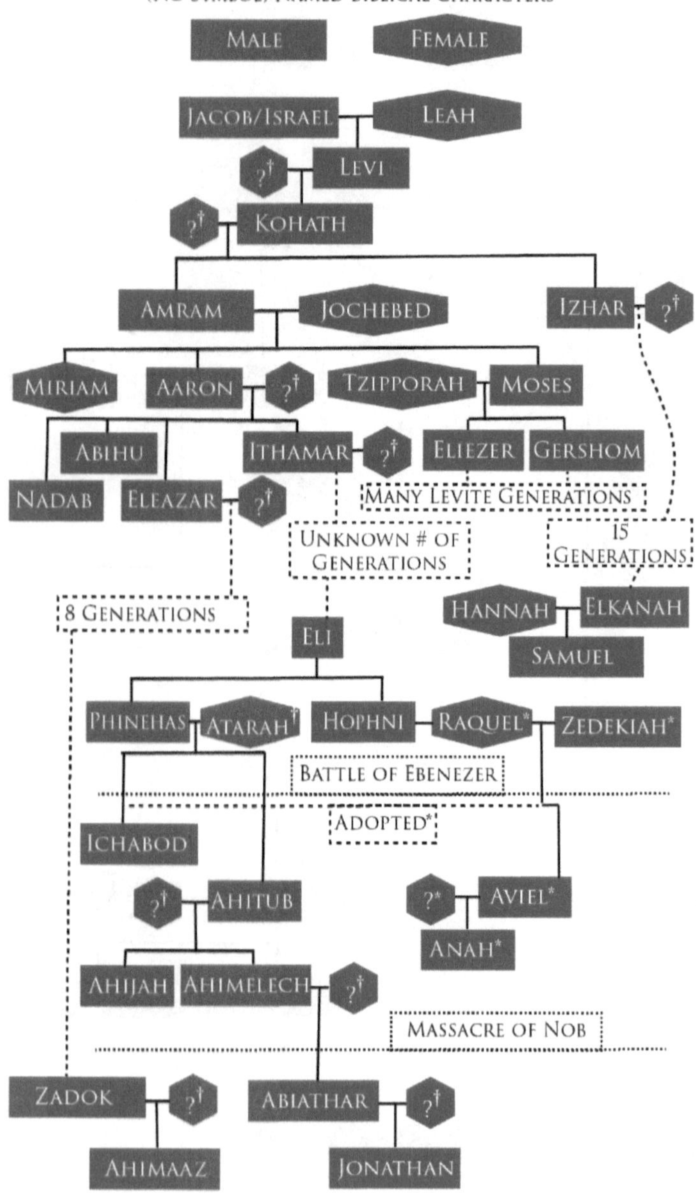

Gary L. Ivey

ANCIENT ISRAEL

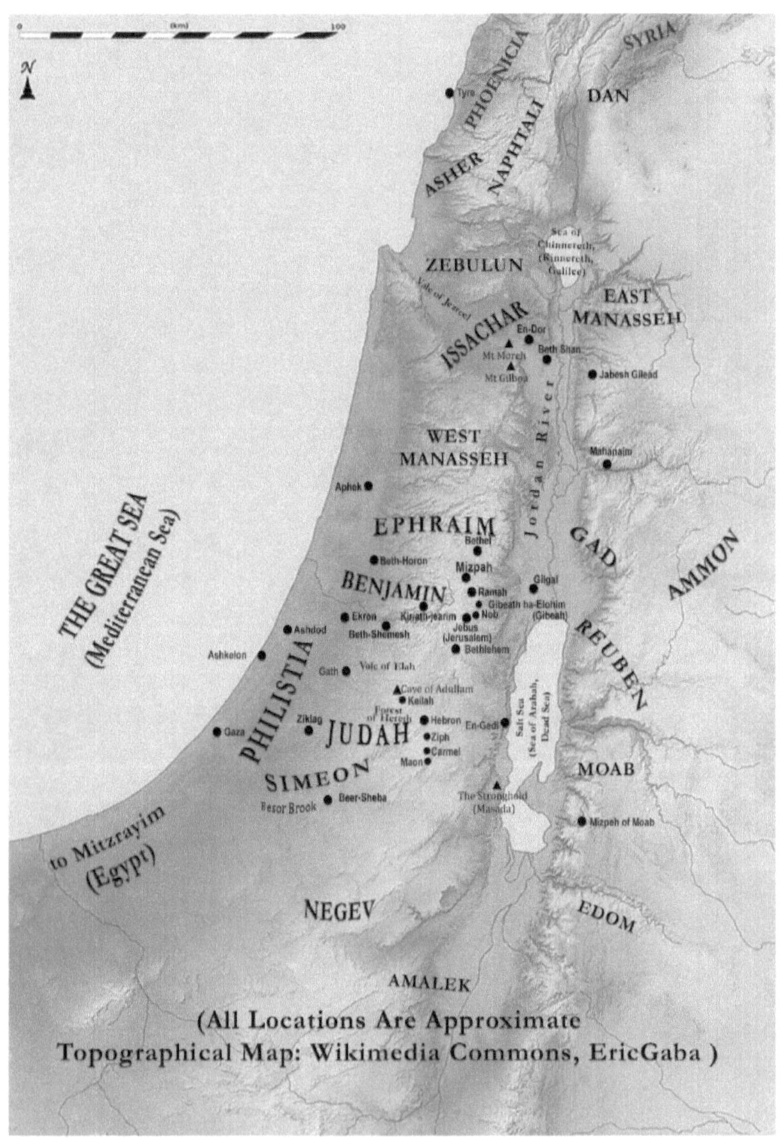

❧ 1 ❧

He prepareth a table before me,
In the presence of my enemies...

He had often sung the words sweetly – words he himself had written – but tonight he muttered them in irony and anger.

He had been thinking of Philistines or Canaanites or Aramaeans when he wrote "my enemies." Who would have thought his "enemy" would now be the king of Israel?

Anger.

It had flashed white hot when the spear had flown toward him. The fire in his own eyes had answered the madness in the eyes of the king.

Now, the cold night air having calmed him, he reasoned that anger had saved his life when the king's spear narrowly missed, enabling him to move quickly to avoid death. Now he repented and sent a silent prayer of thanks to Yahweh, for He had preserved him in the face of enemies before.

Anger.

Yes, but behind the anger was something else.

Fear.

Fear of the unknown.

It had all been so clear on the day the prophet had proclaimed that God had selected him – an obscure shepherd and the youngest in his family – to be king over all Israel. With the anointing oil had come God's Spirit, which had sustained him when he challenged the giant.

He had not known fear that day; only courage, in the certain knowledge that Yahweh was surely with him. And He had been. The demoralized army of Israel had rallied because of HIS courage; courage based on faith and the knowledge that God was with him.

But now, stumbling in the dark, still carrying his lyre, without sword or sling, he knew fear.

What would tomorrow bring? Was he to return as if nothing had happened? Was he to continue pursuing the reward of the king's daughter's hand in marriage as had been promised him? Or must he flee like a common criminal?

When would God's word be fulfilled and how could it happen? How could he become king when the throne was occupied by a man who now appeared mad, with four strong sons well able to succeed him?

And there it was.

Anger, yes, and also Fear.

But behind them lurked another emotion. Another sin.

Doubt.

He had never doubted God's plan and purpose since that day when the pungent olive oil ran down his scalp through his curly hair and dripped from his chin.

But tonight, in the darkness of his soul, he felt doubt; doubt born of fear.

> *I will fear no evil,*
> *For Thou art with me...*

He again repeated the words of the song he had written when he was young and innocent, before he understood how dark the human heart could be.

> *The Lord is my Shepherd,*
> *I shall not be in want...*

Did he truly believe that? Could he act as if it was true in the face of uncertainty and threats and delay? Could he have faith to believe Yahweh would keep his promise?

Doubt.

He shook it off, his mouth forming a tight, thin line on his determined face, and turned around on the road which led to Bethlehem and home. He faced instead Gibeah, returning to where his future lay.

❧ 2 ❧

"Jeriah!"

Shelomith stood with her arms crossed over her breasts, her feet planted far apart as she called her husband's name, standing over his sleeping form.

He stirred and moaned, sure to be upset at being awakened before dawn, but Shelomith would wait no longer. Belatedly he opened his eyes.

"What is going on with you and your brother?"

He looked at her with confusion, then finally spoke.

"My brother is a fool!"

"Or does he have a fool for a brother?" she said, certain it would provoke him.

"You heard?"

"How could I not hear? It's a small house."

Jeriah roused and sat up, lowering bare feet to the floor of the upstairs bed chamber. At 42, he moved slower than when Shelomith had become his bride. Though his shoulders were still broad, hardened as they were by work in the forge and in the service of the king, gray now tempered the black hair at his temples.

"Azel puts our whole family in jeopardy."

"What? How?"

"He favors David over the king," Jeriah explained, rubbing his eyes.

"What do you mean? Isn't David King Saul's champion?"

"Events yesterday may have changed that."

"What events?"

"Saul tried to kill David."

"What?! Why would he do that?"

"Rumors. Rumors the king apparently believes: that Samuel has anointed another to rule over us. One not of the house of Saul, or even of the tribe of Benjamin."

"And Saul believes David is the one?"

"Evidently, and so does Azel."

"But why would Samuel anoint another?" Shelomith asked, her anger turning to perplexity.

"You were not there in Gilgal when Samuel told the king that the kingdom would be taken from him and given to another with a heart like God's own."

"No. Why didn't you tell me?"

"I didn't want to worry you. I didn't think it would affect our family."

"That's what you and Azel were arguing about last night?"

"Yes. He said if it comes to it, he will support David against the king."

Shelomith could not speak. Words of treason had been spoken in her own house. Her husband daily stood before the king. Would King Saul spare Jeriah, his wife and their children if Jeriah's brother was a traitor?

❦ 3 ❦

The pink light of dawn was just beginning to lift the gloom from the city of Gibeath-Saul when Azel left his house by the front door. He looked over at the door marking the entrance of his brother's house right beside his own inside their family compound. Then he left through the gate to go out into the street which lay on the other side of the mud-brick wall that formed the perimeter of their property.

He was not as tall as his older brother, but hard work had made him just as strong, though he often lost patience with Jeriah's affection for traditions and rules.

They had bought the compound a few months before and moved their growing families from their ancestral home in Mizpah, so their wives and children would be near. The decision had been made after their father, Eldad, died.

Since both brothers were now part of King Saul's permanent fighting force, they would be spending most of their time in Gibeah, the capital of Israel's fledgling monarchy.

Jeriah had confirmed the rumors which were now widely known: that Samuel had rejected Saul and his house and had anointed another. Now it was clear that Saul believed David was the rival Samuel had selected.

The battle in which David single-handedly killed the towering champion from Gath of Philistia had been a paradigm-shifting moment for Azel. He had joined the army out of patriotism and zeal for Yahweh, but it was clear that God's Spirit was with David.

Azel had immediately applied for a transfer to David's unit when he was given his own command as reward for dispatching the giant. Since then, Azel had been on many campaigns and knew that David was a charismatic leader of men and a natural military strategist. In short, he was everything King Saul was not.

But when the news spread that Saul had tried to kill David, throwing a javelin at him before the whole court, Azel knew things could not remain as they had been. Now it appeared David had left.

Azel was on his way to the permanent base camp of the army, just outside the city, to see for himself.

He made his way to the square of tents that housed the men of David's cohort and went to the small stone house that had been provided for the hero of the battle of Elah.

Azel was relieved when he arrived to find David sitting outside the house, mending the leather strap of his shield.

"Commander? I was afraid you had gone."

"Good morning, Captain. I left only to clear my head, but Yahweh wants me here."

Azel smiled, but he knew there was still cause for concern.

Arriving back home, Azel knew he was only there to get ready to leave again, this time to fulfill his daily duties as an officer in the army of King Saul.

As he swung open the gate to the family compound, his mind still on David, he came face to face with Jeriah, who was on his way out.

"Uh, Shalom," Azel muttered.

"Yes, Shalom." For an awkward moment neither of them spoke, their altercation of the night before still fresh. Finally, Jeriah broke the silence.

"I'm thinking of building a forge."

"Here? In Gibeah?"

"Yes, Misha'el needs to begin learning our trade."

"That is true. He is, what? 14? Eliel will also be of age before we know it, too."

Azel's and Dani's firstborn had originally been named Erel, but as he had grown, they had begun calling him Eliel, which meant "my God is God." They liked it better and had decided "Eliel" should be the name he would be given for his bar mitzvah, which would mark him as a man of 13.

"They do grow fast," Jeriah said, relaxing a little. "I was thinking of putting it there." He pointed to a corner of the compound where the ground was empty.

"That would be a great place for it. Let me know when you start building. Eliel and I will help."

"All right," Jeriah said. "Well, I need to get to court."

"David came back."

"What?"

"He just left to clear his head. He's back."

"Good," Jeriah said as he went through the gate, out into the street.

Azel let out a long breath when he was gone.

❦ 4 ❦

There had been so much to do for so many years with the establishment of the kingdom that Jonathan had barely had time for himself. So, he was taken by surprise when love found him.

The firstborn son of King Saul saw her the first time quite by accident, while riding his donkey at the head of a company of men on maneuvers. They had marched to Gilgal, where they had trained for a week and were returning to Gibeah, when they passed through a small village near Jericho. She was there in the marketplace, buying wool for weaving.

She had turned to look as the men went by and when her eyes passed Jonathan's, they locked for several moments before she demurely looked away.

Jonathan was unprepared for his own reaction to the look they had shared. He immediately called over his lieutenant.

"Please go and inquire for me as to the name of the father of the young woman buying from the wool merchant."

"Yes sir," the man replied, leaving the formation and going to follow the order of his commander without question. He shortly returned.

"Her father's name is Eliphaz," the lieutenant reported.

"Thank you," Jonathan replied, and he and the column of soldiers continued on their way.

However, Jonathan did not forget the encounter, if it could be called that. A week later, he was able to get away and he went again to the village, which was within the borders of Benjamin, and he went to find Eliphaz to get permission to meet and talk with his daughter.

I don't know her name, he suddenly realized, but he was determined to find her, so when he found Eliphaz' house, he introduced himself.

"Eliphaz, I am Jonathan, son of Saul, son of Kish."

Eliphaz' eyes grew wide and his jaw went slack, then he stooped low, as if to worship.

"I am humbled by your presence, my prince. I will do anything you ask of me."

"No, no sir! I am here on personal business and it is I who must ask a favor of you. Rise so we can discuss as equals."

The older man straightened up, putting one hand on his back as he did so. Jonathan, with height inherited from his father, was much taller than Eliphaz, so even standing, it was difficult for them to stand eye-to-eye.

"Please, come into my humble home. What business could you have with me?"

"If you will permit me, I wish to meet your daughter," said Jonathan, as he took a few steps into the small house.

"That would be wonderful! Of course, you have my permission, but which one?" Eliphaz asked. "I have three."

That stumped Jonathan, of course, but he wasn't about to give up.

"I'm sorry, I do not know her name. I only saw her from a distance in the marketplace buying wool a week ago."

Now it was the old man's turn to be stumped. Then, his eyes lit up.

"Ah, it must have been Mara. She is the oldest and an excellent bargainer! Wait here and I will get her."

Jonathan stood alone in the house's main room, but he didn't have to wait long. Eliphaz appeared shortly from another room pushing Mara before him.

"Mara, this is prince Jonathan, the son of the king! He wishes to meet you!"

It was the young woman he had seen in the market. Her eyes were dark with suspicion, but when her eyes met his, he once again felt what he had a week before. She was tall for a young woman, and she held her head high with a confident air and her face was beautifully proportioned. Jonathan was smitten all over again.

Her face relaxed as recognition came, but her eyes still had questions.

"But why would you want to meet me?" she asked.

"I saw you in the market last week and I just felt I would like to get to know you."

At last, she smiled and for Jonathan it was as if the sun had broken through the clouds.

Mara's mother and two younger sisters joined them as well and they invited Jonathan to stay for the evening meal. Mara joined the other women of the family in making the necessary preparations while Jonathan and Eliphaz got acquainted, but occasionally, Jonathan would see Mara moving about with a dish of some food or other and she would again lock eyes with his, and then, embarrassed, turn away.

Four months later, Ahijah, the grandson of the patriarchal high priest Eli, was summoned from Nob to Gibeah to pronounce a blessing on the union of Jonathan and Mara.

After that, there was a feast which lasted several days, with members of the royal court in attendance and Eliphaz and his wife as star-struck guests, but Jonathan and Mara only had eyes for one another.

They spent much of the time talking of what their life would be like when the marriage feast was done: where they would live; how many children they would have, and more.

Jonathan's sister, Michal, was there for the ceremony and the celebration, taking it all in like a sponge soaking up spilled goat milk. She watched wide-eyed as her brother and his bride made their promises to one another and watched some more as the couple graciously welcomed their guests, but when no one was near, talked in whispers with their faces close together.

Then she saw him: the hero of Elah; the champion who slew the great giant whom no one would face. He congratulated her brother and embraced her new sister-in-law, Mara.

David had a rosy complexion and curly hair, and his ready smile made him always look handsome to Michal.

She tried hard not to stare at David, but he wasn't looking at her anyway.

❧ 5 ❧

Jeriah's work moved forward on the construction of the forge, with his son, Misha'el, taking an active role. Azel was also helping, and even eight-year-old Eliel helped where he could. Jeriah and Azel agreed the boys should have a part in seeing how a forge came to be. It would be part of their apprenticeship.

The furnace was of course central to the forge and had to be built to withstand great heat. The fire would be made hotter by bellows fashioned from goat skin. Both Jeriah and Azel had learned to make bellows from their father, Eldad, because they had to be replaced periodically, for they would become brittle and break over time as the heat from the furnace dried them.

The other thing that was necessary to the forge was an anvil, and Jeriah was able to find a stone close enough to the right shape to serve the purpose with minimal chiseling.

When all was ready, Jeriah taught Misha'el how to bargain in the market for materials which could be refashioned into useful items. He gave the young man a few pieces of silver and some extra tools he could barter for what was needed.

On days when Jeriah was not assigned to the court, he began training Misha'el in the basic skills he needed to master the smith trade, just as Jeriah's father, Eldad, had taught him.

Ten months had passed since the giant had been killed by the young man David in the Vale of Elah. Jeriah passed his days in the king's court aware of tension that seemed to grow with each passing day. After the king threw the javelin at

David, the young commander rarely appeared in the court but stayed with his men in their encampment when they were at Gibeah and not on raids against Philistine villages.

"Father, you must keep your word to David!" Jonathan insisted to King Saul as Jeriah stood at attention to one side of the throne. "You must give Merab to him."

The king had not forgotten that one of the rewards offered to the man who would face the giant was his daughter's hand in marriage. Merab was his oldest daughter, so she was the obvious choice, but Saul was now second-guessing his promise.

"Why should I reward the one who threatens our throne?"

"He defeated the Philistine when no one else would even try," Jonathan argued, "and he continues to win battles against them."

"And so, you defend him. Don't you know you will be the loser if he takes the throne from our house?"

"Yahweh will decide who sits on the throne," Jonathan replied. "The kingdom is God's, not ours, but the point is, you made a promise to him. He is your champion. The people love him and know he is to be rewarded."

The king looked at the stone floor and sighed, "Bring Merab to me."

Jonathan smiled and left the court. It only took a few minutes for Jonathan to return with Merab, the king's oldest daughter. The young woman was beautiful at perhaps 18 years of age, Jeriah thought, but she did not look happy.

"Father, you sent for me?"

"Your brother insists that I honor my promise to give you to David as wife."

"Yes, father?"

"So, make yourself ready," Saul said with a wave of his hand.

"When will this be?" Merab was biting her lip.

"That will be up to the son of Jesse," Saul replied bitterly.

❧

Azel was drilling a squad of his men in the use of the spear in the army encampment at Gibeah when he saw Prince Jonathan enter the camp, heading for David's house. Momentarily, David and Jonathan emerged and were smiling broadly and talking excitedly, then they embraced warmly and Azel watched as they left to go to the King's quarters.

Azel wondered about the embrace. He didn't have to wonder that Jonathan would become David's friend, because everyone admired David, but he was also acutely aware of the conflict that his relationship with David might create with his father, the king.

"What's wrong?" Michal asked when Merab ran into their bed chamber wailing uncontrollably.

"Father has given me to David!"

Michal's eyes narrowed. "When?"

"Whenever he wants!"

"And you don't want to marry David?"

Merab stopped crying and looked at Michal as if she had suddenly turned into a goat. Then she resumed wailing uncontrollably. "I love Adriel!"

"Maybe you don't have to marry David," Michal suggested.

"Why? How?" Merab stammered.

"I'll think of something," Michal said, looking far out the window.

⪽ 6 ⪼

There was tension in the air, but Jonathan ignored it, believing the best about everyone present and preferring to focus on his joy. It was a private meal with all the members of his family and the one who was to soon join the family: David, the hero of Elah.

Jonathan had not had a friend he admired and liked as much as David in a long time. David was much younger than he, but his confidence and bearing belied his youth. It was one of the things that drew Jonathan to him.

And now they would be brothers-in-law. Jonathan was sure that, after David and Merab were married, his father would realize that David was not a threat to the throne.

Around the table was Jonathan's wife, Mara, Jonathan's younger brothers, Abinidab and Malchishua, now in their early 30s, and the youngest son, twenty-nine-year-old Ish-ba'al, sometimes known as Ish-bosheth. Then there were Jonathan's sisters: Merab, the bride-to-be, and the youngest sister, Michal. Also at the table were their mother, the queen, Ahinoam, and father, King Saul, and his concubine, the young and beautiful, but shy, Rizpah, and her toddler, Armoni, another son of Saul.

Jonathan watched as David laughed and joked with the others around the table and as Merab looked at him curiously, but not happily. Then their father spoke.

"I brought the son of Jesse here, because I promised my daughter's hand to the one who slew the giant."

"Hear, hear!" Jonathan said, raising his earthenware cup. David gave him an appreciative look, but his words were deferential.

"Who am I, and my father's family, that I should become the king's son-in-law?"

"However, something has caused me to change my mind," Saul said, causing the noise of the table to abruptly stop.

Jonathan froze in the middle of a bite of roast mutton. *What can this mean?*

"Melchar, the father of Adriel has offered a large bride price for Merab," Saul continued matter-of-factly. "So, I give her to him."

"What do you mean?" said Jonathan's mother.

"You can't do that!" Jonathan protested.

"I can and I have."

"Why would you go back on your promise, father?" Jonathan demanded.

"Oh, thank you, father!" was Merab's response, which caused everyone to stop talking again and look at her. The attention caused her to jump up and run red-faced from the table and up the stairs, but Jonathan was also puzzled by the sly smile on Michal's face, which apparently only he noticed.

Jonathan then looked at David, whose face was flushed, displaying a mixture of embarrassment and anger. He arose from the table and stalked toward the door.

"Don't go, David!" said Michal.

Jonathan looked at her, surprised and not understanding his younger sister any more than the older one.

David looked at Michal for a long moment, but then turned and went out the door.

"Father, what are you doing?!" Jonathan demanded.

"Yes, lord, what have you done?" Ahinoam said, her own face showing her embarrassment for the sake of their guest.

"I have done what I have done," said Saul, with a wave of his hand.

❦ 7 ❦

Azel was sitting in camp, eating a cake of raisins, when he again saw Jonathan in the encampment, striding toward the house of their commander.

"David, come out!" Jonathan called, pounding on the door.

Slowly David emerged from his house.

"I'm sorry!" Azel heard Jonathan say, both of them talking loudly enough he had no trouble hearing.

"Why did he do that?" David demanded.

After a pause, Jonathan said, "I don't understand my father's motives in this. His promise must be kept."

"What of Merab?"

"She has left the house already and gone to the house of Adriel."

"So soon?" David exclaimed. "Was this all planned to humiliate me?"

"No, no!" Jonathan hastened to say. "I don't fully understand what happened, but I'll find out."

"Don't bother. Your father intends to dishonor me. And he has."

"No, I'm sure that's not his intention."

"So how do you explain it?"

"I cannot," Jonathan said, hanging his head.

Azel realized he was eavesdropping and turned to look away, though he was drawn to the scene. He didn't require more than he had heard to know that the king had withdrawn his promise to give his daughter to David, though this had been promised to whoever killed the giant. Azel wondered what would happen now that the king had broken his promise and dishonored his champion.

After his attempt to mend things with David, Jonathan returned to his parents' home and immediately confronted his father.

"Whatever was that about? How could you humiliate David that way?"

"You have no say in this!" Saul shouted. "I am the king! I will do what I will do!"

"How will anyone believe you if you go back on your word so easily?"

"I AM THE KING!" Saul shouted again. "I do what I think best!"

"I will go."

Both men turned to see that it was Michal who had spoken.

"What?" Saul said. "What did you say?"

"I will go. I will be David's wife."

"Why would YOU want to be the wife of the son of Jesse?" Saul asked his young daughter.

"I love David," Michal said. "And if I marry him, you will have kept your pledge."

Saul and Jonathan didn't know what to say immediately. Jonathan looked at his little sister as if he had never seen her before. She was still quite young at 15, but had grown into a beautiful young woman, with womanly curves and shining dark eyes framed by lustrous, black hair. Her declaration of love for David was a complete surprise.

Finally, Saul spoke.

"My dear Michal, are you sure you want this?"

"Yes, father, I do."

"It *would* allow you to keep your promise," Jonathan chimed in.

"Then make it so," Saul answered with a sigh. "Tell the son of Jesse he has his bride."

Michal skipped over to her father and threw her arms around him.

"Oh, thank you! Thank you, father."

"Perhaps if you are his wife, you can keep me informed of his activities."

"Yes, yes father, whatever you wish." Michal skipped out of the room.

Jonathan looked at his father through narrowed eyes, then turned and went out the door without another word.

❧ 8 ❧

Azel was with his men in the headquarters camp, preparing his midday meal. He looked up to see his commander standing over him. He jumped to attention, turning over a pot of soup in the process.

"I need you to accompany me to the throne."

"What?" Azel was puzzled by the cryptic statement.

"I have been summoned to appear before the king," David said. "I need you to come with me as a representative of the men."

"Oh, all right. I mean, yes, commander."

David smiled, apparently amused by his officer's confusion.

On the way to the royal court, David ordered a couple more of his officers to accompany them. Azel saw that he intended to make sure the king remembered he was a man with men under his command. As they entered through the door into the throne room, he saw his brother Jeriah to the right of the throne, as Azel knew he stood before the king almost daily, but he had rarely actually been in the court to see him.

David nodded to the guard outside the door, who nodded back and stood aside to allow the champion of Israel to enter. Azel and the others followed closely.

Saul briefly looked in their direction but did not turn his attention from the elder from far away Zebulun who was recounting the news from that region of the kingdom, including atrocities committed by the Philistines who still occupied much of what should be Saul's kingdom. Azel stood with David and his men with their backs against the wall, wondering how long it would be before they could have their audience.

Then Jonathan appeared and saw David. Immediately he came over and greeted David warmly. They spoke happily but silently, through mouthed words and hand gestures, not wanting to disturb the court business being conducted a few cubits away.

Eventually, the king's cousin and right-hand man, Abner, called for David to stand before the king. David waited for the king to speak first.

"David my son, I have wronged you in that I have not kept my promise to you, to give my daughter to you as wife. I have now decided that my second daughter should be your wife and you must only provide the bride price."

David smiled, but there was questioning in his voice. "Lord, I am immensely grateful for your generosity. You are most kind. However, I am but a poor shepherd and soldier. What bride price am I able to provide?"

"It is nothing," Saul began. "All you must do is circumcise 100 Philistines and bring the foreskins to me as surety."

Azel almost gasped aloud but was able to stifle himself. *Was not the price to wed the king's daughter the slaying of the giant, which David had already done? What is the king doing?*

But David only bowed and backed away, prompting Azel and the others to do the same.

"As you wish, majesty." David replied.

Then they all went out.

The day was ending and Jeriah was finishing a clerical task concerning the king's business. All the courtiers had been dismissed so only Jeriah, the king and his cousin, Abner, remained. Abner then spoke, not trying to prevent Jeriah from hearing.

"That was an odd dowry you requested of your hero."

Saul stood from the throne where he had sat all day and stretched. "Yes, perhaps, but it occurred to me that I might best let the Philistines take care of what is needed."

"'What is needed?'" Abner repeated, a question in his voice.

"The son of Jesse is a threat to my throne. If he dies at the hand of the Philistines, my hands will be clean."

Abner looked at the floor and simply said, "As you wish."

He then walked away, out the door toward his office on the periphery of the court and the king walked to his own door, which was the way to his home.

Jeriah was left alone to reflect on what the king had said.

❦ 9 ❦

The men of Azel's company had been ordered to assemble on the parade ground in Gibeah. Azel knew that this mission would be different from the routine raids on small Philistine towns to which they had become accustomed.

They marched to the west to a small town that was satellite of Ekron, arriving in the middle of the night. The plan of attack was reviewed by David with Azel and the other officers as they stood on a small knoll overlooking the town while the men waited. No substantial changes to their accustomed attack plan were required but there would be a new wrinkle.

Azel returned to his men and called one of his trusted squad leaders.

"I have a special job for you and your men," Azel began, giving the man a rough, woolen sack. "We are to fill this sack with at least 20 Philistine foreskins."

Seeing the questions in the man's eyes, Azel explained, "Our commander has been asked to provide evidence of the circumcision of 100 Philistines as a dowry, so we will kill the men of this town, but we will then circumcise them and put the foreskins in this sack. Each company in David's cohort will provide 20 foreskins."

"That will make 200," the squad leader pointed out.

"Yes, David plans to leave no doubt that he has fulfilled the bride price."

"It will be done," the squad leader said, saluting and turning to go back to his men.

After their bloody business was done, David and his cohort marched back to Gibeah and arrived in the morning just as the king's court was beginning its daily business. Azel and the other company officers dismissed their men and each of them accompanied David to the royal court bearing the blood-soaked sacks with their grisly contents. They were ushered in and David interrupted the proceedings, loudly saying, "May the king live forever, I have done what the king required."

Azel and the nine other company officers came forward wordlessly, not raising their eyes to look at the king, and laid their 10 sacks before the king in such a way that their contents partially spilled out on the stone pavement, then they backed away and stood as a rank behind David.

"The king asked for 100 Philistine foreskins as dowry for marrying his daughter. I have brought 200. Now the king may honor his promise."

Azel watched as the two men looked at one another without flinching, Saul frowning and David looking back resolutely.

The king summoned the priest Ahimelech, son of Ahitub and younger brother of Ahijah, from the nearby shrine of Yahweh at Nob to bless the union of his daughter to David. There was feasting for three days as the house was readied for the new couple. At the end of the feast, David took Michal to the second-story chamber of the house Jonathan had found and bought with money from the royal treasury. There they began to live as husband and wife.

Michal was indeed in love with David and showed her love enthusiastically from their first encounter as husband and wife. Because of the culture, they had had almost no time to talk before they were married; they had only seen one another at meals and in the king's court. But now they were alone and Michal was able to revel in David's kisses. While neither of them were experienced in love-making, love itself showed the way as they explored one another's bodies during the passionate nights of their early marriage.

Her heart thrilled as his strong hands caressed her and pulled her flesh to his. His strength and authority were the perfect counterpart to her young softness and willing love. Afterward they would lie beside one another, spent and sated, but Michal would already be looking forward to the next night or to the night when he would return from battle.

And she often thought of what it would mean when she gave David a son.

❧ 10 ❧

It was later than usual when Azel arrived home. He entered through the front door to see that nine-year-old Eliel was playing in a corner and his wife, Dani, was sitting facing the door, as if she had been that way for hours. At first, Azel feared he had missed some appointment or was late for the evening meal, but there was no food on the table and Dani's face did not show anger.

Instead, she appeared serene and peaceful.

"What's going on?" Azel ventured.

"Come close, my dear."

Azel walked toward her, his curiosity now thoroughly aroused. "You're worrying me."

"Not to worry, my love. My news is good."

"What news?"

"Eliel," she looked at the boy as she began, "will have a new brother or sister."

Azel rushed the few remaining steps to embrace her and lift her from the chair, swinging her in a circle before setting her feet on the floor again.

"Praise Yahweh! A baby?"

"Yes. In the Spring."

They kissed and stayed in one another's arms for a long time.

Eliel took scant notice, preferring to continue with his toys in the corner.

Azel paced nervously from one end of the courtyard to the other. The midwife had come and Shelomith was aiding her while Dani was in labor.

"Papa, why can't we go in the house," asked Eliel, a growing nine-year-old.

"You remember that we told you that you would be getting a baby brother or sister, don't you?

"Yes."

"Well, it looks like today is the day."

"That I get a new baby brother?!"

"Well, it could be a sister, but it looks like it will happen today."

Eliel smiled broadly and Azel was glad he didn't press the questioning further. Then Jeriah came through the gate.

"What's going on?"

"Dani's in labor," Azel replied. "Shelomith and the midwife are in there with her."

"How long has she been in labor?"

"About six hours now."

Jeriah nodded, knowingly. "So, it could be any time."

"Yes, Eliel and I are both anxious."

"I'm getting a baby brother, uncle!" Eliel told Jeriah.

"That's wonderful!"

"I've told him it could be a sister, but he seems to ignore that possibility," Azel said, smiling.

Jeriah nodded, returning the smile.

Azel was glad that things had settled down, with Saul seemingly at peace with David for some time now. It had made a difference in his relationship with his brother. They hadn't talked about the rumors that Samuel had anointed David for quite a while. Azel hoped things would resolve themselves without further conflict.

Then Shelomith appeared at the door. She motioned to Azel to come inside.

"What about Eliel?"

"He can come too," Shelomith said, smiling, and she waved at Jeriah.

"Come, Eliel, let's go see the baby!"

Eliel ran to join his father and they both went through the door.

The main room of the house was relatively dark. Dani lay in the middle of the room on a stack of bedding and covered with a thick blanket. In her arms she held a small baby, wrapped in a white cloth.

"It's a boy," the midwife said.

Azel and Eliel knelt on either side of mother and child. Azel looked at the small face lying against his mother's breast and was flooded with a feeling of happiness and love even greater than what he felt when Eliel was born. He looked at Eliel, who was transfixed, looking at the baby brother he knew he was getting, but not seeming to know what to do or say now.

"What do you think, Eliel?"

"He's little."

"You were that little once," Dani said. "He will grow just like you have."

"What's his name?" Eliel asked.

"Well, we get to give him a name," Azel answered. "What do you think of 'Adriel?'"

"'Adriel' is what Papa and I decided to name the baby if it was a boy," Dani explained.

"That's a good name," Eliel said.

"I think so, too," Dani said, smiling down at her second son.

❦ 11 ❦

Months had gone by and now became years, with King Saul being mostly sane and peaceable, yet David rarely came to the court. Instead, he ranged far and near, wherever there was a threat to the security of Israel. There were many towns with Philistine presence, which David and the men in his command freed. This served to raise David's stock with the people of Israel and cement his reputation as a military leader and champion.

In other cases, David and the men under his command raided and looted Philistine towns. Not the large royal capitals like Gath or Ashdod, but the satellite towns, where he could completely destroy the town and all its inhabitants in one night.

Azel marched with him and did his duty, burning town after town and killing all survivors, so no one could live to tell the tale.

In the spring, the Philistines once again moved against Israel, this time to the north of Gibeah, in western Ephraim.

The night before the expected battle, Azel sat at a campfire with fellow soldiers from David's company.

"Have you fought before?" asked a man younger than Azel, who said his name was Ulam.

"I was at Elah," Azel answered.

"So, you saw Commander David kill the giant?" Ulam said, wide-eyed.

"Yes, it was a great day for worshippers of Yahweh. We praised Him as we pursued the Philistines all that day."

"I wonder what tomorrow will bring?"

"We'd all like the answer to that question," laughed another man, also a veteran, named Maroth. He was a big man with pre-mature gray streaks in his full beard. "None but the prophets know what tomorrow may bring."

All the men about the fire remained silent, looking into the flames, each with his own thoughts.

Jonathan made David and his 1,000 men the vanguard in the campaign, so the next day, as the armies faced one another across the field, Azel and the 50 men under his command were on the front lines of the assault.

Jonathan had generously allowed David to plan the strategy for the entire battle. David's plan called for the main body commanded by Saul to mount the initial attack.

Azel knew Jeriah would be there, commanding a thousand men before the king.

As the main body began the assault, David's men and the rest of Jonathan's cohort waited behind a ridge out of sight. Azel could hear the din of battle beginning and was itching to move forward, eager to aid their brothers, but David continued to wait, Azel assumed, for the right time.

Finally, the order did come. Azel and the others quickly moved forward to the crest of the ridge and before them where they could see the battle raging in the valley below. Their vantage point was a little behind the end of the Philistine lines.

They left their flank exposed, Azel realized, and he understood David's strategy for the battle.

The order was given to "Charge," and Azel and his men ran down the slope toward the Philistines, many of whom faced away from them, focused on the main body of the Israelite army before them. Just before David's cohort reached them, the Philistines realized what was happening and turned to meet the unexpected threat, which meant their right flank was soon crushed between the pincer that David had devised.

Azel's voice joined the roar of his men and the many others in David's company and the larger force under Jonathan behind and beside them. They crashed into the Philistine lines with the sound of choked cries of pain, metal on metal and weapons tearing human flesh.

Azel's sickle sword flashed again and again as he dipped it in Philistine blood. He raised his shield when one of the Sea People swung his straight, short sword toward him, then swung back at him, catching him in the shoulder, which caused the man to stumble, but the wound was not fatal, so Azel swung again, this time dealing a fatal blow to his neck.

There was no time to be sure the man was dead, because there were more Philistines just ahead. One of them rushed toward Azel with a spear aimed at his midsection. Azel jumped aside and struck the spear shaft with his sword, causing it to fall and strike the dirt, leaving the soldier defenseless against the next swing of Azel's blade, which ended him.

Azel looked up to see the fighting moving away from him as the Philistine flank collapsed and the soldiers left alive tried to run away, only to be found by other Israelites in the main body coming from the other direction.

When it was over, the Philistines withdrew, greatly weakened, and the Israelites gave chase and were able to continue inflicting casualties on stragglers for several miles. When the Philistines reached the coastal road, they regrouped and began marching south back toward their five royal cities.

"By the gods, we should turn back and fight tomorrow!" King Achish of Gath said angrily, but a council of the five kings had voted to retire from the field and return home for now. Achish's chariot driver did not comment.

Achish did not further voice his frustration that the land they had abandoned was won years before in the battle of Ebenezer, when his father, Maoch, had been king.

What a waste to have given it up so easily.

Instinctively, Achish knew David, the hero who had vanquished his champion, Goliath the giant, at the battle of Elah, had a hand in their defeat.

As evening came, the Israelites gradually found their way back into camp, having left off their pursuit. There was general rejoicing as the men settled once again around campfires and ate the provisions available to them from King Saul's stores.

As Azel joined his men around the fire where they had been the night before the battle, Azel said, "Our commander's plan for the battle worked well."

"Yes, he is a born master strategist," Maroth answered.

It was obvious to Azel the execution of David's plan had inspired admiration in the foot soldiers in Israel's army.

Maroth, the big Benjamite, asked, "Has anybody seen Ulam, the new recruit?"

Azel shook his head and no one else volunteered anything.

"Ah, well, hopefully he just hasn't returned from the field yet," Maroth said, but Azel knew it was more likely the inexperienced soldier had fallen by a Philistine sword or arrow.

The next day, David and Jonathan ordered a detail of soldiers to build a stacked-stone monument to commemorate the victory and mark the border of the land claimed by the tribe of Ephraim.

After that, the army was allowed to strike camp and march toward the land of Benjamin.

Jeriah was marching with the king's troops, returning home after the battle. The day before, he and his men had seen Jonathan's division, using David's company as the tip of the spear, crush the Philistine flank, which turned the tide of the battle and sent the enemy into a rout, ending the invasion.

Exile of the King

King Saul's division mostly played a supporting role, *almost as a decoy*, Jeriah thought.

All around him, the men in the ranks rejoiced at the victory, but they didn't see what Jeriah and Abner did: that Saul was not rejoicing with them, rather he sat sullen and silent on his donkey as it plodded along.

❦ 12 ❦

It had been several years now since King Saul had allowed David and Michal to marry, and the king had been relatively docile and reasonable. However, on this day the king's moods swung toward depression once again, causing him to be paranoid and to command everyone within hearing to kill David. Jonathan realized he needed to warn him.

Coming out of Gibeah on a donkey, he saw the forward ranks of David's men trudging home after a raid in the Philistine rural area near Gath. They were pushing prisoners and captured sheep and goats along with them.

"Where is your commander?" Jonathan asked the first soldiers he encountered.

"Back there," a weary foot soldier answered with a gesture over his shoulder.

Jonathan looked in the distance at the column of troops and kicked his donkey to get him moving again. About halfway down the column he caught sight of David.

"David, I must speak to you!" he said, dismounting and drawing David off to the side of the marching men and their curious eyes.

"What is it, Jonathan?"

"My father is afflicted with the evil spirit today," he whispered. "He ordered me and all present at court to kill you! You must go into hiding."

"Don't you think he will shortly relent and be in his right mind?"

Jonathan thought for a moment before answering. "See that field?" he said, pointing to a golden field of barley on the side of a hill nearby. "Tomorrow I'll bring my father to this field and question him about you and try to reason with him. If you hide in the field, you can hear his answer."

"All right," David agreed.

"But don't come to court today. Remain here in hiding until tomorrow."

"All right, my friend."

Jonathan then helped David retrieve his gear from one of the pack donkeys so he would have the necessary equipment to sleep in the country one more night.

"I will bring my father as early as I can get him to come out in the morning."

The two friends grasped each other's forearms up to the elbow in the warrior's pledge of solidarity and parted.

"Do one more thing for me," David said.

"Anything."

"Tell your sister why I didn't return with the men and that I will see her as soon as I can."

"Of course."

While he was accustomed to sleeping under the stars ever since he was a young boy, watching his father's flocks for weeks at a time, David would have so much preferred to be home in his soft bed with his loving wife.

He woke with the sun and hid in the tall grain of the field a few cubits from the road where Jonathan had found him yesterday.

As he lay on his back, hidden by the barley stalks, David thought how thoroughly he was enjoying married life with Michal, who lavished him with love in so many ways, but the proximity to his unpredictable father-in-law definitely had its disadvantages.

The only other thing that hindered their relationship was that she had yet to give him a child. He did not hold it against her, but he was concerned for his future legacy. The prophet had said he would be king, and he knew kings must sire future kings.

Yet Samuel had anointed David to be king after Saul, and while this was not supposed to be widely known, David knew that his marriage to Saul's daughter would be an important piece of the puzzle in establishing succession. There were many other pieces that must fall into place and sometimes David questioned God's intentions and how he would overcome the obstacles which lay in his path to the throne.

Chief among the obstacles was Saul's suspicion that David posed a threat to his family's dynastic succession. David knew he had to survive the dangerous mood swings of King Saul if he was to eventually sit on the throne himself.

David also puzzled over how he would follow Saul as king when he had four sons perfectly capable of ascending the throne. Yahweh's plan was truly difficult to discern at times. *Yet I will trust him.*

As he waited, reclining in the field, the sun climbed to what he estimated to be the third hour since dawn. He had no idea if Jonathan could even induce his father to come out to the field, but then he heard something and raised his head to look down the road. There he saw two figures on donkeys approaching on the road from Gibeah.

When they reached the spot where Jonathan had found David yesterday, Jonathan motioned to his father that they should rest under the shade of a tree.

David lay as close to the ground as possible, hidden by the ripe barley, for the king and his son were resting their donkeys but a dozen cubits away from him.

"Please do not do wrong to your servant, David," David heard Jonathan plead with his father. "He has not wronged you. He has repeatedly taken his life into his hands in your service since killing the Philistine. The Lord won a great victory for Israel that day and you were glad of it."

Through the barley stalks David could see the king was solemn and considering what Jonathan was saying.

"What offense has David committed that you would sin against an innocent man like David by killing him," Jonathan continued, "when he has done nothing but serve you faithfully?"

His father did not immediately answer, so Jonathan pressed on, "Now that my sister is married to him, she will be hurt, caught in the middle by this. Both of us would mourn him, but she would then be faced with a life of widowhood. Please change your mind. David has done nothing but serve you faithfully."

Saul looked off in the distance, then turned to Jonathan and said, "You are right. As the Lord lives, David will not be killed."

"Thank you, Father."

They once again mounted their donkeys and spurred them onto the road back toward Gibeah as David watched from his hiding place.

An hour later, Jonathan returned alone to the barley field with an extra donkey for David to ride.

"Did you hear?" Jonathan asked.

"I heard him relent. Do you think it's safe for me to return?"

"My father won't harm you now. I made him promise several times as we rode along together."

"All right, because you say it," David said.

❦ 13 ❦

Michal was sitting on the steps in front of their house when David finally arrived home.

"Where have you been?!" She ran to embrace him, but her face showed her worry and desperation.

"Did Jonathan not tell you I had to wait to be sure your father would not act against me?"

"He did – that's why I was worried – but why is my father against you?

"He believes I am against HIM."

"Well, just tell him it wasn't you whom Samuel anointed."

David looked at her solemnly but said nothing. Michal took a moment to understand what the silence meant.

"It WAS you?!" she whispered.

"It happened before I met the king; before I slew the giant at Elah."

Michal struggled to wrap her mind around this revelation. She had thought her father was just paranoid concerning David, as he often was with others; fearing first one, then another would take his throne from him.

"Why did Samuel choose you?"

"He said Yahweh told him to pick me. God speaks to him, you know? And that time He first told him to go to my family. He examined all my brothers and finally, God told him it was to be me."

"How can you be king? Even if my father was not on the throne, I have four brothers."

"I know."

"How long will you have to wait?"

"As long as God chooses."

Michal paused to carefully choose her words for the next question.

"Will you take the throne by force?"

"That would not be God's will. Your father was anointed king, as surely as I was. I have already waited several years. I will wait on the Lord."

"Do you ever just wish all this would go away?"

"All what?"

"All the fighting, the struggling, the conflict? With the Philistines, the Canaanites, the Ammonites, whoever? But also, the political strife?"

David put his strong, tanned arm around her.

"I don't know if a world without struggle is possible. I just seek to do God's will, whatever my plight."

She laid her head on his shoulder. Presently he spoke again.

"It's unfair to you, to be between me and your father, when we are at odds."

"That is not a difficult choice for me," she whispered.

❦ 14 ❦

Raquel prepared breakfast for her grandson, Anah, as she often did, because her widower son, Aviel, was often gone to assist in the morning sacrifice at the Lord's Tent.

She had lived in Nob for well over 30 years now, and her beloved Zedekiah, Aviel's father, had succumbed to a fever a couple of years before.

Aviel had replaced his father as the foremost Levite serving the Tent. Zedekiah had been instrumental in bringing the Tent to Nob, but more importantly, he had rescued Raquel and her two nephews, Ahitub and Ichabod, the heirs to the priesthood. Now Ahitub's sons served as the priests of the Tent, and each of them had families.

Unfortunately, Ichabod had been a sickly child and before he reached his fifth birthday, he was overtaken by a fever and died. To Raquel, it seemed the priests in the line of Eli had suffered more than their share of tragedy. She herself had been married to Eli's son, the oafish Hophni who, with his brother, had died in the catastrophic battle of Ebenezer, her father-in-law, Eli, died on hearing the news and her sister-in-law died in childbirth. All four died within a 24-hour period.

Raquel set a plate of date cakes and a cup of goat milk in front of seven-year-old Anah.

"Thank you, grandmother."

"Eat the roast lamb, too," she said. "You need to grow up strong and tall."

"Yes, grandmother."

She smiled down at him as he eagerly ate.

❦ 15 ❦

Only yesterday, Jeriah had thought to himself that the king had been remarkably lucid and calm of late. He had let his daughter marry David and had even made David the captain of his personal guard.

It seemed the new bride and groom were very happy, although Jeriah only heard of them second hand. David was often away on campaigns against the Philistines and neither of them frequented the king's court.

As far as the king's court was concerned, out of sight, out of mind, and that helped to keep the peace with the king, so uneventful months went by.

But that was yesterday, and today Jeriah could see the dark mood of the king had returned. It was never clear what set him off, but Jeriah surmised that word had reached his ears of the growing popularity of David with the people.

Jeriah understood the appeal of the young man from Bethlehem. His charismatic personality and keen, strategic warrior's mind were everything the king, with his dour, paralyzing moods, was not. Indeed, Jeriah's own brother Azel had become a fiercely loyal officer in David's cohort.

For some reason, Abner thought it would be a good idea to have David come to the throne and play his music for the king. Jeriah realized that had been effective before, but since the king had thrown his spear at David, he hadn't been back.

David, ever the loyal servant, obeyed Abner's request and brought his lyre and stood under the portico until Abner waved him forward.

Jeriah then watched as David took a seat in front of the throne, eyeing the king warily. Saul's eyes were dark and his mouth was turned down.

As David began to play, the king took note and raised his head, focusing on David. Jeriah suddenly realized that Saul's spear was beside him, as it usually was. He had a fleeting thought that he should have removed it while the king was distracted, but it was too late.

Saul grabbed the spear and in one quick motion sent it flying toward David.

David nimbly jumped to one side and the spear stuck in the chair, which tumbled over with the force of the blow.

David hurried from the throne room, scowling at Abner as he went.

Abner seemed surprised, which didn't make sense to Jeriah. It seemed to him that anyone should have seen this coming.

David burst through the front door of the house he shared with Michal.

"What's the matter?" Michal asked as she laid aside the garment she was mending.

"Your father, the king, has once again tried to kill me!"

"What?! How?"

"As he did before, to impale me with a spear while I sang to soothe him."

"I'm so sorry!" Michal exclaimed.

"Oh, it's not your fault, but what am I to do?"

Michal didn't have a ready answer.

It was late in the day when Saul startled those gathered before his throne.

"Why do you betray me, men of Benjamin?" said Saul loudly and suddenly. Those in the throne room stopped their business and turned to face the king, fear and uncertainty on their faces.

"Why do you favor the son of Jesse, my enemy?"

"Oh king," ventured Abner tentatively. "We have neither favored David over you, nor is he your enemy."

Then Saul looked directly at Jeriah.

"Take your guard and lie in wait outside his house. Then kill him when he comes out in the morning!"

Jeriah froze momentarily. Then, remembering his duty, turned and motioned to another soldier standing guard by the door and they went out, where Jeriah recruited other men guarding the perimeter of the king's royal court to join his mission.

"We have been ordered to lie in wait, to kill Commander David when he leaves his house in the morning," Jeriah told the soldiers as they looked at him with shock and dismay on their faces.

It was a short walk to the house of the king's daughter and son-in-law, but Jeriah and his hastily assembled squad of soldiers were in no hurry. Finally, they reached the street at dusk. A man bearing a baby goat passed by as they approached.

"Where is David's house?" Jeriah asked.

The man looked at them suspiciously and slowly turned. "There," he said pointing to a stone house at the end of the row of connected dwellings. It was inside a mud-brick wall which rose to the height of a man's head. The man then turned and went on his way.

Jeriah looked around and then pointed to a narrow street nearby that rose high enough to see over the wall into the courtyard. "There, we will wait until morning."

The men settled in for the night, two taking the first watch, where they had a line of site on David's front door, and the rest sleeping as best they could against the rough, mud-brick walls, out of sight of the compound.

But Jeriah could not sleep. He couldn't see an easy way out of his predicament. The king had given him a direct order, but how could he kill an innocent man, especially when many, including his own brother, believed the Spirit of God was with him?

Yahweh, he prayed silently, *please provide a solution that saves David, but allows me to honor the king.*

He had no idea how Yahweh could answer his prayer.

Darkness had fallen an hour ago. Michal was cleaning up after the evening meal while David waited for her upstairs. They had considered various courses of action since her father had demonstrated again that he wanted to kill her husband, but they hadn't arrived at a conclusion.

She opened the front door holding a bowl of dirty water and threw it onto the ground beside the steps. She was turning to go back inside when she noticed something. Over the wall, she saw two men in soldiers' garb, looking toward her in the moonlight.

Strange, she thought. *What are they doing?*

Then the thought came to her fully formed: *My father has sent them to kill David when he comes out in the morning.*

Michal knew what she had to do.

"You're right," David said, when Michal told him about the men outside. "I must flee."

"I will come with you," Michal said.

"No," David said. "I don't want you be the object of your father's anger. It's enough that I must flee. You must keep good relations with him if you can. Tell him I threatened you if you didn't let me escape, so he won't blame you."

Michal couldn't bear the thought of being without him, but he was right that she needed to keep on speaking terms with her father.

"All right, I will stay. Perhaps I can find a way to inform you of my father's movements."

"Don't do anything to endanger yourself. I must leave now and put as much distance as possible between me and the men outside."

He began gathering a few things for the trip.

"You must not go out the front door," Michal said. "They are watching."

"Then how?"

"I will help you down from the window and you can escape behind our compound."

The house had a walled courtyard in front, but the back wall was on a street. Unfortunately, there were no windows on the lower floor.

"Yes, that is a good plan," David agreed.

Michal then gathered bed clothes to use as ropes by which he could lower himself from the second story. When she had twisted them into rope-like forms, she looked at him, with his bag thrown across his shoulder, ready to go.

"Be careful!" she said, starting to cry.

"And you as well," David answered, kissing her.

Then he went to the window. She put the bedclothes around the bedpost to give her leverage and held them with all her strength, as he disappeared through the window and began climbing down the back side of their house.

Suddenly she felt the bedclothes go slack and she almost fell backward. She ran to the window and looked down onto the darkened street but could see nothing.

❧ 16 ❧

The next morning, when the sky was just turning gray in the east before changing to pink, Jeriah woke the men and motioned to them to follow as he went through the gate into the compound and pounded on the door of David's house. "David!" he shouted. "Your king requires your presence."

Jeriah and his men tightened their grips on their weapons. It took a couple of minutes before there was a response. Michal opened the door only slightly.

"What do you want? My lord David is sick."

"The king requires his presence."

"He is too sick to see the king just now."

Jeriah did not like being in this position, but he knew he could not come back to the king without having learned if Michal was telling the truth.

"We must see David," Jeriah said, and he pushed Michal aside and led the men through the open door and into the house and up the mud-brick stairs where the bed chamber would be.

There was no door, but only a 90-degree turn to enter the room. There were drapes covering the windows and no lamps were lit. Jeriah paused to allow his eyes to adjust to the darkness.

Suddenly Michal brushed past and stood between him and the bed. "I tell you he is too sick to see the king. He sleeps. Please let him sleep so he can recover!"

Jeriah looked past Michal in the darkness and could make out the outline of a body lying in the bed, covered with a robe, dark hair being the only thing visible above the robe.

"Please let him sleep!" Michal pleaded. "My father will understand. He will come before the king tomorrow."

Jeriah looked into the earnest, young eyes looking up at him and decided he could do no more without turning daughter against father.

"Come men. I will report to the king."

The troops left again by the front door.

"I told you to kill him!"

"Yes, my king, but the champion is very ill." Jeriah replied nervously as he stood before the throne. "His wife, your daughter, assured us he would appear before you tomorrow."

"Go back and bring him and the bed too, if necessary! I demand he be brought before me now! I am the king!"

"Yes, your grace," Jeriah said, icy fear choking him.

Jeriah took his squad back the way they came, and they entered David's house without knocking, noisily mounting the steps to the upper bed chamber once again.

"But you cannot! He is ill!" Michal protested as she tried to get ahead of the rapidly moving men.

"Your father was very clear that we must bring him, even with the bed," Jeriah replied, looking into the frightened eyes of the young woman.

"David!" Jeriah shouted as they arrived at the bed chamber, but there was no response. He strode over to the bed and threw aside the robe. All the men gasped.

"What is this?" Jeriah said, but he knew what it was. In the bed was a household image, a stone teraph of a Canaanite god, nearly life-sized. On the head was a dark, goat-hair pillowcase Michal had put on it to look like hair. Earlier, it had been enough to fool them in the darkened room.

Jeriah spun around and gripped the slender wrist of the king's daughter, barely controlling his anger. "You have deceived us! You have played us for fools! You will explain yourself to your father."

"No, please!" Michal cried, sinking down and becoming dead weight as Jeriah pulled her toward the stairs.

"The king will put us to the sword if we fail to bring your husband before him. You must explain yourself to him."

"How could you plot against me in my own house?!" Saul demanded of Michal when Jeriah's men brought her before the throne.

"David threatened me," Michal insisted. "He said 'Stay out of my way. Why should I kill you?'"

Saul rose from the throne, his face purple with rage, and Jeriah feared he would strike his daughter, but gradually he seemed to settle down and sank once again onto his seat.

"Remove her!" he shouted, and Jeriah had no choice but to take her by the arm again, leading her away.

"Father, I'm sorry!" she said, but Saul ignored her.

❧ 17 ❧

Samuel's bones creaked as he arose to answer the knock at his door. *Who can it be at this hour?*

He answered the door to see the young man from Bethlehem whom he had anointed as king, looking as if he had run all the way from Gibeath-Saul. How he had matured since that day years ago when he had to be called in from keeping the sheep!

"David! What are you doing in Ramah?"

"Lord Samuel, I'm in danger," David said breathlessly.

"What has happened?"

"Saul is determined to kill me."

"Surely not!"

"He knows," David whispered.

"He cannot know," Samuel assured him. "He can only suspect."

"You have not seen him recently; you don't know how he is. He sent soldiers to take me. I only escaped because Michal helped me climb down from the upstairs window and escape in the night."

"You're sure they were coming to kill you?"

"Michal saw them as they lay in wait for me."

Samuel considered what David said and decided it was not too difficult to believe that the melancholy, paranoid king would suspect David would be his successor and would be threatened by his presence.

"Come let us go to the school of the prophets. You can have bread and a place of refuge there."

The slender man pulled his cloak over his head against the chill of evening and started the walk to Gibeath-Saul. The journey would take a couple of hours on his thin legs, but the silver from Abner's treasury would make it worthwhile.

This was Uzziel's first opportunity to give real, valuable intelligence to the king's viceroy as he had promised to do when he was first recruited to be part of Abner's network of spies. The prospect of spying for the king had been exciting, but years had passed and there was nothing to do but report on the comings and goings of Samuel, which the king wanted to know about because they were on the outs, but which were routine at most. Finally, Abner had told him only to inform him if something unusual happened. Tonight was the first time something truly unusual had indeed happened.

Rumors were plentiful that the king feared David was his rival and wanted to eliminate him. Now he had seen David and Samuel together on the streets of Ramah after dark making their way to the school of the prophets, which seemed to Uzziel a perfect place to hide.

Arriving in Gibeath-Saul, he stopped to sleep on the street in the marketplace for a few hours, reasoning he wouldn't be able to pass on his intelligence until morning light, when Abner and the king began their day.

Abner did not wait for the king to take the throne in his court but went directly to his home to give him the news that Uzziel, one of his many spies, had brought. David was in Ramah, hiding at Samuel's school of the prophets in the Naioth sector. This was exactly what he had cultivated his network of spies to do. He finally felt that it had been money well spent.

"Detail some men to go kill him immediately!" Saul said on hearing the news.

"It will be done," Abner answered, bowing and backing toward the door.

⇜ 18 ⇝

"Come, eat."

David accepted the invitation gladly. The young man offering the fresh pita and lamb stew was a student in Samuel's school. He had an infectious smile and was dressed in a simple, shapeless tunic made of wool, similar to what all the students wore. They were seated on the ground in a small square between buildings. He encouraged the fire by adding a couple of small sticks.

"What do you do here?" David asked before dipping the pita in the stew and putting a bite in his mouth.

"I learn the law at the feet of the prophet and the senior students, and we learn what it means to be anointed with the Spirit of God."

David's attention was even more attuned after he said that.

"How does that work?"

"The Spirit of God?"

"Yes, the anointing."

"It is not something you can 'work.' The Spirit is a gift which God chooses to give."

"But were you given the gift by Samuel? Or someone else?"

"Others may be used by the Spirit of God, but the Spirit only comes to those He chooses."

"How do you know you have the Spirit of God?"

The young man considered the question without answering for a moment, then spoke.

"You submit and wait on the Lord. Some never really receive it. Others receive it with power."

"Samuel must have the Spirit of God with power," David said.

"Very much so. Samuel hears the Lord's voice."

"Not everyone does?"

"It varies. It depends on the calling."

"The calling?"

"God calls us all, but each to different purposes in his plan. The Spirit is given to fulfill God's purposes for us."

David considered what the young man said, applying it to his own experience. He too had been anointed and felt God's Spirit move in him, but it wasn't like the work that Samuel and these students did.

"Thank you for helping me understand. What is your name?"

"I'm Nathan."

"I'm pleased to have met you, Nathan."

Suddenly there was noise near the gate of the school compound. David leapt to his feet, for he recognized the sound of bronze weapons striking wood. He began running in the direction of the gate, but was stopped when Samuel grabbed his arm.

"Come this way!"

David followed Samuel into a building where they could look out a window to see what was happening.

Outside, five of Saul's soldiers were demanding to be allowed in but one senior student was holding them at bay by simply holding both his hands outstretched. The soldiers were obviously frustrated, but seemed unable to move forward.

"They are here for me," David said.

"Don't worry, nothing can happen to you here," Samuel assured him.

Then a group of students approached the gate and began singing praises to Yahweh. Samuel left David and went out to lead the students in singing and shouting about God's goodness.

David watched in amazement as the soldiers dropped their weapons and began praising God. They lifted their arms and shouted things like:

"All glory to Yahweh, maker of all things."

"Praise be to the Lord of hosts."

"The Lord is good and righteous always."

The soldiers gradually turned and began walking back the way they came, continuing to praise and prophesy.

"What happened?" David asked when Samuel returned.

"The Spirit of God came upon them as a shield," Samuel said. "See, I told you nothing can happen to you here."

After King Saul's men left, Samuel encouraged David to lie down and rest. He was happy to do just that and slept deeply, until there was noise outside once again that woke him. He arose to see that it was dark outside; seemingly the middle of the night.

In the dim light of a torch, David could see more of Saul's men at the gate, again being refused entrance by Samuel's student prophets, who began singing and praising God. Once again, these men were overcome by – David could only guess it was God's Spirit – for they began praising God and gradually turned away from their mission, leaving the school of the prophets in peace once more.

⤜ 19 ⤛

"Must I do everything myself?" Saul demanded of those before the throne the next morning, when the second group of soldiers returned without their weapons. "I go to Naioth myself," Saul said. "All others are against me. Who will go?"

Jeriah was there, beginning his day before the king. "I – I will go, my king."

He didn't want to go, but he felt duty-bound. On the way out, Jeriah recruited a half dozen of his men who were available to serve as a royal guard for the short trip to the small town where Samuel's school of the prophets was located.

They were almost there, when suddenly Saul dismounted his donkey.

"Lord King, what is wrong?" Jeriah asked, concerned, but the king ignored him.

"Great is Yahweh, God of Abraham!" Saul exclaimed, and he raised his arms toward heaven. "Great is Elohim Sabaoth and greatly to be praised. His mercies are everlasting."

Jeriah and the others looked on with concern as Saul continued down the road toward the school of the prophets.

"My King, please come and take your mount again," Jeriah pleaded, but Saul seemed not to hear.

"From everlasting to everlasting, You are God!"

Saul then started to sing a song that Jeriah knew from the feast days. He was seemingly oblivious to all that was around him, continuing to sing and shout praises.

Then Jeriah looked ahead and, standing in the road, was the unmistakable silhouette of the prophet, near the gate of a walled compound Jeriah assumed was the school of the prophets.

Saul saw Samuel then, and his voice became louder and higher and he took off his crown and threw it to the dusty road. Horrified, Jeriah ran and picked it up, trying to get the King to put it on again, but the king was now unclasping his purple cape and then unbuckling his armor, letting it fall to the ground.

"King Saul, please," Jeriah pleaded in vain.

Jeriah could not prevent Saul from removing his tunic, leaving him exposed except for the cloth around his waist. By now, Saul was face-to-face with Samuel. He again said, "Great is Yahweh…" then he collapsed, falling backward, his tall frame stretched out on the road. He was still uttering sounds, but Jeriah couldn't make out words. He ran to the king and bent over him, not knowing what to do.

"Let him be," Samuel said. "The Lord's Spirit has stripped him of his power for his disobedience."

Jeriah looked down at the man who wielded so much power, now rendered stripped of his crown, his armor and even his clothes, babbling incoherently, vulnerable as a baby. Then he thought of the man who was rumored to be Saul's replacement, hiding even now a few cubits away, under the protection of the prophet. Jeriah truly didn't know what to do.

Hours passed and still the king lay on the ground. Occasionally he would speak, sometimes intelligibly, sometimes not. Jeriah and the other men sat off the side of the road under a tree, out of the sun, where some of them slept a little.

Samuel had gone back through the gate. Then the gate opened again and, to Jeriah's surprise, Samuel and David came out together.

Alarmed at seeing the person they had come to kill, Jeriah started to rise, but Samuel raised his hand, and Jeriah sank down again, feeling more than hearing, "God is protecting him."

Jeriah and the others watched helplessly as David and Samuel walked down the road.

Saul finally became aware of his surroundings during the early hours of evening. Jeriah was startled awake when Saul tapped him on the shoulder in the dark.

"We should be going," he said. "The Spirit of God is strong here."

Jeriah and the others roused and began the trip back to Gibeah.

The sun was low in the west and Jonathan worried that he might not be able to find his way in the dark if he didn't find who he was looking for soon.

He topped a small hill and saw a level field stretched out before him with a rocky slope to the right. He did a double take, thinking he saw movement, then decided he was wrong. But then there was movement again and David stood from behind one of the rocks. He walked briskly to meet him.

The two friends embraced briefly.

"What have I done? Why does your father want to kill me?" David asked.

"There's no way you will die. My father tells me everything. I would know if he really meant to kill you."

"I swear, your father knows I have your approval, so he won't tell you his plans. As the Lord lives, there is just one step between me and death!"

"What can I do?"

David's face betrayed his concern, "Tomorrow is the feast of the new moon. Everyone is expected to be at the meal. If he misses me, you could tell him my brother called me to celebrate the feast in Bethlehem with my family and I begged you to let me go.

"He may say, 'That's fine,' then I'll know I'm safe," David continued. "But if he becomes angry, we'll know he intends to harm me. You must be loyal to me, we have a covenant! If I am guilty, kill me yourself!"

Jonathan was alarmed at how distressed David was. "Why would you even suggest that?! If I thought my father wanted to harm you, wouldn't I tell you?"

"How will I know if your father intends me harm?"

Jonathan thought for a moment.

"Let's do this: you hide here day after tomorrow and I'll come to practice archery. I'll bring a servant with me to fetch the arrows. If my father has repented of his desire to kill you, I'll tell my servant, 'The arrows are this way from you,' and if my father truly will kill you, I'll say, 'The arrows are beyond you.'"

"All right. That's fine," David said.

"I assure you my father would not kill you."

"We'll see."

"Everything will be resolved and you can return. I want you to be there. I am to be a father!"

"You are? Congratulations to you and Mara!"

"Yes, and I want you to be there when my first child is born. You will be a second father to him or her! I am determined to convince my father to honor his promises to you and not to harm you."

❦ 20 ❦

The next day would be the feast of the new moon, when there would be feasting and sacrificing for three days. Jeriah, in his clerical work for the court, had been occupied with arrangements with the king's cooks and bakers to ensure that all would be ready in the king's recently completed banquet hall.

When the day arrived, the first events included a parade of the king's professional soldiers. Jeriah noted that David did not ride at the head of his men. Later there was a noon meal where the highest-ranking government officials gathered to feast. The royal family would be there, along with prominent elders who stood before the king.

Jeriah stood guard near the king as always, a javelin in his hand, its shaft resting on the floor, as the men of the royal family and the officers of the court gathered to eat the evening meal on the first day. Jeriah had overseen the seat assignments and saw that David's seat remained empty. The king, however, didn't seem to notice.

On the second day of the feast, that would change.

"Where is the son of Jesse?" Saul asked when the revelers sat at table the next day. Jeriah saw that Saul looked around the table for the answer, but his gaze stopped on Jonathan.

"O King," Jonathan answered. "David asked me for permission to go celebrate the feast with his family in Bethlehem. His brother commanded him to go. He said, 'If I have your approval, let me get away to see my brothers.'"

Saul brought his fist down on the table with all his strength, causing all those gathered to jump. Saul shouted at his firstborn, "You stupid son of a whore!"

All those in the room gasped as the king continued.

"Don't you know you have sided with the son of Jesse to your own shame and that of the mother who bore you? Don't you understand it will be your throne he will take? As long as he is alive your right to the throne is in doubt! I demand that you bring him to me; he must die!"

"Why? What has he done?" Jonathan was shaking and had turned white.

Jeriah looked first at Saul, then back at Jonathan. They were sitting across the table from each other, now staring without blinking at one another, as if the first to look away would lose some contest only the two of them understood.

Finally, Saul turned away and Jonathan looked down in relief, but when he looked up again, Saul had risen from his seat. Jeriah was startled when Saul jerked the javelin from his hand and, in one quick motion, threw it across the table at Jonathan.

Jonathan ducked and fell backward at the same time, turning over his chair. The javelin barely missed him and clattered against the limestone plaster surface of the wall behind him. As soon as he could compose himself, Jonathan stood to his full height, his face red with anger and surprise, but unable to speak.

Jonathan then turned and stalked out of the room.

❧ 21 ☙

Jonathan hurried to avoid being seen by anyone as tears streamed down his face. Finally, around a corner and out of anyone's sight, he clutched his chest with the confusion of grief that came from finding out that, not only would his father truly kill David, he would even kill his firstborn son!

How could I have been so wrong?

Still finding it hard to believe that his father had tried to kill him, he leaned against the wall and let out a long sigh.

He had struggled to ensure that David would be safe ever since he had killed the giant four years ago, but it appeared he had ultimately failed. He had no choice but to face that fact.

It was then he remembered what he had told David he would do.

Azel was returning home when he encountered Jeriah and a platoon of very intense looking soldiers headed the other way.

"Where are you going, Commander?" Azel asked Jeriah. Barely acknowledging him, Jeriah said loudly, "Out of the way, soldier! We are on the king's business!"

Azel was a bit peeved at his brother's impersonal response, but understood that Jeriah was probably protecting him by not revealing their relationship at that moment. Curiously, Azel followed the fast-moving column. Soon he realized they were headed to David's house.

Azel continued following into the courtyard and saw that the front door was standing open. Jeriah paused only a moment before entering, while pounding on the open door. The men with him followed him into the house.

"David! Michal! The king requires your presence!" Jeriah called loudly.

Azel heard no answer. Not wanting to incur his brother's wrath at being sent on a fool's errand, he backed out of the gate and slipped around the corner. He peeked around at the gate of David's house periodically as he listened for muffled sounds of the soldiers tramping up the stairs to search every room.

It wasn't long before the soldiers emerged from the gate, apparently having failed to find David or Michal. They marched away, though not as urgently as they had arrived.

Azel then entered the gate once again and slipped into the house, seeing chaos in every room. Apparently, the occupants had departed quickly, or maybe the soldiers just departed had made the mess for no reason. He knew the feast of the new moon was going on and all the king's family and top officers were expected to be there. Was it possible that David had finally fled once and for all?

Then there was movement. A curtain shifted in the sunlight.

"Who's there?"

As Azel watched, the slight figure of Michal emerged from the curtain, fear showing on her face, her eyes red and swollen.

"Michal, where is David?"

"I don't know, Captain. I hoped you might know."

"How long has he been gone?"

"Since three nights ago. He left to escape the men my father sent to kill him. Could you find out where he went? I would join him, if I knew where he was."

"I can try, but your father already has men looking for him and if they find him first..."

Neither of them needed to finish that thought.

❧ 22 ❧

The next day, Jonathan took a young servant boy to the field where David was hiding, just as they had planned. He played out the little drama with shooting the arrows for the boy to retrieve like he had told David he would. He couldn't see David, but he knew he was there.

"Aren't the arrows beyond you?!" Jonathan called loudly. When the boy brought the arrows back to him, he said, "That is all I feel like doing today. Here, take my bow and quiver. You can return to town." The boy left.

Jonathan then stood looking around, wondering if David would show himself. They had arranged the signal so David would know whether it was safe to return. The call "the arrows are beyond you" meant it was not safe. David might not come out of hiding but simply slip away.

Probably, if David had had his way, he would have already been gone, but Jonathan had insisted that his father would come around and that he ultimately meant David no harm.

How wrong I was!

Presently David signaled tentatively from behind a large boulder at the edge of the field. Jonathan looked one way and then the other to ensure no one was watching, then ran to where David was.

David bowed down to the ground, but Jonathan pulled him to his feet and embraced and kissed him on both cheeks. They both wept, knowing that Saul's jealousy would keep them apart and perhaps even pit them against one another.

"I was sure my father would listen to reason," Jonathan said through his sobs. "But, when the question of your presence came up, he even threw a javelin at me!"

David pulled away and looked at Jonathan with wide eyes. "If he would kill you, then he will not hesitate to kill me."

"I fear that is so," Jonathan answered.

"Go in peace," Jonathan said after bit, trying to be positive, "for we have sworn friendship to one another in the name of Yahweh, who will bear witness between your descendants and mine forever."

Without another word, David embraced him again and left, leaving at a trot, going south.

Jonathan wondered if he would ever see him again.

David had stayed in the field all day without eating and now hunger became a real problem. His strength began to fail just when he needed to move with great speed.

Now, on the road, he hardly knew what direction he had been running, although he was vaguely aware that he was tending southward. He had not gone far when he realized that, in his haste, he had left his gear behind. He had neither cloak to ward off the cold of night, bread to sate his hunger, nor sword to fend off enemies. Saul had spies everywhere and, if he was seen, Saul would order him apprehended or perhaps even killed right there on the road. He had told Jonathan as much.

Barely three miles down the road, he came to Nob. He went immediately to the Tent to find the priest. Ahimelech, who had close ties to Samuel, being the grandson of Eli and, since Ahimelech had sanctified his marriage, David believed he could find help there.

Nob was a small village of merchants and weavers that had grown up around the shrine near the king's city; it was not a walled city with soldiers guarding. Yet David could feel eyes watching as he hurried through the narrow streets to find Ahimelech, although he was probably just being fearful, he reasoned. After all, no one here would have heard Saul's outburst to Jonathan; although the word would undoubtedly spread.

"Lord Ahimelech!" David whispered loudly with obvious urgency when he reached the shrine, the Tent of Meeting which they had brought from Shiloh.

"My son!" Ahimelech emerged through the tent flap, appearing genuinely surprised to see him. The priest, who had his great-grandfather's rotund belly, eyed David curiously. "Why have you come? And why are you alone? Where are the troops in your command?"

"I am on a mission for the king and I cannot share the details," David lied. "My troops will be meeting me later. Do you have a few loaves of bread?"

The priest answered slowly. "We only have the sacred bread which has been removed when fresh bread was put in its place. Perhaps if the men have not slept with women recently, they could be ritually clean and may receive the sacred bread."

"Women have indeed been kept from us, as always when we prepare for battle," David said, at least telling the truth about himself. "Our gear is holy even when we are on missions that are not. All the more so today!"

David thought the pitch of his voice had been a little too high on his last false assertion, and the wise priest looked at him sideways, but said nothing. Yet, slowly he arose and went into a tent near the shrine and soon returned with several loaves of bread wrapped in a white cloth. Solemnly he handed them over to David who took them eagerly.

"Do you also have a sword or a spear I could take with me, for I left so quickly I did not take a weapon, the mission was so urgent."

Ahimelech regarded him with the sideways look once again, while David maintained his gaze without blinking and attempted to smile.

"We have no weapons here, except the sword of Goliath, the Philistine, whom you slew in the Vale of Elah. It's stored in a cloth behind the ephod. You could take that if you want."

"There is no sword like that one!" David exclaimed, a little too enthusiastically he realized. "Give it to me!"

Again, the priest turned slowly and went into the Tent of Meeting. When he returned, he bore the great sword of the giant and David took it and left wordlessly.

ᏇᏥ 23 ᏥᎧ

As he hurried away from the Tent, David saw him.
What is his name?
Doeg. An Edomite responsible for the royal herds. David had only seen him a few times, for he was often away with the flocks and cattle. He tried to avoid making eye contact, but it was too late.

The thin, dark man's black eyes followed him until he rounded a corner and was out of sight. Doeg could tell Saul that he had seen him in Nob and Saul would deduce his direction of travel. David realized he had to hurry and perhaps change his route.

He was out of Nob in less than five minutes and on the road again. He looked to the right, to the left and behind him, then hurried out of town.

Doeg watched through the leaves of a tree as David left Nob by the road that went southwest toward Kiriath-Jearim. He followed a little distance down the road and saw that David was moving very fast, eating from the bread he had gotten from the priest as he went and carrying a large sword. Certainly, King Saul would want to know this. He wondered what had transpired to cause David to be hurrying so.

There could be no doubt that Doeg could benefit by sharing this information with Saul. Abner had made it clear that anyone passing on information about David's movements would be rewarded and anyone aiding David would be viewed as an enemy of the state and treated accordingly.

Doeg wasn't sure what benefits would come to him, but as the chief keeper of the king's cattle, he was not unknown to the king and could hope for a great reward. As an Edomite, his fortunes were at a disadvantage compared to other close servants of the king, who were Hebrews, mostly from Benjamin, the king's own tribe. His responsibilities now were limited to overseeing other non-Israelite herdsmen who kept the royal herds, temporarily centered near Nob. Perhaps this would be his opportunity to garner greater honor.

Doeg saw no reason to continue following David. It was more important that he relay the information to the king in a timely manner. Saul would then marshal troops to deal with his enemy and rival. Besides, night would soon fall, and Doeg had no desire to challenge the champion of Israel, now armed with the sword of the giant.

As the chill of midnight settled around him, David was acutely aware of his aloneness on the road, and he puzzled what his course should be. After seeing the king's herdsman in Nob, he had changed his direction, away from his family home in Bethlehem, where Saul's men might look for him first. Instead, he turned toward the southwest, hurrying to put as much distance as possible between himself and the royal throne in Gibeah. But now, past Kiriath-Jearim and soon to come to Beth-Shemesh, he found himself on the blurred border of the Philistine lands. If he continued on his present course, he would come to Gath by morning.

"Perhaps they will not know me and at least Saul cannot pursue me there," he reasoned to himself. And so, he continued on his course. He left the road and skirted Beth-Shemesh, fearing that other eyes would note his passing. Few in Israel could be trusted now, because Saul's reach was long and his resources deep. Anonymity in Philistia was preferable to celebrity in Israel just now.

David's shepherd's eyes and feet found sure footing in the dark as he passed by the city that was Israel's main outpost against the Philistines. Soon he was back on the road west of the town and passing through the no-man's land of the border between his old enemy and the land of his new one.

❦ 24 ❧

The next day, Jeriah was out on the parade ground and was surprised to see Michal riding in a cart pulled by oxen. She was weeping unconsolably. A driver was with her, one of Saul's shepherds. There were personal belongings in the cart. The driver struck the hindquarters of one of the oxen and the cart slowly rolled away.

"The king is sending her away."

"What?" Jeriah turned to see that it was Joash, his fellow guard who often stood with him beside the king.

"Yes, marrying her off to a man up north; far away from here."

"But how?"

"How can the king just cancel her marriage to David? It's what kings do," Jeriah's fellow soldier shrugged. "Anything they want."

Jeriah continued watching as the cart slowly moved into the distance, Michal's sobs growing faint.

David slowed his pace once he crossed into Philistine territory, knowing that Saul and his troops would not follow him there. He did not expect to attract attention as a lone traveler, so perhaps he could find a place in the bustle of Gath in which to rest and hide.

The terrain was very different from what he was used to. Gradually, the ground had flattened out and was obviously fertile as each step took him closer to the Great Sea. Along the way he saw Philistine farmers in their fields with teams of oxen, plowing in the cool of the morning. They paid him scant attention and he passed slow enough that they would not give him a second thought.

He went through a couple of small villages, even passing one he and his men had destroyed. Few stopped to note his presence. David hoped none would think of him again. He paused only to drink from a well in one of the villages and kept moving.

Finally, he saw the spires of Gath in the distance. The city had formidable walls on which stood soldiers with spears in their hands and iron swords at their sides.

Then he thought of the sword of the Giant, which he was carrying. He stopped, the realization coming to him that to enter Goliath's city with Goliath's sword would certainly prevent him from remaining unnoticed. So, he left the road and, down an embankment, found a stone behind a bush where he felt he could hide the sword until he could return for it. Ironically, he felt less need of it in Philistine territory than he would have in Israel. Confident that the sword would not be found, he returned to the road.

David kept his head down and slowly but steadily walked toward the open gate of the city. Merchants, craftsmen and farmers were passing in and out, beginning a day of commerce, and smoke ascended from several temples of various gods in different parts of the city.

As he entered the city, he noticed the huge wooden gates and remembered the story told by the old men, how the Israelite judge Samson had torn these gates from their hinges with his bare hands and carried them on his back to a hill a mile away, where David supposed many men and oxen were required to bring them back.

David joined the people threading their way both directions on the narrow street which stretched from the gate to the central marketplace. Warily he looked ahead and from side to side, but few noticed him.

He slowed in front of an inn that seemed neither prominent nor the haunt of undesirables. Here, he thought, he might be able to go unnoticed. He had only a few pieces of silver in his pouch and little to trade, but he entered the inn and paid the first night's price.

Once in his tiny room, he set down his scant belongings on the small table. The room was barely big enough for the table, single stool and bedroll. The only air was from a high window which would let in sunlight for only a couple of hours a day. One oil lamp sat on the table.

David still had three loaves of bread from Nob. He unwrapped them and took several bites from one of them, then lay down on the bedroll and slept, though it was still early afternoon.

❦ 25 ❦

Doeg arrived in Gibeah to the court of Saul late in the afternoon. He first found Abner and gave him a report of his activities, then Abner accompanied him into the court. Others in the court looked up to note their arrival, curious about the presence of the king's chief herdsman.

There were but two seats in court: besides the royal throne, a backless chair sat at a table where the royal recorder was taking down the proceedings for the official record. The ground was covered by a variety of colorful rugs and the portico was draped with bright scarves which were gifts of the various tribes of Israel and neighboring kingdoms desiring to curry favor or cement alliances. Torches of bronze ringed the center of the portico around the throne, the most opulent object in view. It was made of polished wood with golden accents which caught the torchlight and seemed to glow with an inner light, even in the daylight streaming in intermittently through the leaves of the Tamarisk tree waving in the breeze.

Doeg watched Abner sizing up the gathering of jealous courtiers, each scheming to gain favor with the king, who sat listening to one subject droning on about some slight.

He was rarely present for the royal court, but Doeg knew a few of the people. He recognized Sheba, a Benjamite like Saul, who was dressed in threadbare finery beyond his means. He was whispering loudly to a couple of men who were listening closely as if they weren't sure of his meaning, but were eager to be close to one who was close to the king.

Also present was Shimei, another of Saul's Benjamite advisors, standing more or less alone, looking furtively toward the throne and toward the others gathered nearby.

Doeg also knew Saul's third son Malchishua, dressed in his military uniform as a newly minted Captain of a thousand in the army of Israel. The young prince, who had inherited much of his father's good looks and kingly stature, might have a promising future in the young monarchy, but was just now having his ear bent by some old man Doeg didn't know.

King Saul, though now in his sixties, had lost none of his regal bearing and commanding presence, Doeg saw. He watched him for a while, trying to judge the mood of the king. Doeg had heard enough to know that Saul could be volatile, and he felt a sudden flush of fear, but his news would be good, so he reassured himself that all would be well.

When Saul finished the business with the subject who had been before him, he suddenly addressed the entire court in a loud voice. All the men involuntarily took a step back.

"Why have you all conspired against me you men of Benjamin?" Saul began. "Will the son of Jesse give you all fields and vineyards?"

The king spat the words "son of Jesse" out of his mouth. Rather than say his son-in-law's name, the king contemptuously referred to him as the son of his father, as if the champion of Israel was a child. The assembled courtiers were unable to speak out of fear and uncertainty about what Saul was referring to, exactly. Doeg was especially confused since he had not been present for the feast from which David had fled, but he had known something was amiss when he saw David in Nob, absent from the royal festivities.

"Will he commission you all commanders of hundreds and commanders of thousands?" Saul continued, looking around at the men standing before him. No one dared answer.

"My daughter hides the son of Jesse from me and my son makes a covenant with him and no one tells me! Not one of you is concerned about ME or tells me that my son abets the son of Jesse, who certainly lies in wait for me this very day!"

Doeg felt a nudge from Abner. When Doeg looked at him, Abner motioned for him to step forward and speak. Doeg's eyes widened with unspoken questions about Abner's wisdom, but Abner silently insisted that now was the time Doeg should speak.

"I saw the son of Jesse!" Doeg's voice sounded far away to his own ears. "Lord king…" he added, bowing belatedly.

"Where?" Saul demanded.

"He came to Ahimelech at Nob. The priest gave him bread and the sword of Goliath the Philistine and he inquired of the Lord for him."

Doeg waited nervously while Saul digested the information. It seemed to Doeg that a dark shadow passed over Saul's face and his eyes flashed. His face grew redder with each passing moment.

"Bring Ahimelech here to me!" the king commanded loudly. "And bring the whole family of his father Ahitub the priest. Bring them all here!"

Abner took Doeg by the arm and they left the tent. Doeg was shaking.

"You did well," Abner said. "Now you can ingratiate yourself to the king further by carrying out his command to bring the priest and his family to Gibeah. I can detail some soldiers to serve you."

"Lord Abner, I can use my shepherds," Doeg replied. "They are perfectly capable of rounding up priests."

Abner regarded the Edomite a moment then said, "Very well. See to it."

⇜ 26 ⇝

Doeg was soon on the road to Nob. He was excited that he had been the one to convey the message to the king that David had fled to Nob and been aided by the priests. Soon he had covered the short distance from the king's court in Gibeah to Nob, where he called his shepherds and herdsmen together, all that could be spared from the fields.

"The king has given us a job to do," Doeg told the assembled shepherds, most of whom were descendants of Esau, like himself, or Bedouins from the eastern desert. "We must bring the priest Ahimelech and his father's whole family before the king in Gibeath-Saul." Doeg purposely called the Benjamite town by the name that was common now to honor Israel's king.

"And do not fail to strap on your swords!"

"Where is Ahimelech?" demanded Doeg of the first white-clothed Levite they encountered near the cult Tent in Nob.

"He is in his house," the man replied, with a curious look on his face.

"Take us to him immediately!"

Wide-eyed, the Levite beckoned for them to follow him and turned to pass by the Tent. They stopped in front of a low stone house.

"Ahimelech! Come out! Your king calls!" Doeg shouted, his fist loudly pounding on the door.

A long moment passed before there was any movement, so Doeg pounded on the door again. Finally, the wooden door opened slowly on its leather hinges. Ahimelech's heavy-set frame appeared. He looked out, taking in the scene of the large number of men in front of his house.

"What brings the king's servants to your servant's humble home?" Ahimelech said, deferentially.

"The king commands you to appear before him, with all your father's house as well."

Doeg then motioned to a couple of herdsmen, who happily grabbed the fat priest by the arms and pulled him from the doorway. Doeg nodded again and more herdsmen entered the house and drew out all that were within. They were a pathetic group of mostly women and children, whimpering and balling. Doeg already disliked them.

By now it was late afternoon, and the members of the priest's family were herded by Doeg and his men as they might drive stubborn cattle, giving them no time to wander off or stop for refreshment and letting them taste the end of a crooked staff if they got out of line.

Ahimelech tried to encourage his family, but he knew his worst fears were likely to be realized. His wives and children clung to one another and scarcely made a sound. Ahimelech knew it would be him whom the king would question.

Abiathar's heart was pounding, even as he gave his weeping mother an arm to lean on. Though the men from Saul had not stated the reason they were called before the throne, their demeanor could only predict the worst. His father, Ahimelech, was being rushed forward at the head of the procession and Abiathar didn't know why, although he had seen his father's face display an uncharacteristic fatalism when the men from Saul appeared.

Abiathar, himself a priest though barely 20, did not have the extra weight his obese father had, and he worried about his father's ability to withstand the trip of three miles at the pace they were being forced to walk. His younger brother and sister were in tow, along with his mother's servant girl and nanny. Also with them were Abiathar's cousins, the sons of his late uncle Ahijah and their wives and children.

The men driving them had their swords at the ready, so to try to slip away in the trees close to the road would be suicide, but Abiathar continued to look for an opportunity to save his family.

None would come.

⤐ 27 ⤏

"Grandmother, why did they take my papa away?"

"I don't know, Anah," Raquel answered her small grandson. The elderly woman struggled to rise from a low stool to look out the window at the empty street in Nob. "Let's pray he will return soon."

Anah's papa was Raquel's son, given to her by her husband, the late Zedekiah, the Levite who had served at Shiloh so many years ago. Anah's mother was also dead, and the young boy spent most of his time with Raquel, his grandmother, while his father was busy with the work of a Levite ministering in the Tent. He had been included in the group that had been forced to walk to Gibeah by the rough men who had come looking for High Priest Ahimelech.

Though her words and tone to her grandson were positive, Raquel worried because of the threat posed by the armed men who forced their men to leave, walking to the king's court.

She had no idea what this was about.

The shepherds forced the priest and his family to cover the three miles to Gibeah in record time and were ushered into the king's court with their captives as the sun was setting.

"Listen now, son of Ahitub," Saul began with a nasty sneer.

"Yes, my lord king," Ahimelech answered meekly, yet he feared nothing he said would make any difference.

"Why do you conspire against me and aid the son of Jesse? Did you and he not work together against me, giving him bread and a sword and asking guidance of the Lord for him?"

Ahimelech was not sure he heard Saul correctly.

"Who of all your servants is as loyal as David, the king's son-in-law and captain of his bodyguard and highly respected and loved by all the king's family," Ahimelech answered. "How would I know I should not help him? And do you think that day was the first time I inquired of the Lord for David? Of course not!"

Ahimelech thought his answer very reasonable, but he could see little of reason in the king's dark eyes. He continued anyway: "Let not the king accuse his servant or any of my father's house of any wrongdoing for your servant knew nothing of the whole affair."

Ahimelech saw he might just as well have saved his breath.

"You will surely die, you traitor, and everyone in your father's house!"

There was a weak cry from the knot of his family behind him, but Ahimelech could think of nothing to do or say.

"Jeriah, kill them all!" Saul ordered the soldier standing at his right side. Doeg saw the man's eyes grow wide as he turned and looked first at Ahimelech in his white linen priest's tunic and then back at Saul.

"But my lord king, he is a priest of Yahweh!" the frightened warrior, Jeriah, said.

Saul turned from him in frustration.

"Then you!" he said, pointing at Doeg. "You and your shepherds are not sons of Jacob. You do not fear Yahweh's priests!"

Doeg recognized instantly that this was his chance to establish his reputation in Saul's kingdom. He drew his sword and looked at his herdsmen who stood by.

"Kill them!"

The other herdsmen drew their swords and attacked the little knot of terrified, defenseless people in the center of the court. One by one they fell and Doeg himself ran Ahimelech through, which pleased Saul, he saw.

❦ 28 ❧

When Abiathar saw his father fall, he turned to protect his mother, standing nearby, but he was too late. Another of the king's shepherds had struck her and she fell. Other members of his family were set upon by still other of the rough men.

Realizing there was nothing he could do and knowing he must act, he picked up a colorful rug from the floor and threw it over the head of a shepherd who was coming toward him with sword raised. He rushed past the confused man, through the curtains and into the dark porch. In the confusion, he was able to find the door.

Once outside, he startled other guards, but they did not know enough to try to stop him, so he was able to run past the gate and into the darkness.

Abiathar's young legs carried him swiftly back over the road whence they had just come, where he acted with a singleness of purpose he hadn't known before.

He knew exactly where it would be; where it always was. He wasted no time going to the Tent where he scooped up the ephod with its magical stones through which God spoke his will. He didn't take time to get anything else.

As he exited the Tent, he could hear commotion on the road into the town and could see torchlight illuminating the taller buildings.

He turned and fled in the other direction, out of the town which had always been his home; the town that was the home of the cursed line of priests, descendants of Eli, of whom he was now the last. He knew he must get as far away as he could, but did not know where he should go.

Only when he was far enough away that he knew he was safe did he stop to weep for his family.

At that late hour, Doeg and his herdsmen went again to Nob and dragged men, women and children out of their houses and ran them through with their swords. Many screamed and tried to run, but Doeg's men caught them and cut them down until no resident of Nob was left alive. They did not even spare their livestock. They finished by burning the town at dawn, all its buildings and the bodies of its inhabitants, in order to permanently erase all traces of these descendants of Eli from the earth.

Not all were descendants of Eli, Doeg realized. One old woman lay on the ground with the body of a young boy beside her. Doeg assumed they were Levites, the second-class citizens of the religion of Yahweh.

❦ 29 ❧

David had slept long and well and awoke before dawn. Shortly, he went out of the inn and down the street to one of Gath's outdoor markets, hoping he could trade a loaf of bread for some dates or raisins, something to give some variety to his diet, which was likely to continue being lean for some time. If he could find employment, he would look forward to being able to afford mutton.

How he missed the abundance and variety of food in the king's house: the beef and lamb; the onions and the bread and pita, sopped in olive oil, the figs and dates without number and wine in abundance. He nearly swooned as he remembered, and his stomach complained bitterly.

The sun shone brightly on the plain so near the sea, and it cast hard shadows against the cloth canopies and baked-mud walls of the market where scores of vendors hawked their wares. He hurried past a booth with the carcass of a pig hanging from a post. Pork was forbidden by the Torah, but there was no need to consider it, for the aroma of roast mutton was strong in the air. But he knew he would not be able to trade his loaf of bread for much meat at all. Better to trade for dried fruit that could sustain him for several days than a morsel of flesh that would be gone in one meal.

His eye was caught by a farmer's booth which displayed large bunches of grapes and figs, some fresh and some dried. As he approached, he could almost taste the sweetness of the fruit, so he didn't see that someone in the market had noticed him.

"Isn't that the one who killed the champion?"

David whirled around to see a couple of soldiers, one of whom had a sword drawn.

"Yeah, this is the one of whom they sing, 'Saul has slain his thousands, but David his ten thousands,'" said the other. "Doesn't look too tough now, without his sword, does he?"

David thought of Goliath's sword which he had hidden so it wouldn't attract attention. Panicked, he then turned to run through the crowd but was stopped by another soldier standing behind him. Something crashed into the back of his head and all went dark.

❦ 30 ❦

The report was difficult to believe, but the messenger assured King Achish that it was true: David, the champion of Israel, was in his dungeon. He had been recognized in the marketplace by soldiers who had served in the Hebrew campaigns.

Achish had given orders that when the young warrior awoke from the unconsciousness administered by his alert soldiers that he should be immediately brought before the throne. Achish had many questions for him, if this was indeed the David that made his most hardened soldiers nervous when they heard his name. Why was he here in Philistine territory, alone and unarmed? David was known to be a skillful commander and had been a valuable asset to Achish's enemy, Saul, king of the Hebrews.

Achish didn't have to wait long. Soon word came that David was awake and Achish confirmed his order to bring him immediately before him.

When the throne room door opened, Achish looked with ill-concealed curiosity. The man that was brought before him did not inspire confidence. Instead of the proud bearing of a warrior, he cowered and simpered and mumbled incoherent babble. His hair was mussed as if it had not been attended for days and the smell of dust and sweat were upon him.

"Are you David, champion of the Hebrews?" Achish asked.

The man before him did not answer. In fact he did not appear to have heard, so Achish repeated the question.

"Are you David, who slew the giant at Socoh in the Valley of Elah?"

At that the young man dropped to his hands and knees and began a nonsensical chant in a sing-song voice that was high-pitched and scratchy while he moved his finger over the stone floor as if writing something.

Achish watched in curious amazement, as did the soldiers who had brought him from the prison cell. As the King watched more closely, the man kept his head down, singing and writing on the floor. Then incredibly, a sticky, shiny substance strung down from the man's face.

Is he drooling?

Suddenly, he jumped to his feet and shouted something Achish didn't understand, then ran over to a pillar and began writing with his finger again. Getting more and more agitated, he ran to another pillar and sang more rapidly as he continued to write, sometimes on the pillars, sometimes in the air.

"Bring him back!" Achish shouted to his perplexed guards.

When the soldiers approached him, he jumped past them and mounted a platform where a knot of courtiers sat. They scattered as he climbed over the seats, continuing to sing and gesture with his hands. The soldiers followed him and, with difficulty, brought him back before Achish, somewhat subdued, though they couldn't stop him from his high-pitched singing of nonsense.

"Once more," Achish said loudly and slowly. "Are you David?"

The young man looked up, but seemed to be looking past Achish and now became subdued to the point of being transfixed on something no one else saw. His singing now was just an occasional high-pitched dip and slur.

"Look at this man!" Achish demanded of the soldiers. "He's insane! Do I not have enough madmen around me that you bring me another? Throw this wretch out into the street and trouble me no more!"

Achish kept a stern look on his face as his men took David away, but he was smiling on the inside.

❧

David continued to feign madness until he was down the road some distance away from the door of the royal court of Gath, where the soldiers had unceremoniously dumped him. They had been especially rough, since they were still certain they knew who he was, but the king had ordered them to eject him from the royal palace. Though they had provoked him, David knew better than to react, and had continued his ruse to preserve his life.

He returned to the inn and gathered his meager belongings. *How foolish I was to think I could remain anonymous in the home of Goliath!*

He still needed food, but he must return to the road where potential enemies were surely looking for him. David knew that he would now have to find a place to hide deep in the wilderness where Saul would be unlikely to look.

That meant Judah.

Among his own tribe, where he was a favorite son, fewer people might be eager to ingratiate themselves to the throne by revealing his location and movements. He might be able to receive aid and sanctuary in Judah more than anywhere else, since his idea of being anonymous in Philistia didn't work out so well.

Ironically, in passing from Gath through the heart of Judah in search of a hiding place, David passed very near Elah Valley, the site of his triumph over the Philistine champion, Goliath. How different was that day from his plight now. He was praised and was able to lead the pursuit of the panicked Philistine army as they fled in disarray all the way back to their borders. But now he was on the run himself, like a hunted animal, not knowing who he could trust or where he could find refuge.

He remembered a place near Adullam that was a good possibility. It was in a thick wood in the western edge of Judah, many miles from the territory of Benjamin and the court of Saul. The area was full of caves. He could surely get lost there.

❦ 31 ❦

Word of the massacre of the priests spread throughout Israel quickly, so that the next day it reached the ears of Samuel in Ramah. It had now been years since he had seen Saul or had a word from the Lord for him.

And so, he thought, *the old prophecy given to me when I was but a boy concerning the sons of Eli is fulfilled once again.*

Jeriah stood looking at the smoldering rubble that had been the town of Nob. There were burnt bodies everywhere. He struggled to keep from gagging. Doeg and his Edomite shepherds had done a thorough job of punishing this Levite town for the crime of aiding David.

The men under his command were performing clean-up operations. It was slow going, so Jeriah walked the perimeter of the town to survey the damage. As he rounded a corner, he was shocked to see the Tent of Meeting. It had not been burned! There was perhaps some singeing of some of the outer covering, but it was surprisingly intact. He would relate this information to Abner or Saul himself. Surely, they would want to relocate the Tent to another Levite city.

"There is a Levite city, and it is near to Ramah," Abner did not need to tell Saul that Ramah was where Samuel lived, but Samuel had not been to Gibeah to stand in the king's presence for years. "Gibeon. Perhaps moving the Tent there would be to Samuel's liking," Abner suggested, knowing that his cousin was desperate to hear from Samuel and his messages from the Lord.

Saul considered the suggestion. "That is a good idea. See it done!" As Abner turned to leave, Saul spoke again. "But you must rid Gibeon of all Gentiles. It won't do to have it contaminated by those who are not of Israel. And that way we will avenge their deception of Joshua."

"It will be done," Abner said.

Nobody needed any explanation. The ruse of the Gibeonites, pretending to be from a far country to avoid being overrun by Joshua and the invading Hebrews, had put him in an impossible situation. He kept his word to not attack the town in the shadow of Mizpah, but Israel had long forced the Gibeonites to labor for them. Now Saul would take revenge on Joshua's behalf.

Two days later, Abner led a company from Saul's army the handful miles north and west to Gibeon. They had to march through Ramah to get there.

Once there, they drove the non-Israelite population to the town square and put them to the sword. Every Gibeonite they could find, they killed, to exact retribution for their deception of Joshua hundreds of years before; at least that justified it in Abner's mind and that was enough.

Samuel watched with mixed emotions as the men Saul sent brought the Tent of Meeting through Ramah on their way to Gibeon. The town was one of the Levite cities set aside by Joshua, but it had always had a large non-Israelite population because Joshua had sworn to them they would not be harmed. True, they had deceived Joshua in order to extract that promise, but Samuel felt that didn't warrant the massacre that Saul and meted out to them.

He had grown up around Yahweh's Tent when he was raised and mentored by Eli, and by some miracle it had now survived the burning of both Shiloh and Nob. He would be glad to close his life as it had begun, ministering at the Tent.

❦ 32 ❦

David was aware of a cave in a tangle of forest well east of Gath that was so remote he hoped he would not be found by Saul and his spies. He was able to make the trip from Gath overnight, but had to wait until it was daylight to find his way under the dense canopy.

The huge sword of Goliath came in handy as he hacked his way through thick underbrush to the place where he believed the cave was. Along the way, he noted sources of water and places he could likely snare birds and deer for meager meals.

It was about midday and a rare gentle snow had begun to fall when he found the cave. Its mouth was partially covered with underbrush and tall grass. It appeared no one had been here for months, which made it perfect for his needs. He gingerly pushed aside a branch of a large bush in front of the mouth of the cave and looked into the darkness. He stepped inside, being very quiet because he didn't want to startle any animals that might have made the cave their home.

Then he was startled himself by a sound outside the cave. It sounded like two animals fighting. He was drawn to the noise, following the sound through the falling snow with the sword stretched out before him.

The sounds of struggle drew him to the side of a depression in the ground that looked like an old animal trap. He looked down and saw a lion with a male's short mane in desperate combat with a man. They were rolling on the bottom of the pit and both were crying out in desperation. Before David could speak or do anything, the man scrambled onto the back of the lion and stabbed him multiple times in the neck and shoulders with a long-bladed knife. When the lion finally stopped thrashing, the man fell back, breathing rapidly and deeply.

"Shalom. Are you all right?" David called to him.

The man was suddenly alert again and held the knife up as if to defend himself, if the owner of the voice was a threat.

"Don't be afraid. I won't hurt you. Are you all right?" David repeated, seeing blood on the man's clothes. "You're hurt. Let me help you."

David began climbing down the steep sides of the pit where the man lay beside the lion he had killed.

"I'm David. Who might you be?"

"Benaiah, son of Jehoiada."

"Looks like the lion got you on your leg."

"It's nothing."

"Perhaps, nevertheless we should clean the wound. I saw water nearby," David began. "But I have nothing to carry water in. I'll have to think of something."

The man shivered. It wasn't terribly cold, but the light snow had made him damp.

"Come to the cave. You need to be out of the weather," David said.

"That's where I met this fellow," Benaiah said, gesturing to the lion's corpse.

With difficulty, David helped the man climb out of the pit and hobble over to the cave.

"Wait here," David instructed him when he had helped him just inside the mouth of the cave. "I'll return shortly with water and perhaps food as well."

"You said you are David?"

"Yes."

"Saul's champion?"

David paused before saying, "I was, but no longer. I am not welcome in the king's house."

"You, too?" Benaiah laughed. "My family is not approved by the king as well. Something about our being of Judah and not wanting the king to be the king. We never said any such thing, but the king would not be persuaded."

"I know all too well what you mean," David said. "I guess I'd better go get that water."

❦ 33 ❦

They left the grass and the brush in front of the mouth of the cave, but over the next couple of weeks, David and Benaiah made the cave livable as best they could. There was plenty of game in the forest and there was fish in nearby streams, as well as berries and figs in the forest, so food was not a problem.

When Benaiah was able, David sent him on an errand. Even though Benaiah's family was not favored by the king, he was not a threat to the throne the way David was perceived to be, so he should be able to travel without much danger.

Benaiah wasted no time getting on the road.

After being alone for several days, David was just coming out of the cave when he was startled by the sound of someone trudging through the leaves on the forest floor.

He drew back into the cave to see who – or what – was there. Presently three figures came into view, one of whom was riding a donkey. Suddenly he recognized the person leading the donkey.

"Father!" he called as he came out of the cave.

David ran and embraced his father, then lifted his mother off the donkey and gave her a bear hug. Then he turned to his new friend, Benaiah.

"Thank you," David said, grasping his hand.

David ushered his elderly parents into the cave to the area he had prepared for them and invited them to sit on rough-hewn benches or stones.

"It's very rustic, I'm afraid," he apologized. "But before much longer I want to move you out of the country."

"Oh, where?" Jesse asked.

"I thought you could find shelter with our cousins in Moab. You will be safe there until Saul is no longer a threat."

"I don't know if they will know or remember us. My grandmother left there when she was a young widow."

"I feel sure some distant cousin will have a place for you," David said confidently. "Anyway, I fear it isn't safe for anyone close to me as long as Saul is alive."

"Speaking of that," Benaiah said.

David looked at each of them, wondering what was next.

"Your brothers and sisters will be coming soon," David's mother said.

"Coming here?" David responded.

"And they may bring others with them," Benaiah said. "There are many who feel it is no longer safe for them in Saul's kingdom."

David looked around them at the cave and said, "How big is this cave? I guess we're about to find out how many it can accommodate."

❦ 34 ❧

Jeriah left the court for the day, going to the family compound he and Shelomith shared with Azel and Dani. He went through the gate and saw that the door to Azel's house was standing open, which seemed odd.

"Azel! Dani!"

Getting no answer, he went inside. There were things strewn about the floor as if they had departed in a hurry. The furniture was all still there, but many other items, such as food containers and clothing, were gone.

"What's happening?"

It was Shelomith, who followed him through the open front door.

"It appears they are gone."

"Gone? Where? Why?"

"Gone to join David, I suppose. Wherever he is."

"I wondered why I hadn't seen Dani today," Shelomith said, looking around. "But I was busy enough I didn't stop to check."

"They must have left during the night. I wonder if Azel is the only one of David's cohort to desert?"

"What will happen to him?"

"If he's caught, he'll be executed as a deserter."

Shelomith looked as if she would cry. "What can we do?" she asked.

"I don't know. I guess I need to find him and try to talk some sense into him."

It was the beginning of the next day and King Saul had not yet entered the court. Jeriah was finishing a few clerical items before the scheduled petitioners were allowed in, when Prince Jonathan entered the court.

"My prince, the king has yet to arrive from his home," Jeriah said.

"I'm not looking for him. I need to talk to you."

Jeriah feared he knew what Jonathan wanted to discuss.

"It isn't widely known, but several members of David's command deserted last night," Jonathan began, then quickly continued as if he knew what Jeriah was thinking. "Your brother was one of them. Don't worry. I've taken care of it."

"What? How have you taken care of it?"

"I signed hardship passes for each of them."

"What kind of hardship?"

"For most it was a death in the family or the family needed them for the harvest," Jonathan shrugged as if his lie didn't matter. "The king doesn't bother with day-to-day transactions among the men. The only person who might notice is..."

"Abner," Jeriah finished his sentence for him.

"Right, though he walks on eggshells as much as anyone around my father. I hope he'll prefer not calling attention to one more thing that would upset the king."

"I need to go to try to bring him back."

Jonathan looked at Jeriah through narrowed eyes. "Is he likely to want to return?"

"He needs to return! My brother can't be a deserter."

"I wish it was that black and white, but things are a good bit more murky than that. If you want to try to find him, I'll make your excuses to Abner and assign someone to stand before the king in your place. I give you my word I'll make sure no one is sent to bring the deserters back."

Jeriah was mystified by this statement, but he didn't feel like he could pursue it further with the prince.

Jeriah took the prince up on his offer of leave, so as soon as he could get away, he went to Mizpah, assuming Azel would go to their ancestral home. He found his uncle Jacob in the forge, along with his oldest son, Elihu. He was surprised how much his uncle had aged.

"Have you seen Azel?" Jeriah demanded.

"He came here, but only to gather some things they still had here, then he, Dani and the boys left yesterday."

Jeriah scowled. "Did he say where they were going?"

"No. I assumed they were going back to Gibeah."

"That's not likely. He's likely joining David in hiding."

"The giant killer?"

"Yes. The rumor is Samuel anointed him to be king in Saul's place."

"Why would he do that?"

"Samuel made a very public pronouncement that Saul was rejected by God, because he didn't carry out the ban on the Amalekites."

Jacob's face betrayed that he didn't fully understand, so he went back to working on the tool he was shaping. "I don't suppose the king is very tolerant of rivals?"

"No. Not at all," Jeriah answered.

"So, if you find Azel," Jacob said, "tell him his Uncle Jacob said to watch his back."

Jeriah nodded and left the forge.

Jeriah stayed with his extended family for the evening meal. It brought back a lot of memories for him of nights spent there around the table when he and Azel were boys and their mother and father were still alive.

But now Jacob was the patriarch, at least for a while longer. He moved slowly and Jeriah noted that his legs would not bend like they needed to.

Ophrah, Jacob's first wife, was quiet. Her daughter, Talia, had married long ago, and lived in another town.

Tzipporah, Jacob's second wife, was obviously favored, and with her two strong sons, dominated the conversation.

"How is the business?" Jeriah asked, referring to the forge that had been built by his grandfather.

"We are still hampered by the Philistine presence," Elihu answered. "But they don't bother us too much. We are able to do pretty much what we want."

"Do they still require that you pay them taxes?"

"Sometimes, but they have reduced the number of soldiers stationed here. I guess it became too expensive to maintain a full garrison."

"We are able to hide some of our activities from them," Shallam, Tzipporah's second son, added. "We simply transact certain business at night."

"And where is your sister?"

"Aisha is married," Tzipporah answered. "She lives in Beeroth, near to Ramah."

"It's hard for me to think of her married," Jeriah said. "I still remember her as a little girl."

"And I remember when YOU were born!" Jacob laughed. "Such is the circle of life, nephew."

❦ 35 ❧

Azel was accustomed to marching long distances, so the trip was not a problem for him, but some of the women and children were suffering with weariness and thirst or hunger. They had left with short notice and he knew Dani was bound to be weary and little Adriel was whining. Their second son was likely as bored as tired, for he had boundless energy, but the trip was long for a seven-year-old.

At 15, Eliel was well able to help his parents manage his younger brother, but the younger sibling would only regard Eliel's commands as suggestions, considering himself to be just short of Eliel's equal. Eliel's attempts to discipline his brother usually devolved into fighting. Azel then had no choice but to step in.

Their party was almost 50 people, all of whom believed they would be in danger from Saul if they remained in their homes.

David's brothers and sisters and their spouses and children were the core of their band, but there were also several like Azel, who had served in Saul's army, but feared their loyalty to David would cause the king to kill them as he desired to kill David. Azel saw the massacre of the priests at Nob as proof that Saul would kill anyone connected to or helping David.

They were deep in a remote forest and Azel wondered how anyone could find the way, but David's older brother Eliab seemed confident in where they were going.

"There," Eliab said more than once along the way, pointing to a piece of brightly colored cloth on a tree limb. "This is the way. Father has marked it for us."

The group was slowed by the donkeys and goats they had brought with them, which were loaded with whatever they had been able to bring, ranging from eating utensils to clothing to carpentry tools. Azel and the others had also brought their weapons. Azel figured there were at least 15 experienced fighters in the group, including David's brothers and nephews. That could be important if Saul decided to pursue them.

About when Azel believed they were getting close, David appeared. He stepped from behind a tree and stood in front of them. Azel saw that he was lean and tanned and more muscular than before. He didn't look hungry, but his life here was obviously not as comfortable as before.

David embraced his brothers and sisters, and then acknowledged Azel and others from his former command.

"It is good to have all of you. I feel safer already," he joked. "I'm afraid I don't have very luxurious accommodations, however."

"God is with you," Azel called out, "and we are with you, wherever you lead."

Some of the party cheered and applauded, but David turned toward Azel and, to his surprise, looked solemn as he answered, "Thank you. Thank you all. And it's good to see you," he said, looking directly at Azel. "I now have someone who can keep our weapons sharp and in good repair!"

Azel smiled at that.

"Now let us see your new home!" David said loudly and led the way to the cave.

The Cave of Adullam turned out to have a lot of space, with passageways going in many directions and little natural rooms to the side of the passages, making natural places for the refugees to settle.

Azel and Dani found a corner of the cave that they and the boys could call home for whatever time they would stay there.

It was indeed rustic, as David had said. They were still arranging their bedrolls, when the hero of Elah appeared.

"Azel," he whispered, and Azel turned to face him.

"What is it, commander?"

"I have heard nothing about Michal since I left. Is she well? Is my father leaving her in peace?"

"You haven't heard? I am sorry to be the one to tell you, the king sent her away to be the wife of Paltiel of Gallim!"

David's face fell. Azel was unsure if he saw sadness or anger in David, but the hero quickly recovered.

"Well, thank you. I guess I shouldn't be surprised."

David turned and slowly walked away, but as he went, he kicked a loose stone that was in his way.

<h1 style="text-align:center">❦ 36 ❦</h1>

Jeriah had thought he would try to find Azel to talk some sense into him, but as he left Mizpah, he realized he had no way of knowing where David would be hiding. Presumably it would be in Judah somewhere, because he was from Judah and had sympathizers there, but that was a huge area to search. And some of the terrain was very forbidding, with harsh deserts and thick forests and almost every conceivable climate in between.

No, he couldn't just go looking without knowing where to look, and that meant he needed intelligence. Then he realized that Abner had foreseen this need and he would have spies reporting to him. This made him turn back toward Gibeah, for he had no doubt that Abner's spies would be able to pinpoint David's hiding place before long.

Somehow word spread and more people found their way to the cave of Adullam until there were more than 100 men, plus wives and children, camped in and around the cave. All of them had some reason for fearing Saul and favoring David.

The men hunted most days, for keeping all these people fed was a constant crisis. David organized division of labor for both men and women, so everyone knew their jobs and everyone was taken care of.

David assigned Benaiah to begin training the men in the ways of war. Azel took a supporting role in training those who had not already been in the army.

No one asked why they needed such training.

"But why does Eliel need to be trained in war?" Dani asked Azel at one point.

"Because if Saul pursues us, we will need every available hand on his sword."

"But isn't it enough that you are in danger? Must our firstborn be exposed as well?"

"It is the responsibility of a man to defend his family and his community. Eliel needs to learn this lesson as much as anyone else."

Dani didn't protest again, but her mother's heart ached as she watched her husband and son attend to training for war. She pulled Adriel a bit closer.

"We cannot continue without supplies," Benaiah said as David, Azel and a few others held an impromptu council under the forest canopy one day. "We need tools and weapons and foodstuffs we cannot obtain from the land."

"We could raid some Philistine towns," David suggested, recalling the raids they had made when in Saul's army. "They often have surprising wealth."

The others nodded. They would be able to get many things they needed that way.

"Locate a good candidate and we'll plan a raid for day-after-tomorrow," David said.

"It will be done," answered Benaiah.

The raid on the small Philistine town close to the border claimed by Israel's tribe of Judah yielded tremendous supplies and equipment which the growing band of outcasts needed. More people joined David's fugitives every day.

With the wealth of supplies and pack animals acquired in the raid, there was much to do to prepare for the journey. All day they labored to pack and prepare, but when night fell, the women prepared a fine feast and, as the men sat around the fire, David took a lyre which was part of the booty from the Philistine town and sang a song that had been on his heart.

Plead my cause, O Lord
With them that strive with me:

Fight against them that
Fight against me.

Take hold of shield and buckler,
And stand up for mine help.

Draw out also the spear,
And stop the way against them
Into my soul,
You are my salvation.

Let them be confounded and put to shame
That seek after my soul:
Let them be turned back and brought to confusion
That devise my hurt.

For without cause have they hid for me
Their net in a pit,
Which without cause
They have digged for my soul.

David finished singing and coughed a little. "Oh, how I would love to drink from the well near the gate of Bethlehem right now!"

No one said anything, so Azel wasn't sure if David was homesick or thirsty. He decided he could be both.

❧ 37 ☙

That night, when all the others had gone to bed with full stomachs, Eliel and two of his friends about his age sat on their bedrolls and talked in low whispers.

"I'm thinking we should go to Bethlehem and get the water for the commander," said Adino.

"It would be dangerous," warned 17-year-old Shammah. "The Philistines are camped there right now."

The others knew it was true. The Philistines had recently invaded Judah and were at this moment camped between Jebus and Bethlehem, very near the well which David had mentioned.

"But we could do it," insisted the 18-year-old everyone called Adino, though his name was Jashobe'am.

"It would honor our commander," Eliel commented.

A few minutes later, the three young men slipped away from the encampment.

The three young men, dressed in cloaks to hide their weapons, went north and east in the valley of Rephaim, skirting very near the Philistine encampment.

Dawn came quickly and they dared not go all the way to Bethlehem in daylight, so they stopped in a small village to barter for some fresh raisins to go with leftover dried mutton they had brought with them and then went north. When they came to the approach to Bethlehem, they found a place where they could rest in the shade of a large rock. They would continue on only when it was dark.

In the darkness, they could see the fires of the Philistine camp, perhaps 500 cubits away. They were north of Bethlehem, and they knew the well was near. That is why the Philistines were camped there.

Silently they looked at one another in the light of the quarter moon. Adino nodded and they began to walk. There was a single tree beside the well, but they saw no one.

"Who's there?" came a deep voice from a dark hulking shape walking toward them.

"Weary travelers needing water," Eliel answered in his weakest voice. Eliel and Shammah walked in the direction of the questioner. They had already discussed what they would do in precisely this circumstance. As they approached the Philistine sentry, Eliel put his right hand on his sword under his cloak and spoke again, "Is this the well?"

But the Philistine sentry didn't answer, instead his eyes grew wide, their whites showing through the darkness, and he fell forward, A dagger protruding from his back. Adino retrieved his knife from the lifeless body and the trio continued on as silently as possible.

When they reached the well, Eliel carefully picked up the clay jar from the stone wall surrounding the opening, making the slightest scraping sound, which caused the others to look this way and that, nervously. Eliel lowered it by its rope into the cool water below. Adino and Shammah faced outward in opposite directions, each of them scanning the distance for other sentries who might approach.

It took Eliel three times filling and pulling up the jar to fill the waterskin they had brought. When he was through, he gave a quiet "whoosh" through pursed lips. It would have been a whistle at some other time, but the puff of air was all that was needed for the others to hear and know their mission was accomplished.

The evening meal was just concluding, and David once again was tuning his lyre, preparing to sing another psalm, when Adino, Eliel and Shammah appeared, entering the mouth of the cave.

"Friends, where have you been?" David asked. "We missed you at table." He used the word "table" euphemistically, since they had few tables in the cave, except for some they had obtained in the raid.

"We brought this," Adino said, slinging the heavy waterskin from his shoulder and setting it on the ground in front of David.

"What is this?"

"Water from the well near the gate of Bethlehem."

David's eyes grew wide, and he touched the cool, bulging waterskin. He looked up at the three young men.

"You went to Bethlehem?"

"Yes."

"But the Philistines are there."

"Yes, but you desired the water, and we live to serve you," Adino said.

David could not speak for a moment, but he rose to his feet and picked up the waterskin, holding it at arm's length in spite of its weight.

"You men are mighty, indeed. You honor me by your courageous act. But Yahweh forbid that I should drink this water that was purchased at the risk of your lives! It would be like I was drinking your blood!"

With that, he uncorked the waterskin and poured the water on the ground. Everyone watched in amazement.

As one man, Adino, Eliel and Shammah knelt down and bowed to David. The entire camp was silent as a tomb.

❦ 38 ❦

"We need to move," David said matter-of-factly at a council the next night. "We have become so many we can't keep our location secret much longer."

"That's true," said Joab, David's nephew, the oldest son of his sister, Zeruiah. He was a strong, young man in his early 20's. The two of them had grown up together and David trusted Joab implicitly. "Where do you propose we go?"

"I promised my parents I would take them to Moab to stay with our distant cousins," David answered. "It will keep them safe and will allow us all to stay a long way away from Saul. We would go to the south, through the desert, around the Salt Sea."

"A difficult journey with so many," commented Benaiah, "but the king would not likely follow."

"Then let us prepare to travel." David said, slapping his thighs. "We leave day-after-tomorrow."

The refugees were uncertain how to go about moving everything they had, plus animals, but they finally were underway.

The journey was indeed hard, down south through the Judean wilderness toward the Negev and then across the Arabah south of the Salt Sea. It was difficult, desert country.

Finally, they reached the land of Moab.

David had two connections to Moab. With all Hebrews, he shared the fact that Moab and Ammon had been sons of Lot, Abraham's nephew, born of incest with his two daughters after the destruction of Sodom and Gomorrah, when they thought they might be the only people left alive. So, the

Moabites had been cousins to all the Israelites for a thousand years, but, more importantly, David's great-grandmother was Ruth, a widow who came to Bethlehem from Moab with Naomi, her mother-in-law. She had married the Bethlehemite Boaz, and they would be David's great-grandparents. For this reason, David felt sure they would find a welcome in Moab.

Upon arriving in the country, David was directed to the king in the city of Mizpah of Moab, who received him and his entourage out of curiosity, because he had heard of the Hero of Elah.

"Your majesty, would you allow my father and mother to stay in your country until I learn God's will for me?" David asked the monarch of the desert kingdom.

"They will be welcome and well cared for here," the king answered. "We will locate the relatives of your family and make arrangements."

"Thank you, your majesty."

So, David saw to it that his parents, his sisters and their husbands were settled in Moab, but his brothers, experienced warriors like Eliab, Abinidab and Shimea, and his sister Zeruiah's sons, the serious Joab, carefree Abishai and young, impetuous Asahel, returned to Judah with David.

❦ 39 ❧

After a few months in Moab, the band of misfits and outlaws which had attached themselves to David left and returned to Judah, making their way back around the southern end of the Salt Sea and going north along the coast.

The sun beat down mercilessly on the travelers here in the place with the lowest elevation in the world and the dust seemed to never stop blowing. To the west was a barren wilderness and to the east the deep, dead waters of the Salt Sea. The coast was lined with white salt deposits which encouraged industry based on that invaluable commodity to flourish.

Azel and Asahel were walking faster than the rest of the group, so they fell into conversation.

"I am tired of this barren country!" Azel said. "There's nothing but yellow-gray, rocky soil where nothing grows and rugged hills rising from the desert floor, not to mention the lifeless sea, with its salt deposits along the shore. I can't wait until we are back in the hill country."

"Yes, it would be good to see a tree again," Asahel answered. They both laughed at that.

"And to drink from a cool brook!"

"Yes! I think there is an oasis somewhere ahead."

"Look. What's that?" Azel asked, shading his eyes.

Asahel looked into the bright sunlight where Azel was pointing. "Is it a mountain? Let's go see!"

Asahel began running toward the horizon. Azel looked back at the closest members of their party in the distance, then turned and sped away after Asahel.

"Wait for me!"

Azel caught up to Asahel after some distance because he had stopped and was looking at the gigantic rock formation that looked like it could be one thousand cubits above the desert floor. It rose almost straight up and appeared to have a broad, flat top.

"It's a natural stronghold. From the summit you could see an enemy coming for miles from any direction," Asahel said, obviously in awe. "A small group could defend it against a large army."

"But could we even get up there?"

"I say there will be a way. Let's find it!" And Asahel began running forward again.

Azel was older than Asahel, but he tried to keep up. They were at the base of the mountain on the side toward the Salt Sea. Suddenly, Asahel stopped and Azel caught up.

"Here! I found it," Asahel shouted and he started to climb.

Azel saw it was a narrow path with steps hewn out of the rock. When it had been done was impossible to tell, but Azel assumed it would have to be very ancient. He started upward behind Asahel.

The path snaked one way and then the other to make it possible to scale the steep sides. When they had gone to a height of perhaps 100 cubits, they looked back toward the south and Asahel called out to the rest of their group, which had finally gotten close enough to hear.

"Hello! Look what we found! It's a natural stronghold. We are going to the summit to see what it's like."

David and Joab waved at them. "We will stop here for the night," David shouted, partly for the benefit of the weary travelers behind him. "Come tell us what you find."

David looked at Joab and he volunteered, "It does appear to be a natural fortress. No one could approach it without being seen."

"Yes, that's true," David agreed, "but is there adequate shelter up there? And water? There may be no food nearby in this desert; we know there are no fish in this dead sea."

The heat was very nearly unbearable here, where the elevation was so low.

"Maybe it will be cooler at the higher elevation of the stronghold," David continued.

"Asahel will report the answers to those questions," Joab assured him.

"Make camp here," David called out to his men and their families. "We will camp in the shadow of this mountain where at least we will have cooling shade for the rest of daylight today, then we would see what tomorrow would bring."

The weary travelers began obeying David's directive to set up camp.

"Joab, have someone search for a water source, if one can be found," David said.

"Right away."

The next day, David made the decision to stay there at least for a while. They all scaled the mountain to camp on the summit the next night.

Azel, Asahel and other young men were tasked to find water and food in the coming days. They had brought supplies and gifts of food from the king of Moab, but with their company having grown to 300 men, plus women and no small number of children, a tremendous amount of food and water was required.

Other men worked with the loose stone that was everywhere on the mountain to construct some basic shelter over which they stretched cloth or animal skins. There were no tree boughs or tall grasses from which to weave a covering over their huts, but some protection was needed from the relentless sun.

⧼ 40 ⧽

Azel, Asahel and others, including Eliel, ranged far to the north in search of food. Asahel carried a spear and wore a sword at his side, plus a dagger in his belt. Azel also had a dagger and sword, plus a bow and quiver of arrows.

Azel suddenly grabbed Asahel's arm and held his finger to pursed lips. Asahel was obediently quiet and looked where Azel pointed.

In the shade of a large boulder was a lion, evidently a male because of his short, dark mane, sleeping in the heat. They did their best to avoid waking him, tip-toeing on the stony ground. Finally, they felt they were safely past him.

They had been out all day and had found nothing. The heat was terrible and they were about to turn back when they heard a sound coming from a cave high on a shear rock wall facing the Sea.

"Listen!" Azel said. "What was that?"

"It sounded like a goat."

"It came from there."

"Let's go," Asahel said.

They scrambled up the steep rock face, something they had become adept at doing, and soon were able to look into the dark cave. They waited a moment to allow their eyes to adjust to the darkness after the bright sunshine. Then they ventured inside, where it was cool and dry, drawing daggers to be prepared for whatever awaited.

Then they heard it again, definitely in the cave. Suddenly, a four-legged animal came rushing at them with its head down and huge, curved horns forward. They each jumped aside and then pounced on top of it, all three of them falling to the ground. With one purposeful motion, Asahel slit its throat and both of them held it down as it bled out and gradually stopped struggling.

Once the animal was dead, they could see that it was indeed a goat, though not the same as the domesticated goats they raised in their towns to the north. This was some kind of mountain goat.

"This will provide food for a number of our people," Azel said, "and there are likely more of them."

Just then, another sound came from further back in the cave. They looked at one another and rose to go toward the sound. Soon they found a female and two kids. Asahel raised his knife.

"Wait," Azel said, touching Asahel's arm. "If we take her alive, she can provide milk."

"Good idea. This is all I have to tie her," Asahel said, taking a sling from his leather shoulder bag.

He approached the goat carefully, tying a loop in the leather thong as he went. The goat backed up slightly, and when Asahel tossed the loop at her head, she brayed and tossed her head. It appeared she would throw the leather loop off, but Azel jumped to hold her still and Asahel made the loop go over her head and around her neck.

Before long, they had scrambled down from the cave. Azel carried the dead male on his shoulders and Asahel pulled the female along while the kids followed, crying pitifully.

"There are sure to be more in those crags," Asahel said, gesturing toward the sheer rock formations.

"I'm sure of it," Azel said with a smile. "Tomorrow we should bring more men and tomorrow night we will all eat well indeed."

The smell of meat roasting over open fires wafted over the flat top of the stronghold as David's people ate their fill. The men had killed enough goats during the day for each family to eat for a week and others, directed by Joab, had found water. There was a small amount of greens to go with the goat meat. Various women had gathered and hoarded edibles since their time in Adullam. Now they brought them out to go with the meat and it became a feast; improvising dressings from flour, oil and wine, it was the best meal they had had since leaving Mizpah of Moab.

Eliel was off with friends, as he often was. Azel and Dani made sure little Adriel had his fill and he was soon nodding off as they sat under the explosion of stars in the cloudless sky. As Adriel fell asleep, Dani lay down with him to ensure he slept deeply. Then Azel heard something. It was the sound of David's lyre in the center of the camp.

Azel got up and walked over to where their champion was singing one of his songs, the soft notes of the lyre cascading in melodic arpeggios in beautiful concert with the tune he was singing. Azel saw Eliel among those listening and he stood beside him, putting his hand on his shoulder and smiling as they listened to the warrior that they had risked all to follow sing one of his psalms.

<h1 style="text-align: center;">❧ 41 ❧</h1>

The fugitives were gradually able to make a life for themselves in the forbidding desert around the Salt Sea. It turned out, mountain goats were plentiful and provided meat, milk and skins, as well as gut for bowstrings. They also found a herd of gazelle nearby, which were more difficult to hunt, but were an additional source of food.

Gradually, they were all changing. The dry air and sun dried and darkened their skin and they became lean and muscular, especially the men, who spent every day foraging.

The biggest problem was water.

They could look out at the expanse of the deep, blue Salt Sea, but it was worthless to provide the fresh water they needed. There had not been a single drop of rain since they had entered this desert on the way to Moab.

David solved this problem by detailing different men every other day to make the trip to the oasis at En-Gedi to the north to get water. They took a dozen donkeys with them and each returned bearing two heavy clay pots of water in a sling on its back. It was punishing in the heat and the trip there and back took most of the day. After all that effort, it was hardly enough water for each person and their animals to have a little a few times a day. Azel and Eliel were both in the rotation to go for water.

While they were at the cave of Adullam, a prophet had joined them and had accompanied them to Moab. His name was Gad. One day he came to David.

"Do not stay here," the prophet said, cryptically. "Go back to the land of Judah."

David considered what the prophet said. He knew the word of the Lord could not be taken lightly. While this desert was technically Judah, David knew Gad meant to return to civilization. They were well situated strategically at the stronghold and Saul would be unlikely to look for them there, but returning to the towns of Judah would make it infinitely easier to find food and water. He decided they should do what the prophet said.

"Have the people prepare to travel," he told Joab, who had become his right hand. "Tomorrow, we return to Judah."

But on the way they would stop at the oasis of En-Gedi for a few days to be refreshed and drink their fill.

❧ 42 ☙

Mara strained to push when the midwife finally gave her permission, the contractions having come ever closer together. She had no idea how long she had been in labor, and at the moment she wanted nothing more than to give her husband, Jonathan, a son and heir.

"Push, Mara, Push!" the midwife cried. Mara's mother and sister were also there.

And with the last of her strength, she pushed and then collapsed back, vaguely aware that a new life had slipped from her body.

Presently, she heard a baby cry. She raised her head and looked, seeing the midwife with the baby in her arms. Mara's mother and sister had huge smiles on their faces.

"You have a son!" the midwife said, and she placed the crying infant on his mother's breast.

Presently, Jonathan was allowed in to see his wife and new baby.

"I gave you a son," Mara said, smiling. He kissed her forehead and cupped the baby's head in his hands.

"He's wonderful," Jonathan said, obviously moved.

"What will you name him?" Mara's sister asked.

"Now, now. They may want to wait until his personality reveals itself," Mara's mother cautioned.

"We agreed, if it was a boy," Mara began, "we would name him 'Mephibosheth.'"

"So he will be a breaker of idols?" Mara's mother said. "Couldn't it also be 'Mephi-Ba'al?'"

"Yes, it could," Jonathan answered. "But we prefer 'Mephibosheth.'"

Mother and child, exhausted after the ordeal of birth, closed their eyes to rest and the other tiptoed out, except for Jonathan, who remained to just sit and look at his new family.

❦ 43 ❦

One day Saul, seated on his backless throne, called his generals and the elders of Benjamin before him.

"Our law states that there must not be any witch or sorcerer or necromancer among us," he began, "but we all know these black arts thrive in the land. It would please Samuel if we destroyed all practitioners of the occult arts.

"As such, I have planned a campaign to rid us of this scourge. I will lead a contingent of our army to the north and Abner will lead a division to the south into Judah. We will eradicate all the witches from among us. Only Yahweh is to be worshipped in Israel. We leave tomorrow!"

Jeriah was surprised that he had not heard of this plan before. Those assembled mumbled, "Yes my king."

"As you wish."

"It shall be done."

Jeriah rode his donkey with Saul's division. About a thousand of Israel's professional soldiers went north to Bethel and then beyond toward Ophrah to the east. The place was remote, but with one of Abner's spies guiding them, they arrived at a cave in the highlands of Ephraim which, according to the spy, was home to a witch and necromancer, one who communed with the dead.

"Take your men and bring her out," Saul said to Jeriah.

Jeriah dismounted and obeyed the order, calling to the men under his command, "Come."

Jeriah drew his sword and burst through the cave opening with his men close behind. He had to pause to allow his eyes to adjust to the darkness inside the cave, then he moved forward.

The cave had improvised sconces of oil lamps on the rough walls, but only a few were burning. Jeriah took one of the lamps from its stone perch and held it aloft as he led his men deeper into the cave. There were a few pieces of rude wood furniture, but no person was to be found. Then Jeriah saw something that made his blood run cold.

A human skull sat on a rough table. Beside it were polished stones and other bits of bone, but Jeriah couldn't be sure whether they were human or animal.

This must be the divining room, he thought.

A nearly burned-down candle also sat on the table, casting long, flickering shadows on the cave wall.

Pushing on deeper into the cave, Jeriah and his men came upon the man and his wife, a thin, elderly couple dressed in ragged, old clothes, sitting huddled near a cook fire on the packed-earth floor, looking at the intruders with wide eyes.

"Come with us!" Jeriah demanded, grabbing the old man by the arm and jerking him up. Another of his men did the same with the weeping wife. They quickly moved the frightened couple toward the mouth of the cave and out into the daylight, presenting them before Saul, still mounted on his donkey.

"You are the sorceress of Ophrah, are you not?" Saul asked the weeping woman. The old man looked at the hundreds of heavily armed soldiers and his knees nearly buckled.

"Is this her?" Saul asked the spy when she didn't reply.

"It is, my king."

"The law of Moses states clearly that mediums and witches must be put to death," Saul said loudly enough for all to hear. "As the king of Israel, I defend the law."

Then turning to the trembling couple, he said, "You have been condemned to die by your wickedness.

"Stone them!" Saul commanded, looking at Jeriah.

Jeriah nodded to his men, indicating they were to carry out the execution. There were plentiful stones at the mouth of the cave where someone in the distant past had hollowed out areas of the natural cave to make it habitable. These stones Jeriah and his men made use of now.

Jeriah cast the first stone and his men followed, all of them raining down a shower of heavy rocks that caused the couple to scream and raise their hands in a futile effort to shield themselves.

"Curse you Saul, son of Kish!" the woman shouted suddenly, in a shrill, trembling but surprisingly loud voice. "You are cursed because Adonai has rejected you!"

Jeriah and his men were startled and stopped throwing stones for a moment.

"Stone them!" Saul shouted, irritated by the vaguely prophetic words. Jeriah and his men began again to execute the sentence prescribed by the law. Eventually the couple fell to the ground with bleeding wounds opened by the countless stones. They lay still, but Jeriah and his men continued to pelt them with stones, until they were sure they were dead.

"Burn them and everything they possess," Saul ordered one of his soldiers who was a commander of 10. The men set about gathering dry sticks, which they lay on top of the old sorcerer couple. Other men went into the cave and brought out all their pitiful belongings, piling them on top.

Then a fire was started and Saul and the men stood by and watched, mesmerized by the yellow flames as they consumed everything but bones and stones.

The contingent of soldiers found and executed several other witches before arriving at another cave near the ruins of Shiloh. The spy had been certain that another witch lived there, but when they arrived, they found nothing but shards of broken pottery and a trash pile, which included animal bones, smooth stones and bits of spent candle wax.

"It is enough," King Saul declared. "We return to Benjamin. Any witches who survive have been sent a clear message."

Jeriah was relieved that Saul had declared their persecution ended and he rode beside the king as they spurred their donkeys on the road south to Gibeah of Benjamin and home.

As he rode, he remained alone with his thoughts and none of the other men broke the silence either.

❦ 44 ❧

The old woman cursed the slow donkey which was overburdened with the totality of her belongings. Some things had to be left behind, but they were no big loss. She could easily find or fashion the charms she needed and animal bones would be plentiful after she found a new home and had prepared a few meals.

Word had come just in time that King Saul had declared war on witches, which was strange because he had tolerated them up until now. Why had he suddenly decided to enforce the prohibition of the Torah?

She could divine many things, but not the mind of the king. She only knew that she had needed to abruptly flee to a place too far away for the king to find her. She would also need to be more discreet in her efforts to procure customers for her special gifts.

Fortunately, there would always be grief and people desperate to communicate with the dead.

She crossed the Vale of Jezreel and climbed the plateau to the north as the sun was speeding toward the western horizon. She inquired of a couple of farmers who happened along on the road. They told of an abandoned house nearby. She decided she was far enough away to be out of the reach of the murderous king, so she slapped the rump of the donkey and guided it toward the village of En-Dor.

When Jeriah and the rest of Saul's men returned from their bloody purge of the practitioners of black arts, he was all too happy to take his leave and spend some time with his family, away from court.

As he approached his family home, he saw a head looking at him above the wall. The head then disappeared and the gate flew open revealing his daughter, Zaina, running toward him at full speed.

"What is wrong?" he shouted, alarmed.

"Nothing is wrong, Father," Zaina answered. "Ithiel wants me to marry him! He can pay the bride price. Will you give me to him, Father? Will you?"

Jeriah was speechless. *My baby daughter to marry?*

But he looked at her. She was a woman of 15, with womanly curves he had hardly noticed, being gone so much.

Of course, she is able to marry.

"Do you want to marry Ithiel?" Jeriah asked, even though her eagerness made the answer unnecesary.

"Yes, Father, I want to marry him, please!"

"Then tell Ithiel to come with his offer and we will sit together to decide."

Zaina threw her arms around her father's neck. "Thank you, Father. Thank you!" Then she turned and ran through the gate again, no doubt to inform her mother.

Jeriah knew that Ithiel was the grandson of a man of Mizpah his father had done business with for years. There was no question in his mind about the family. He just didn't know Ithiel that well.

When Ithiel came, Jeriah was reminded of the awkward meals at the home of Shelomith's family when they were contemplating marriage. Conversation at the meal was stilted, as Jeriah asked about Ithiel's father and he gave respectful answers. Jeriah didn't hurry through the meal, even though he knew his wife and daughter were impatient that they get to the point of agreeing on the bride price.

Jeriah continued to maintain a somber face during their negotiations, for the sake of tradition and impressing on the young man that he was asking for a great responsibility, but there was never any doubt that he would agree to the union. Ithiel was from a fine family which Jeriah had known all his life. Of course he would make a good husband for his only daughter.

At last the agreement was complete, sealed with a shared jug of wine and the handing over of the agreed upon price. When told of the result, Zaina enthusiastically thanked Jeriah and began packing to accompany Ithiel to his home.

Jeriah marveled at how quickly the generations progressed, so that his daughter was now at the point where he had been, seemingly just a short time ago. He struggled to understand the mixture of joy and sorrow he felt as he and Shelomith bid farewell to his young daughter as she left home to establish her own back in Mizpah.

❦ 45 ❦

The journey was difficult because of the terrain. Azel and Asahel did not run ahead this time, because there was much to do to keep donkeys, women and children moving at the pace that David and Joab had set. Hebron was almost straight west, but the road was brutally uphill; they had to ascend almost 4,000 cubits in only about 25 miles.

Azel knew they would not go to Hebron, the seat of Judah's tribal elders' council. There might be loyalists to the king who would report their whereabouts. Instead they would go to the thick forest to the north of Hebron. They knew there would be abundant game and precious water there. And they could easily hide under the forest canopy in the tangle of undergrowth.

Azel had not been there before, but it seemed to him a good plan. It was not far south of Bethlehem, the home of David and his nephews, Joab, Abishai and Asahel, so they knew it well.

It was dark when they arrived at a place that could be defended. There was no time to set up their tent or completely unload the donkey, but Azel saw that Dani and Adriel were settled comfortably with their bedrolls and he supposed Eliel was off somewhere with friends. Then he went to find Joab or Asahel to learn if he was to stand sentry.

Near the center of the hastily constructed camp, a torch had been set up and Azel made his way toward it, being careful not to step on sleeping women and children in the darkness.

"Azel!"

He looked to the side to see Asahel and Benaiah also approaching the torch.

"We are assigned to the first watch," Asahel told him as he left Benaiah and fell into step with him.

"Where?"

"To the north," Asahel said, pointing.

Toward King Saul, Azel thought sourly. Together they found their way through the scattered bedrolls and went a few cubits outside the camp to locate a hill where they could see into the distance.

Jeriah was on his way to begin his day performing his regular duties in the court of Saul, when Abner caught him.

"Jeriah, the king desires your presence."

"I am on my way there now," Jeriah answered, wondering why Saul would summon him when he should know that he would be on his way to his daily posting.

A cold sweat arose on the back of his neck when he thought about the fact that Azel had disappeared. Jeriah suspected that he had joined David, like many others, wherever he was hiding. Could Saul have heard about Azel's desertion and defection?

He entered the throne room with some trepidation, but strode to the center of the room to face the king, who was up and at court early this morning.

"You summoned me, sire?"

"Yes, Jeriah. You have stood by me these many years. You are a good son of Benjamin; You and your father before you."

Jeriah said nothing, wondering if there would be a "but."

"You know that the son of Jesse was my bodyguard and armor bearer, but he has deserted me."

Jeriah nodded, though he knew David might tell it differently.

"Therefore, I want you to be my close servant, to bear my armor and command my personal guard."

Jeriah blinked, wondering if he had heard right.

"Of course, my king. It is my honor to serve you in whatever you need me to do."

"Good," the king said with a wave of his hand. "Now see to your command and detail one of your men to stand before me in your place today. Abner will have further instructions."

"Yes, sire."

On the other side of the king, Joash stood in his usual place. He smiled and nodded slightly to Jeriah.

Jeriah turned and walked to the portico and saw Abner standing by the door.

"Congratulations," Abner said.

"Thank you," was all Jeriah could think to say.

～§ 46 ＆～

Joab was overseeing a detail of men who were cutting trees out of which to fashion shelters for the fugitives which had now grown to 600 men plus their families. There was an abundance of wood and brush in this forest and they were making the most of it. Joab watched as a tree fell with a tremendous CRASH! The men who had labored to cut it down now set upon it with axes and saws to cut it down to the bare trunk, with heavy, leaf-covered branches set aside to be used for a variety of purposes.

When they had all the branches cut from the straight trunk, they tied ropes to it and began dragging it to the site where it had been decided they would build an assembly hall. This trunk would be the center pole and the best branches would serve as rafters with smaller limbs woven into a roof that would shed rain.

"Man approaching!" a sentry called out. Joab looked in the direction of the call and soon saw a couple of his armed men escorting an younger man toward the camp proper. He was dressed in a dirty tunic that had once been white.

"Stop," Joab called, and he went over to the man. "Who are you and what is your business?"

"I am Abiathar, a priest in the line of Eli. I look for David."

"What makes you think you will find him here?" Joab asked, looking him up and down. It was obvious he had traveled a long way.

"I know he is in hiding in Judah. I asked along the road and was told there were rumors I would find him in the Forest of Hereth."

Joab frowned. *Is our location that well known?*

"Please, Saul has killed all the priests of Nob and our families. I have nowhere else to go."

All the priests killed? Joab now looked at the pitiful eyes of the grieving young priest and saw another refugee from Saul.

"Come, I will take you to David."

David looked up from sharpening his sword to see Joab approaching with a bedraggled young man in the once-white-linen garb of a priest.

"David, this is Abiathar," Joab said. "He says Saul has killed all the priests of Nob and he alone escaped to tell it."

"Oh no! And Ahimelech?"

"My father is dead, as are my mother and all those living in the town," Abiathar choked back a sob.

David looked down. "This is my fault. That day when I stopped to see your father, I saw Doeg the Edomite there. I should have known he would tell Saul."

David then stood and put his hand on Abiathar's shoulder. "Stay with me; don't fear Saul, for he seeks my life also. You will be safe here with me."

David then noticed the bag Abiathar was carrying. "What is that?"

"The ephod. I retrieved it before they burned the town."

"Bless you! We can inquire of the Lord!"

Word came to David that the residents of Keilah were being harassed by the Philistines on one of their regular incursions. Keilah was a town of Judah northwest of where they had camped in the Forest of Hereth and just a little south of Adullam, so they knew it well.

With almost 600 men who could carry arms now, David could mount a serious offensive, and that is what was called for on behalf of Keilah.

Before agreeing to help Keilah however, David had Abiathar consult the ephod to be certain Yahweh would be with them. This was done in the presence of the leaders of the outcasts, who stood in a circle around David and Abiathar, who was holding the ephod.

"Shall I go and attack the Philistines?" David asked. Abiathar waited and watched, then declared the affirmative stone had been illuminated.

"Yes, go attack the Philistines," Abiathar said, interpreting what he saw.

"Commander," said Abishai, David's nephew, hesitating.

"What is it?"

"We have just heard how King Saul killed men, women and children in Nob to eradicate the priests who helped you," Abishai looked around the group and David could see many of them could finish Abishai's sentence. "We are afraid of the king as it is, even though you have supporters here in Judah. Should we also call the Philistines' attention to us? Can we fight both Israel and the Philistines?"

David considered what Abishai said but didn't answer. Instead, he turned to Abiathar.

"Ask again."

Abiathar looked around at the others, then repeated the question and watched the stones for a sign.

"The Lord says, 'Go down to Keilah, for I have given the Philistines into your hand,'" Abiathar confirmed.

With that settled, David gave the order, "Prepare for a journey. We go to Keilah."

The men left the brush-arbor shelter to begin preparing to move again.

❦ 47 ❧

Compared to the trip to Moab, this will be easy, Azel thought.

Keilah was only about 15 miles away. Azel did wonder if moving would expose them, since their total number was well over 1,000 men, women and children, and they had many sheep and goats which they drove along, and donkeys which bore much of their stuff. The amount of baggage they had to carry with them had increased as well, so men, women and children bore shoulder bags and heavy bags on their backs with wide straps across their foreheads. The main body could not move fast on the narrow, rough road.

Azel walked at the head of the column with 100 men under his command to be the vanguard. Dani insisted on walking beside him, though he worried about her if they came under attack.

He supposed their party must stretch a long way behind them. Benaiah and his 100 men were the rearguard.

When they drew near the city, perhaps five miles away, the sun was low in the west and the people were weary. Then Joab and Asahel rode by on donkeys. Asahel waved to Azel.

"We're going to go find the Philistines!" he shouted.

Azel waved back. They were in familiar territory now. They had walked this path before when they were staying at the cave of Adullam.

Shortly after that David rode to the front of the procession.

"We stop here," he shouted. "You may rest until Joab brings back intelligence about the location of the Philistines."

The main body of people stopped walking and took a few steps off the road to sit under the trees. Families began retrieving pita and dried figs from their sacks because the children were hungry.

When they were settled, David called out, "I need to see my captains of hundreds and captains of tens now. Come let us meet under this tree," he said, motioning to a large tamarisk with broad branches.

Azel joined the others as they encircled their leader. The hero of Elah already had a plan, which he now proceeded to share with them.

"The Philistines are harassing our people, taking their harvest, looting the threshing floors. You may remember the threshing floors of Keilah are to the west of the walled city, so unless Joab comes back with different information, I believe we will find them west of the threshing floors.

"Abishai, you will stay here with your cohort to guard the baggage and the women and children.

"The rest of you will lead your men toward the city. Benaiah, you and your 100 will go the farthest, so you can approach the city from the west. Your job will be to prevent their escape to Gath. We will drive them toward you.

"Joab's 100 will also march far around the east and then north of the city to attack from the north. The rest of our body will mount the main attack from the south. Between us we will crush them and make sure they cannot escape.

"We should have the advantage of surprise, for if the Philistines are expecting someone to rescue the people, they will be looking to Saul to come from the north, but he is not moving, as far as we know.

"We will attack before dawn, so get some rest. We will rise very early."

Azel and the other captains walked back to join their groups to give them the word as darkness descended. After a short conference with his men, Azel returned to where he had left Dani and found that she had prepared a meal complete with pita, salted mutton and figs.

"I don't know how you do it," he said, and he gave her a squeeze and a kiss.

"I have to take care of you. You need your strength."

"God did a great thing when he gave me you."

Soon after he finished, Azel folded a cloak for a pillow and lay down to sleep. It would be a short night.

❦ 48 ❦

Benaiah's troops were the first to leave, because they had the farthest to go. He decided not to ride a donkey as he might have in other battle situations, because surprise was paramount to their success, and donkeys could be very unpredictable, braying at the most inopportune times.

Even though they started earlier than the others, they had to keep up a good pace so they could be in position to do what they were supposed to do. This wasn't easy to do in the dark, but they were making good time.

Joab's surveillance had shown what David had expected: the Philistines were camped to the west of the threshing floors, so Benaiah and his men would position themselves to the west of them.

It is a good plan, Benaiah thought.

Azel slept well enough and rose in plenty of time to rouse his men. They were to be part of the main body that would attack the Philistine camp. Joab and Asahel had estimated that there were about 250 soldiers there; apparently just a harassing party large enough to rob the town of its harvest with impunity. The element of surprise and superior numbers would help ensure success, but Azel was also glad that David had been able to inquire of the Lord.

The 100 men under Joab's command had already left and would be in position to the north before the main body attacked.

Then Asahel appeared at Azel's side.

"David wants someone to go ahead to eliminate sentries, if there are any," Asahel said, "I want you to come with me. I have two other men to go with us."

"But what of my command?"

"David will command them personally."

"All right," Azel answered, surprised.

"Let's go," Asahel said, and he began to run ahead. Azel struggled to keep up as usual.

Joab and his men had gone around the north side of Keilah, by way of the cave of Adullam, and now they were lying in wait in a stand of trees where they could see smoke from Philistine campfires as well as the walls of Keilah.

"You and you, go quietly to see if the Philistines are awake and if there are sentries posted." Joab ordered two men.

"Yes, lord," they answered and immediately went forward in the dark.

"Have the men rest. David will attack first and then we will join," Joab told his second in command. He immediately left to fulfill the order.

Azel and the others fanned out to cover as wide an area as possible, but not so far as to be out of hearing of one another. He was moving fast as was possible in the darkened woods.

Soon we will need to slow down and be quieter, Azel thought.

Off to his left, Azel thought he saw a glimmer of light; something reflecting the moonlight. He stopped and looked more closely but could no longer see it.

Perhaps it was an animal's eyes?

He decided he needed to be sure, so he began slowly making his way to where he had seen the light, and then he saw it again. This time he was certain he saw something and he lowered his spear, approaching cautiously.

A shiver went up his spine as he saw the bronze helmet of a Philistine soldier, apparently a sentry, but he was sitting against a tree trunk, asleep.

Azel made his way near the sleeping man and got around in front of him. He pulled back his spear, preparing to run the man through, but the sentry awoke and looked up!

Azel thrust the spear toward the Philistine's midsection, but he rolled aside and the spear stuck in the tree. The Philistine jumped to his feet and came at Azel, tackling him and they both went down to the ground and began rolling and thrashing, each trying to get the upper hand.

The man tried to cry out a warning, but Azel smashed his fist into his face and he fell back, stunned. Azel took advantage and drew his dagger, plunging it into his chest, just above his breastplate. The Philistine went limp and didn't move again.

Then Asahel trotted up. "Are you all right?"

"Yes. They do have sentries. This one was sleeping, but the next ones might be awake, so tread lightly."

Azel retrieved his spear from the tree trunk and they continued on.

❧ 49 ❧

Benaiah motioned for the men behind him to stop, then he turned and motioned with both hands, telling them to "stay." Benaiah knew the weary men would understand they had reached the place where they were to be positioned.

He looked to the east and saw the slightest change in color in the sky from indigo to gray. It would be dawn soon.

"Have the men rest," Benaiah said to a couple of his officers, "We are to catch those who try to escape to Gath. The others will join the battle."

Benaiah found a flat stone which made a good seat and sat down to rest himself.

David was walking to the front of the column of 300 men when he saw four men approaching through the shadows. He raised one hand to stop the marching column. Those at the front with him put their hands on the hilts of their swords.

Then David recognized his nephew, Asahel and those he had taken with him.

"Uncle, we have cleared the way. We found three sentries who will no longer be able to sound a warning and we viewed the Philistine camp with our own eyes. Almost no one is awake."

"Good job. How far?"

"Perhaps a half mile."

"Spread the word, we must now be silent as the deer."

"Yes, lord."

The four men walked down the column as it passed and told them the rest of their journey was to be quiet, because they would soon be in position to attack.

❧

Joab looked toward the east and saw that the sky was pink. If all had gone according to plan, David would be attacking soon. And as soon as they heard the noise of battle, his own men would join the fight as well.

He turned and motioned for his men to get up and be ready.

As the 300 led by David approached the Philistine camp, the ground became flat and spread out before them. There was no forest cover. It was a recently harvested barley field, so they wouldn't even have the thin stalks of grain in which to hide.

David motioned to his officers to array their men in an east-west line. Azel obeyed; through vigorous hand motions he communicated that they must hurry and line up at the place he designated.

When the men were in position they crouched on the ground, awaiting the order to attack. They didn't have to wait long. Soon David stepped out in front of the line, drew his sword silently, raised it toward the encampment and then sliced it through the air.

Instantly, the men were on their feet and running toward the tents. Azel was in front of his men so he reached the camp first. He ran his spear through the first tent he came to and felt it hit a sleeping soldier.

Then a cry of alarm went up and soon soldiers were coming out of the tents. Most did not have their armor and might only have picked up a sword or knife. Azel threw his spear and it went through the midsection of a man dressed only in a loincloth, then he drew his sword and hacked at the neck of another bewildered soldier, who fell backward.

Azel's men ran past him and found their own victims.

Joab and his men heard the first shouts of battle and he stood and shouted, "Forward!"

His men cried out deep, throaty yells and began running in the direction of the encampment. Soon they began meeting Philistines fleeing the surprise attack. Joab's men quickly dispatched them with their superior numbers.

Azel and his men soon found themselves in the center of the camp where the chaos was complete, with panicked Philistine soldiers running every direction, trying to get away, but meeting David's men at every step. The element of surprise was complete.

Azel ran to engage a tall soldier dressed only in a linen shirt but carrying a sword. The man raised his sword and brought it down hard. Azel put his own sword in the way to defend, but the force pushed him back. The man attempted to thrust his sword's point into Azel's stomach, but he parried just in time, knocking the sword from the Philistine's hand. Undeterred, the soldier jumped Azel and they fell backward. The man was on top of Azel and began slamming his sword hand on the ground trying to break it free, but Azel was focused on taking his knife from his belt. He flipped it around in his palm and stabbed the man in the neck. He fell limp on top of Azel, who struggled to push the heavy soldier off him.

He arose to see that most of his men were beyond him and there was no one nearby except for dead Philistines.

❦ 50 ❦

Benaiah stood and addressed his men: "The battle has been joined. Let us march forward and meet our comrades. Any Philistine you meet should taste your sword."

They gave a loud "hurrah" and started moving east toward the sound of the battle. The sun was coming up and made it difficult to see, Benaiah realized, but they had to do what they had been sent to do.

As it turned out there weren't many who managed to escape to flee back toward Philistine lands, so soon Benaiah's men were at the encampment, where the only men standing were David's.

It was all over in about a quarter hour. David looked about and saw that there were no Philistines left alive to tell what happened. Joab was striding toward him to report and Benaiah was approaching from the west, their pincer movement having closed.

He looked to the west and saw a large number of sheep and goats penned on the western edge of the camp, plus a number of oxen and the carts that were pulled by them. These would all be serviceable to their growing company.

"You," David called to a low-level officer standing nearby, "get some men to help stockpile the weapons and other supplies and equipment."

Soon men were scouring the camp and putting all their new-found riches in categories for transport.

David then turned and looked the other direction, toward the rising sun, and saw the gate of Keilah opening and a few men slowly coming out. They were led by an old, white-haired man walking with difficulty but with purpose. When he got to David, he knelt.

"Bless you and all your men for rescuing us from these uncircumcised. Are you David?"

"I am."

"Bless you, bless you. I am Jacob, elder of Keilah. Thank you for coming to our aid."

"The Lord be praised. He told us to come and help you."

"Yes, thank you. We hear nothing of Saul here."

"Perhaps you will permit us to camp in your town," David responded.

"Certainly, certainly," the elder said. "How many are you?"

"Six hundred men, plus women and children and flocks and herds."

The old man's head jerked back at that, but he recovered and said, "You are welcome. We will find lodging for all."

The rest of David's following were summoned from where they had spent the night by the road about five miles from Keilah. Some of the men and their families stayed outside the walls in the cleaned-up Philistine encampment, but Azel and other officers were quartered in the homes of prominent families and treated as heroes.

Azel and Dani luxuriated in the comfort of a straw-mattress bed like they had not had since they fled Gibeah, given up by the master of the house, an elder of the town. For Adriel, they prepared a pallet at the foot of their bed.

Azel hadn't realized how tired he was until he lay down between the soft bed clothes and closed his eyes.

It was still daylight, but sleep came quickly for him and Dani didn't leave his side as he slept deeply and long.

❧ 51 ❧

By the angle of the moonlight coming through the window, Azel judged it must be after midnight. He had slept well and saw that Dani had fallen asleep beside him with little Adriel sleeping against her back. He reveled in the soft curve of her cheek in the dim light.

Then he rolled out of bed and went to the window to look up at the moon. It was full and bright and Azel could see that the house where they were staying was built into the wall. The room was on the second level, so if he looked to the right he could see over the wall to outside the city and if he looked to the left, he could look down the narrow street. Directly in front of him was the parapet that could be used by soldiers to defend the city, if necessary, but doubled as the roof of a single-story building, perhaps a merchant's shop.

As he watched he was surprised to see movement on the street. *Who would be out at this hour?* he thought.

As he watched, a man wrapped head-to-foot in a black cloak quickly climbed the stairs leading to the parapet and went to the wall. Because the cloak covered his head, Azel could tell nothing about his face, hair or beard. He carried a crooked shepherd's staff, which he used to hook to the top of the wall and lower himself over and down to the ground. Then he was gone in the darkness of a nearby line of trees.

Azel thought this was curious indeed.

Ze'ev ben-Yisachar held his threadbare, black cloak tight against his thin body to ward off the chill of midnight and walked briskly with the help of his staff to try to generate heat, but also to try to reach Gibeath-Saul before the sun set tomorrow. He was eager for the three silver pieces from Abner's purse in exchange for the information he had.

The general was indeed wise to foresee the need for informants like myself, Ze'ev thought. David certainly did represent a threat to the house of Saul; everyone in Judah believed it. Many in the largest tribe had long been put off by the upstart king from the smallest tribe, but politics didn't interest him. Ze'ev's main loyalty was to whoever put money in his pouch.

Thank Yahweh for the moon tonight, he thought. It made it easier for him to travel at the speed he wished to go, although the trip would be challenging; uphill all the way as it was.

In the morning, Azel went to a meeting of David's captains in the former Philistine encampment.

"Good job yesterday," David began. "Did we have any killed or wounded?"

"None," Joab said. "Only a few minor injuries. Mostly we outnumbered them almost three-to-one and they had no opportunity to mount an organized resistance."

"That was my hope," David said. "God said He had given them into our hand and He did."

"The people of Keilah now owe us a debt of gratitude," Joab said.

"That is true," David answered. "Perhaps, since this is a walled city, we can stay here a while and enjoy the comforts of their homes."

To Azel that sounded like a very attractive idea.

In spite of his desire to hurry, Ze'ev ben-Yisachar arrived in Gibeath-Saul after darkness had fallen, but he didn't want to wait so he made his way to the court of the king.

"I must find General Abner," he told the first soldier he encountered. "I have vital information to share about David."

"Come with me," the man said, looking Ze'ev up and down.

Though he was exhausted from the journey, Ze'ev shuffled along, following the soldier to a room in the outer wall of the king's compound. The soldier knocked on the wooden door.

"What is it?" came a voice from inside.

"Lord Abner, a man is here who says he has information about David."

The door opened then, and Abner stood there illuminated from behind by candlelight. He looked first at the soldier and then at Ze'ev and the light of recognition came into his eyes.

"Come, tell me what you have for me."

Ze'ev followed Abner to a table and sat down wearily on the chair before it while Abner remained standing.

"You have information about David; where is he?"

"You promised three pieces of silver for information."

"Yes, yes. You'll get your reward. What do you know?"

"David and his men are shut up in Keilah. They defeated the Philistines and are staying in the city."

"How many are with him?"

That stumped Ze'ev, but he answered, "Hundreds. I don't know the exact number."

❦ 52 ❦

Jonathan was walking to the army encampment in early morning when he saw that a large number of soldiers had assembled on the parade ground. Each of them was carrying full battle gear and their packs for a multiple-day campaign.

"What is happening?" Jonathan asked a soldier running by.

"We are marching to Keilah in Judah," the soldier said, saluting the prince.

"Why?"

The soldier shrugged and continued to join the formation.

Jonathan proceeded closer to the assembled troops and saw Jeriah mounted on a donkey.

"Jeriah, why are you going to Keilah?"

"The king has learned that David and his men are there," Jeriah answered. "We are awaiting the king and then we will be underway."

Jonathan scowled and turned away.

Just then, Saul rode up on his own donkey and shouted to the troops, "Let's go, God has given David into our hands. He sits imprisoned behind gates and walls!"

Jonathan watched as the troops marched by, then he hurried to find his household servant boy, Ziba.

When he found him, he drew the boy aside, where no one would hear. "You must take a message to David in Keilah in Judah," he told the youngster. "Say 'Saul knows you are here and is now marching to trap you.' Go quickly! You must not let the army see you, but you must arrive before they do. Hurry!"

Ziba looked at Jonathan with wide eyes and then started toward the door.

"Wait!" Jonathan called, taking a partially eaten loaf of bread from the table. "Take this loaf with you for your journey. Don't let the soldiers see you. Now hurry!"

"David has called the officers together!" Asahel said urgently.

"Now?" Azel had just completed bargaining for a leg of lamb in Keilah's marketplace.

"Yes, it is an emergency!"

Turning to Dani and handing her the leg of lamb, Azel said, "Can you manage this?"

"Yes, you go on," Dani answered, taking the meat and beginning to walk toward the house where they were staying with Adriel in tow.

Azel went with Asahel, and they hurried through the city gate toward the center of the camp outside the city.

"What is happening?" Azel asked.

"I don't know for sure, but I assume it has something to do with King Saul."

"Or the Philistines," Azel said. *We do have enemies in both directions.*

Once everyone was present, David spoke: "We have received word that Saul and his army are marching to Keilah. They somehow learned we are here."

"Did someone from Keilah tell him?" Joab asked with his hand menacingly on the hilt of the dagger in his belt.

No one spoke immediately, so Azel raised his hand.

"I saw something odd night-before-last. I awoke sometime after midnight and saw a man go over the wall."

"Why did you think it strange?" Joab asked.

"Because of the late hour, and it seemed he was trying not to be seen."

Joab looked at David.

"Call Abiathar and have him bring the ephod," David said to a young man standing nearby.

While Abiathar was being fetched the discussion continued.

"We are in a walled city." Benaiah pointed out. "Should we stay and fight?"

"Being inside walls can be good, but it can also be bad," David answered. "We could be trapped here. Saul has enough troops to mount a siege."

"And it sounds like we don't know if we can fully trust the townspeople," Joab added, nodding to Azel.

Abiathar appeared with the ephod.

"Abiathar, I need to inquire of the Lord," David said. "Ask 'Lord God, your servant has heard that Saul is coming to Keilah to destroy the city. Will Saul come, as we have heard?'"

The men around the circle looked at one another.

Abiathar, watching the precious stones on the ephod, finally answered, "Yes, Saul will come down."

"Will the men of Keilah surrender me into Saul's hands?" David asked.

Abiathar again studied the stones, then looked up. "Yes, the Lord says the men of Keilah will betray you."

Everyone was quiet, until David broke the silence.

"I like our chances better if we are outside these walls and able to run." Then he turned to the young messenger Jonathan had sent. "You have done well for your master, Jonathan. Now, I have a task for you. Go back by the road to Gibeah and meet Saul and the army on the road. Tell the king that word came to Jonathan that David has left Keilah and no one knows where he went. Can you do that?"

Ziba nodded and hurried away.

❧ 53 ☙

Jeriah's responsibilities had increased with his promotion to the rank of the king's armor bearer. He commanded the king's personal guard and was personally responsible for the king's security. That meant he was responsible for the administration of funds devoted to the king's personal movements and the detailing of soldiers to scout locations preceding his movements. It also meant he was made aware of potential plots against the king, real or imagined.

The abrupt end of the trip to Keilah had been an embarrassment, because Saul's nemesis, David, had supposedly been in the bag, but halfway there, Jonathan's servant boy, Ziba, had caught up with them and told them the prey had escaped the snare.

Had David been warned? Jeriah had his suspicions. The king himself didn't trust his own first-born son where David was concerned, but it was up to the king to do something, not Jeriah. However, the king didn't seem to want to take action, which unfortunately was often his approach to any problem.

Jeriah wondered about the wisdom of continuing to pursue David, since it was now Spring and there would likely be war with the Philistines once more, but Saul was obsessed.

Now they truly didn't know where David was. They were still attempting to find him and those with him in a tangle of forest north of Hebron. Abner's spies sometimes brought reports, but by the time Jeriah could confirm them, David and his company had moved on.

Sometime later, Abner came to Jeriah with the word of two of his spies.

"David is moving about in the desert of Ziph," Abner told Jeriah confidently. "With these two reports we can tell what direction he is moving and can intercept him."

"Assuming he keeps moving in the same direction," Jeriah commented.

"Well, it's better information than we've had. I'm going to inform the king."

"All right. I'll assemble the troops for the journey."

Ziph was far down into the Judean desert, south of Hebron. It was inhospitable country, both in terms of the climate and the political attitudes toward King Saul. They were getting reports of David's movements, but Jeriah felt sure Judah's hero was being aided by some in that tribe also.

Azel, Asahel and others were returning from a hunting trip and were weary. The heat was oppressive and relentless. They had been back in the desert for a while and, while they still had sheep and goats from the Philistines they had defeated at Keilah, their diet once again was supplemented by mountain goat. They had learned how to survive on the run, but Azel could still remember the soft bed and comfortable home where he and Dani had been quartered during their too-brief stay in Keilah.

They were almost back to their encampment, when they saw two men on donkeys approaching.

"Who's that?" Azel asked absent mindedly as they trudged along, each of them carrying a goat carcass.

"Probably nobody," Asahel answered, barely looking up, then he did a double take. "Prince Jonathan!"

Azel, Asahel and everyone with them dropped the goat carcasses from their shoulders and drew their swords, ready for anything. Azel saw there were indeed only two men. *What could this mean?*

"Wait!" Jonathan shouted. "I come in peace."

"Why should we believe you?" Asahel shouted back.

"David and I are friends and brothers. I don't wish him any harm, unlike my father."

By then, Jonathan and his servant were very close. He drew his sword and Azel, Asahel and the others tightened their grips on their own swords. Then Jonathan threw his sword to the ground so it stuck in the sand and he dismounted.

"Please take me to David. I miss my friend."

Azel and Asahel looked at one another, unsure what to do.

Adriel and a couple of friends about his age were on the periphery of the camp, occupying themselves playing with sticks and rocks to construct a make-believe city, when Adriel looked up and what he saw caused him to suddenly jump up and begin running toward the center of camp. The other two boys looked up and then followed Adriel.

"Lord, the hunting party is returning, and someone is with them!" Adriel told David breathlessly when he found him.

David arose from the small, rustic desk where he was writing and shaded his eyes, looking into the desert haze.

The encampment was atop a hill where the sun beat down upon them, but it was defensible and that was why they chose it. They were now in Horesh, deep in the desert below Hebron. They had been moving at least once a week, not going too far each time, but keeping on the move. There were so many people hiding out with him now, and they had acquired many sheep and goats, and even a few oxen, in their raids on the Philistines. It was difficult to move so often, but it was necessary.

The hunting party was coming into view, goat carcasses on their shoulders, and David could see two mounted figures with the men on foot, silhouetted against the sunlit desert. Then David recognized one of the men and he couldn't believe it.

"Jonathan?"

He began running toward them and when he got close, Jonathan dismounted and they embraced.

"It is so good to see you, brother!" Jonathan exclaimed.

"I'm glad to see you, too!"

"Praise Yahweh you are all right!"

"Here, please sit," David said pointing to a looted Philistine chair outside his tent beside the desk. "Refreshments for our guests!" David shouted to Adriel and the other boys, who took off to find someone to provide hospitality.

"How did you find us?" David asked when they were seated.

"My father has his sources and I have mine," Jonathan said, his eyes narrowing.

This did not make David feel very reassured.

Jonathan leaned forward and spoke in low tones: "Don't be afraid. My father pursues you still, but he won't be able to harm you. God has said you are to be king and I will be your viceroy. I know it and my father, King Saul, knows it too."

David reached out and took Jonathan's clasped hands in his. "Let's agree before the Lord that we will remain loyal to one another, regardless of what others may do."

"I pledge my loyalty to you," Jonathan said. "It's GOD's kingdom, after all. HE will decide who is to rule." He pointed upward as he said it, so there would be no doubt who he meant.

David smiled, understanding.

§ 54 ‰

While David was obviously glad to see Jonathan, Azel
knew that if Jonathan could find him, so could King Saul, so
no one was surprised when, a couple of days later, David
ordered camp struck and they were soon on the move again.

Azel was able to acquire a donkey that wasn't being used
as a pack animal for Dani to ride on. They were just a little
way back from David, Benaiah and David's nephews who
were leading the procession. Azel then noticed something: a
young woman was beside David and he was turning to her
and talking, causing her to look down with a demure smile.

Azel recognized her as Ahinoam, whose father was from
Jezreel and whose family had joined the group in the Forest
of Hereth. Azel hadn't known David to be with a woman since
Michal, Saul's daughter, had been taken from him.

Ahinoam looked up at David with wide eyes and a smile as
they walked along, David talking to the men.

Azel smiled at Dani, and she responded with a smile that
let him know she knew what he was thinking.

It would be good if David found happiness with a woman.

That night they made camp on a flat, barren plain and, as
the campfires were being lit, David called all to gather.

"Our life has been hard and you honor me by following
me. So, I want you to be the first to know that I have paid the
bride price to Othnal of Jezreel," David reached out his hand
to grasp the shoulder of Othnal, who was standing beside
him. "Tonight, I take his daughter, Ahinoam, to be my wife."

The young woman came from behind her father as all the assembled company cheered. She smiled bashfully, her large, dark eyes reflecting the light of the campfires.

Someone began singing a wedding song and dancing about the fire.

"Abiathar!" David called, when the song was done. "Bless our union."

Abiathar prayed, "Yahweh, bless your servant David and Ahinoam his wife. Guard their lives and bring them fully into your will."

That night, David took Ahinoam to his tent and she became his wife.

❦ 55 ❦

Azel was startled awake by a trumpet and the sound of shouting and women wailing. He jumped up from his bedroll and said, "What is happening?"

"Saul is near!" said a woman who was running by.

Azel grabbed his sword and ran toward David's tent, where he found David and his top echelon in a tight knot speaking in low tones. Other men were coming to await news as well.

"How far?" Azel asked Asahel.

"Only a couple of miles we think."

Then David turned to face all those who had gathered.

"Saul has apparently found us," he began. "He is coming from the north. We must move quickly. I say we should move to the other side of that mountain."

Azel looked in the direction David pointed. There was indeed a mountain with many boulders around its base about a half mile away.

"We may not be able to outrun him," David continued, "but on the other side of the mountain we will hopefully find cover from which we can defend ourselves and allow our families to escape.

"Now see to it, we must leave quickly. If you must, leave behind things which would slow you down. Don't wait for a signal. When you are ready, leave!"

Then he turned to Asahel.

"Asahel, take the men who have no families and form a defensive line to our rear as we move out."

"Yes, lord!"

❦

Jeriah was riding his donkey close to the king when a scout approached.

"O King, may you live forever. I have seen David's camp. They are just ahead."

"Then lead the way," Saul said, then turning to the troops behind him, he shouted, "Hurry, we will catch him today!"

The scout took off running and those officers who were mounted on donkeys spurred their mounts to move as quickly as they were able, with the foot soldiers following at a trot.

Jeriah wondered if all this would finally end. He found himself with mixed emotions about the slaughter that might be just ahead; of people whom they should see as their brothers, and quite possibly of his own real brother.

Ahinoam trembled as she packed her few things in a bag in the relative darkness of David's tent. She had only just become the wife of Judah's hero and, while they had been fleeing the king for some time, today there was real danger.

Then David entered. "Ready?" he asked.

"Almost."

"You may have to leave some things."

"Yes, I just can't decide what to take," she said, just starting to cry.

"The Lord will provide whatever we need."

"But what if the king catches you?" Ahinoam sobbed.

"It has been foretold that I will be king. Nothing will happen to me."

Ahinoam looked at her new husband, whom she barely knew. The look on his face told her that he believed what he said, and strangely, it calmed her.

"Then I'm ready. Let's go."

⚘ 56 ⚘

Azel and Dani came out of their tent and threw some of their belongings on the back of their donkey.

"Go on. I'll catch up," Azel told her.

"No, you must come! Saul wants to kill you, too."

"I'll be right behind you. Now go."

Dani grabbed her young son, Adriel's hand, and tugged on the donkey's bridle to get the stubborn beast moving.

Azel turned and looked to the north. He could see Asahel and his men, preparing to defend them. He knew that Eliel was with them, since he was "a man with no family." He thought of joining them, but then realized he did have family responsibilities, so he turned and ran to catch up with Dani and Adriel.

"I see their dust!" Abner shouted, pointing for Saul to see the desert sand being kicked up by David's fleeing refugees.

"Hurry, men!" Saul shouted behind him. "We will catch the son of Jesse today!"

The men did their best to push forward, but they were weary after an all-night march and the desert sun was debilitating.

Abner looked over at his cousin, the king. He was haggard, but doggedly pressing forward. They were pushing their donkeys to move under them as their men ran alongside them, weapons ready.

Then Abner looked forward again and could still see the cloud of dust before them. *Could it be that Saul's obsession with David might finally end today?*

It appeared David's band of outlaws was turning to go around the mountain.

"We need to be careful," Abner shouted to his cousin. "David is a brilliant tactician. We cannot take anything for granted."

There was no response from the king.

"Let's gradually fall back," Asahel told his men, including Eliel. "We will be ready to meet them when they arrive, but we need to stay close to the rear of our group."

The men didn't have to be told twice. They understood that their job was to protect their fleeing friends and family, not to make a stand where they had been camped. They could best do that by conducting an orderly retreat around the mountain.

They had gone about a mile, Eliel guessed. They were part way around the mountain and could see neither their fleeing group, nor Saul's pursuing army. He knew that if they engaged Saul's main force, theirs would become a suicide mission, but it might allow the others to escape.

They kept moving, running backward part of the time with weapons ready, expecting to see Saul's troops come around the bend at any moment. Eliel and the others took turns hiding behind rocks to look into the distance, then breaking and running a short distance before looking again from behind the next pile of rocks.

"Stop," Asahel whispered loudly. "Listen."

The men stopped, looking at him, not understanding what he meant.

"I don't hear anything," said Adino, Eliel's friend and one of Asahel's squad leaders.

"Exactly." Asahel walked out in the open and continued listening. A couple of his men warily came out and stood with him. "If they were still coming, wouldn't we hear them?"

"But why wouldn't they still be coming?" Eliel asked.

"We must go forward; we almost have him!" Saul shouted. He had dismounted and was arguing with Abner, his sword in his hand. The whole army had halted and were watching the argument between the powerful cousins.

"But the Philistines have invaded the land," Abner said, turning to the messenger who had just caught up with them and halted their pursuit of David. "They are in Gezer, didn't you say?"

"Yes, and marching toward Beth-horon," the messenger answered.

"They are at the borders of Benjamin!" Abner said, looking at the frustrated king of Israel. "And Jonathan leads the main body of the army to meet them now. We must join him!"

Saul angrily threw his sword into the sand too close to Abner's feet. Abner had to jump to ensure it didn't hit him.

"All right! Turn! Turn 'round if we must," Saul shouted with a low growl. "We go to fight the Philistines!"

"Turn, men," Abner ordered, speaking to the soldiers standing nearby. "We are going north to intercept the Philistine army."

The men, who had already marched all night, looked a little bewildered and angry, but they turned and began marching back north again.

❦ 57 ❦

"I'm tired!" Adriel whined.

"I'm tired, too," Dani replied, "But we must continue on to a safe place."

Dani knew that a nine-year-old could not visualize a threat that was not right in front of him, but she didn't want to tell him how dire their situation was, because a frightened nine-year-old could be more of a problem than a tired one.

"I'm thirsty."

Dani could do something about that. She had managed to pack a waterskin on the donkey before they had to rush away from their most recent campsite. She gave him a long drink and wondered how long it would have to last.

Azel had been with her and Adriel, but when word came that the king had broken off the search, he had left to confer with the other leaders of their band. Eliel was still away with the fighting men, no doubt still guarding the rear of their ever-expanding group of wanderers. She assumed others were planning the next place they would make camp.

She was truly tired, not just weary from having to leave so hurriedly, but tired of being always on the run, never feeling safe. She had left behind a lot of what she had collected over the past several months, so she figured the men would now make more forays into Philistine territory to raid and pillage their villages for the things their nomadic band needed.

She gauged from the angle of the sun that they were headed more-or-less east. They were already in the Judean wilderness and she knew if they continued on their current path, soon they would descend into the Valley of Salt.

They had been there before and she knew how difficult it was to survive in that desert.

Ahinoam struggled to keep up as David and his cousin, Joab, set the pace for the rest of the group. Her husband ignored her as he and Joab's intense conversation proceeded. She wasn't miffed by that at all, knowing that the situation called for careful leadership.

She didn't know why King Saul's army had stopped following them. The talk among the group, relayed by the men in the rearguard, was that Saul's army had just suddenly stopped, but she also knew that they needed to put as much distance as possible between them and Saul, in case he pursued them again.

The pace was exhausting and she wondered how long they would keep it up. The only source of encouragement was that the ground was tending to slope downward as they began descending into the valley around the Salt Sea.

An elderly man tripped on a stone and fell headlong. Azel rushed to help him up.

"Here, let me help. Are you all right?"

"Thank you, young man. I think so."

The man straightened up. Azel marveled at how light he was. He likely had lost weight during their ordeal. Azel realized he was also leaner and darker than when they had fled Gibeah so long ago.

Azel stayed until the man had his feet under him again and had started forward.

"Will you be okay?"

"I will be fine. I've been taking journeys like this since before you were born!"

"Yes, sir. I'm sure you have."

Azel watched as the old man gathered his threadbare cloak about him and rejoined the group, walking precariously on his thin legs.

Azel looked up and down the long column of dusty, weary travelers.

How long will we have to be on the run?

❦ 58 ❧

This country is indeed a wilderness.

Jeriah and the rest of the king's army were riding deep into eastern Judah to desert country near the Salt Sea. Everywhere were rugged crags and caves in the steep walls of barren ridges.

They had driven back the Philistine invasion, as they had many times before, but it had taken several weeks to do so.

Saul was still obsessed with finding and killing David, convinced that he was intent on taking his throne from him, so Jeriah, as the one who stood at Saul's right hand, and 3,000 soldiers hand-picked by Abner, were once again giving chase.

Jeriah and Abner had been unable to reason with the king or dissuade him in the least. Jeriah wished something would happen to make the king come to his senses and they could go back home to the green, familiar land of Benjamin. The only thing that had been able to steady the king in the past was the singing of David, the warrior psalmist, but it was him whom they sought to kill now.

Laboriously, Jeriah and the other officers rode on poor suffering donkeys while the infantry trudged on the stony ground, over a rise and down a treacherous slope in the merciless sun, seeking David, the brilliant military tactician, as if he could be caught like a truant child.

Jeriah, with a keffiyeh on his head to shield him from the harsh sun, doubted that they would ever see any trace of David in this rocky wilderness with its countless caves if he did not wish to be found.

"Do you think we'll actually be able to find him in this unforgiving country?" he asked Abner at one point in their journey, when they were out of earshot of the king.

"My spies reported they had seen David and his men in this very area, and that with some luck, we will find them yet. They can't elude us forever," Abner insisted.

"But your spies also reported that David's company of outcasts has grown to a size approaching that of his prior command, and I have no doubt that David would train them to fight." Jeriah said. "I fear if we meet them in this wilderness, we would be at a disadvantage for not knowing the terrain, despite our superior numbers."

"Our scouts will ensure that won't happen," Abner replied, "and our superior numbers will prevail."

Jeriah sensed that was the end of the matter as far as he was concerned.

Jeriah's former second in command, Eliab, David's brother, though not a full-time soldier, had resigned his commission some time ago, but when Saul had led his guard on a similar chase to Bethlehem, the family of Jesse was nowhere to be found. Jeriah felt sure that Eliab, experienced soldier that he was, was also in hiding with his brother.

The men were dusty and weary and finally they arrived at the oasis of En-Gedi and Saul gave the order to stop and rest. There was a spring where waterskins could be refilled, date palms without number and grass on which the donkeys could feast. After drinking their fill, the soldiers lay on the sand, looking up through the palm fronds above them, many of them drifting off to sleep.

"I am going to relieve myself," Saul announced wearily and Abner acknowledged with a nod. Saul sauntered off, looking like the old man he was, walking in the direction of a cave in a nearby hillside.

"Shall I follow?" Jeriah asked, starting to arise from where he had sat after dismounting.

"No, I'll be back shortly," Saul said with a wave of his hand. "Be refreshed."

Jeriah watched as the king approached the mouth of a cave, then lay back against the trunk of a date palm and closed his eyes.

Azel couldn't believe his eyes. He had been watching Saul's army pass by from the safety of a cave, when suddenly they stopped and dismounted near the spring some distance away. Then Saul himself began walking alone toward the mouth of the cave!

Azel stealthily stepped back into the shadows and slipped behind a stalagmite, peeking around it to watch as Saul entered the cave.

Amazed, Azel watched as the King of Israel raised his robe above his waist and began pissing against the cave wall. When he was finished, he coughed, cleared his throat noisily and walked a few loud steps further into the cave. Azel's right hand closed on the handle of the dagger in his belt, but shortly Saul found a flat place in the dirt on the cave floor and, with the difficulty characteristic of old age, lay down. Soon his snores were reverberating off the cave walls and Azel relaxed.

❦ 59 ❦

Azel pondered what he should do next. He could simply go and slash the king's throat and end the threat to David, but he wasn't sure he wanted to make that decision. If he killed a king, there would definitely be those loyal to Saul who would hunt him down. His brother might even be one of them.

So Azel slowly stood and carefully picked his way across the dirt, gravel and exposed rock of the cave floor and made his way back into the darkness of the cave's recesses.

There he joined David and a few other men, all sitting hunched in silence. The rest of the refugees were farther back in the cave, where they had been hiding since they became aware that Saul's men were in the area.

"What's happening?" David whispered.

"It is Saul and his army as we suspected," Azel began. "But Yahweh has delivered the king into your hand! Saul is right now alone and asleep inside this very cave. Hurry and you can cut his throat and your exile will be at an end!"

"Let us go see," David said, motioning for Benaiah and Eliab to accompany them.

Azel and the others approached the mouth of the cave until they could see the king in the distance and beyond him the dazzling light of day.

"See, he is alone. You can kill him easily," Azel whispered.

David looked at the man who had once been his father-in-law and said, "I cannot raise strike the Lord's anointed."

Azel and the others looked at him, amazed, then they looked at one another, not knowing what to do.

"Come, quietly," David motioned for the others to follow him. Benaiah's hand was on his sword as he moved ahead silently with the others.

Soon the four men stood over the snoring monarch, who was lying on his back sleeping, his head thrown back and his mouth open, his neck and belly within easy reach of the men's swords.

Presently, David drew his sword and the others started to reach for their own weapons, but David held up his hand to stop them.

As they watched, David took Saul's cloak in his hand and cut a section off the corner of the distinctive garment, with its colorful brocade and bright, golden fringe. That done, David motioned for the men to head back into the cave. After they had gone a short distance, David motioned again for them to stop behind a rock where they could watch.

◁ 60 ▷

It took about twenty minutes for the king to rouse. He sat up slowly and hunched over, coughing several times, then slowly rose and started for the mouth of the cave. As Saul emerged into the daylight, David signaled his men to stealthily follow. They stayed against the walls of the cave as they moved toward its mouth.

Azel could not imagine what David was planning. He could see that the king's guard had also rested and most were now mounted to continue the hunt. The infantrymen had already marched ahead down the trail. Soon the king himself was on his donkey and starting to move with only a few soldiers to bring up the rear of the column.

"Stay hidden and at the ready," David whispered and then he quietly rose and walked toward the cave's entrance. Saul and the others had moved some distance when David broke the silence.

"My lord and king! Why do you listen to men who say I am intent on harming you? What have I done that you hunt for me like a robber?" David shouted, his voice reverberating off the rocks and back into the cave. Azel couldn't believe it. He instinctively drew his sword, certain Saul's men would soon be upon them.

"David?" Saul called out turning his donkey. "Is that you my son?"

"It is. What have I done that you pursue me? Did I not sit at your table? Am I not a true friend to your sons and daughters?"

Saul and the men around him seemed unable to move, so surprised were they that their prey had revealed himself.

"See, father, I cut a piece from your cloak just now while you slept. I could have just as easily cut your throat, as some of my men urged me to do, but I said, 'I will not lift my hand against the Lord's anointed."

Azel could hear pain in David's voice; something he hadn't heard before in the usually strong, unflappable warrior. He also saw the king check his coat and realize David was telling the truth.

"Please understand, I am not guilty of doing wrong or rebellion," David continued. "I have not attacked you, though you are pursuing me to take my life.

"May the Lord judge between you and me and may He avenge the wrongs you have done to me, but I will not lift my hand against you.

"As the proverb says, 'From evildoers come evil deeds,' but have not touched you.

"Who are you pursuing anyway? A dead dog? A flea on a dead dog? May the Lord vindicate and deliver me!"

From the darkness of the cave, Azel saw King Saul's head had sunk down and his shoulders had slumped. When he spoke, his voice cracked in a sob.

"David, my son, you are more righteous than I. You have treated me well, but I have repaid you with evil. The Lord delivered me into your hands, but you did not kill me. Will a man finding his enemy let him get away unscathed and continue on the road? May the Lord reward you!"

Then he choked and seemed to be weeping. The king took a long breath before continuing.

"I know you will be king, and the kingdom of Israel will be strong under your leadership. Just please promise me you will not wipe out my family and destroy the memory of my father's house."

"I promise I will not destroy your family," David answered.

Azel looked on, unable to fully understand the drama. These men were supposed to be bitter enemies, at least Saul had been acting like David's enemy. But now they were talking like long-lost family.

"I will pursue you no more!" the king continued. "You don't need to be concerned. I am returning to Gibeah."

Saul then motioned to the men around him to follow and they rode slowly away.

As the king and his men disappeared around an outcropping of rock, the three men walked out, joining David in the open, looking after them in amazement.

"Does this mean we can go home?" Eliab asked.

"No," David replied. "I know the king. He says he will no longer pursue me, but tomorrow the evil spirit may return and he will again desire to plunge a javelin through my heart."

The three men looked at David, then at one another, then sadly at the trail through the desert outside the cave as the king's men rode away.

Azel couldn't be sure, but he believed one of the men riding with the king was his brother. He suddenly missed Jeriah, but he couldn't dwell on it because David spoke again.

"One thing it does mean, though," David continued. "We must move again. He knows where we are now."

As the army of Saul rode away, Jeriah strained to look back at the mouth of the cave. He could now see four men there. They were obviously unwashed and with worn clothing, due to their long exile.

He wondered if one of them was his brother. If not one of them, certainly he was nearby with his wife and sons; loyal to the man under death sentence from the king Jeriah was sworn to protect.

They rounded a curve in the trail and Jeriah could no longer see them. This was another wasted trip, but at least no blood was shed.

How many times would they pursue David, only to be turned back?

❦ 61 ❧

Jeriah once again stood at the right hand of the king as courtiers and supplicants came before him. The experience at En-Gedi where David had refused the opportunity to kill him had made the king quiet and opaque as he discharged the day-to-day activities of the royal court. Jeriah was glad that Saul seemed stable, but he wondered how long it would last. Still Saul's mood didn't match the sunshine that filtered through the branches of the Tamarisk.

Out of the corner of his eye, Jeriah noticed that Abner had slipped into the courtyard and was standing in the shadow of the portico. Focusing on the general and allowing his eyes to adjust, Jeriah could see that Abner's face showed distress.

When Saul dismissed the courtier before him, Abner came forward and stood before the king.

"May the king live forever," Abner began, bowing slightly, with more-than-usual formality. "There is news."

"Why do you hesitate? Tell it," Saul replied to his cousin.

"Samuel has died."

Jeriah gasped involuntarily, even though this death was not unexpected. Samuel was very old, but he wondered how the king would react to the news.

Jeriah saw that Saul's face had gone white. He lowered his head so far that no one in the room could see his expression. Finally, the king arose and spoke.

"You are all dismissed. I am finished with business for the day. I go to mourn the passing of a great judge in Israel."

With that the king walked to the door behind the throne and passed through to go to his home.

The men who had been waiting to come before the king didn't immediately move, so Abner turned and spoke.

"You heard the king. There will be no more business today. We mourn for Samuel!"

❧ 62 ❧

Azel was preoccupied with providing for the comfort of Dani and Adriel as the large company moved again, led by the charismatic David, like some little, nomadic nation. Eliel was now a man in his own right and marched with others his own age in a separate unit.

After they climbed the steep road from the shores of the Salt Sea, they once again entered the wilderness of Judah. The travelling was difficult and exhausting, so Azel was glad he had a donkey for Dani to ride. Adriel was off with friends, playing the games boys play.

As they emerged from the desert, the land was densely covered with tangles of trees and undergrowth and then, gradually the vegetation grew dry and sparse. The soil grew sandy and dry: They had entered the Desert of Maon.

When Adriel rejoined his parents complaining of thirst, Azel gave him the last of the water in one of the jars and checked the other two, only to find one bone dry and the precious liquid in the other nearly gone.

The sun was setting when they finally stopped in a dry, inhospitable valley where there was evidence of a stream during the rainy season, which was just past, so there was a little water in the stream. Eagerly Azel and the others in David's band of men drank from the trickle of water and filled their jars and waterskins. They moved a little further and the order came down the line to stop and make camp on top of a hill.

It was pretty much dark as Azel helped first Adriel and then Dani down from the donkey and tied the donkey's goat-hide reins to a stake, which he drove into the hard-packed sand with a stone lying nearby. The donkey immediately started munching a pitiful tuft of desert grass within its reach.

Dani took their blankets and tent from the donkey's back and looked for a place that was flat and not too stony to lay them, while Azel took two tent poles and pushed them into the ground temporarily until Adriel handed him the stakes he would use to anchor the ropes stretched over the poles. He pounded the stakes into the hard ground with one of the many rocks which were plentiful all around.

As they had now done many times, Azel, Dani and Adriel soon had their lean-to shelter of black goat-hair cloth erected and ready for a much-needed night's sleep. Adriel returned after wandering off, having found a lonely desert flower for his mother with which to grace their tent.

All around them hundreds of others were doing the same thing, but Joab called several men to take positions to watch the periphery of the camp during the first watch. Azel was glad his name was not called. A decision about whether they would continue on or stay in this place would be made tomorrow, Azel knew.

When Azel awoke in the morning, he looked down into the valley and his eyes grew wide. Below their encampment a large herd of sheep was moving by. He had never seen so many sheep! There were hundreds of them.

"The owner of this flock must be very rich." Azel turned to see that it was Asahel who had spoken. "We should offer our protection to them. It may be that the rich man will reward us with supplies we can use. Let's go talk to the herdsmen."

After Azel strapped on his sword, he and Asahel descended into the valley, having to negotiate some steep places, holding to scrubby bushes as they went. As they drew closer, Azel could see that there were stone walls in the valley forming several pens and the shepherds were moving the sheep into them.

"Good morning, men of Judah!" Asahel called out when they had reached the valley floor and begun walking toward the herdsmen nearest them. The men just looked at them suspiciously.

When they were closer, Asahel spoke again. "We bring greetings from David. He is camped right up there on the ridge with his men. Whose flock is this?"

"Nabal of Carmel," the man nearest answered, still watching Asahel and Azel closely.

"My family and I are shepherds also," Asahel continued. "It is shearing time, is it not?"

"It is. We have come to this valley to shear the flock."

"Well, it looks like you have a big job ahead of you," Asahel said, looking across the valley at the hundreds of bleating sheep. "We will be camped here a few days and would be happy to provide protection from predators, so you may devote yourselves to your work."

"All right," said the man, still looking at them with questioning in his eyes. His gaze fell and rested on the swords strapped to Asahel's and Azel's sides.

"Good, you will not have to worry while you are here," Asahel assured him.

❧ 63 ☙

Asahel and Azel informed David of the arrangement and he was pleased. He directed his men to move their encampment to the valley and set up on the periphery of the shearing area. The day was spent moving their tents, along with their women and children to create several little camps encircling the sheep and the shepherds.

Over the next several days, they developed an uneasy truce as the shepherds gradually came to trust them, realizing that David's men would not hurt them and would make their work go faster because they didn't have to worry about security.

At night, the fires of David's company served to warn off the lions and wolves that would be tempted by the prey within the stone walls. During the day, David would lead two-thirds of his men on foraging trips, while leaving one third to serve as sentinels on the perimeter, guarding their own belongings and that of the shepherds.

Only once did David's men have to act to protect the flock. As darkness was falling, Azel heard a shout from the other side of the sheep pens. There was a short commotion, with shouting and the sound of weapons clashing, then silence.

Azel later learned that men on camels had ridden up fast. They wore the black mohair of desert nomads from the Negev and were probably Midianites. It appeared the men intended to take the flock for themselves, however they were not expecting to find men with swords guarding the perimeter and, after a very short skirmish, the desert dwellers fled.

After that, the shepherds were friendlier and more open, and even shared their supply of food with David's men and their families.

When the shearing was completed, it was customary to have a great feast in celebration. The shepherds had moved the flock to better pasture and most of them had gone to their master's house for the feast. David summoned Asahel and gave him a task.

"I want you to take some of your men and go to Carmel, to Nabal's house, where they are enjoying the feast at the end of shearing season," David began. "Say to him, 'When your shepherds were with us, we did them no harm and nothing of theirs was missing. Ask your men and they will tell you. So please, let my young men find favor and give to your servant and your son David whatever you find at hand.'

"Can you give Nabal that message and bring back whatever he gives you?"

"Yes," Asahel answered. "I'll take several of my men."

"Men, gather 'round," Asahel called out when he was back to his part of the encampment. "David has charged us with going to Carmel to appeal to Nabal to give us supplies from his abundance. We will need pack animals with which to bring back supplies. I need nine volunteers."

Eliel, Shammah and Adino stepped forward immediately and several others joined them, so Asahel had his volunteers, very quickly.

"Good. Each of you get a donkey on which we can carry supplies. We will meet back here and leave within the hour.

Abigail, the wife of Nabal, was in charge of all the arrangements of food and wine for the feast. She had a staff of nine women and two young men, some of whom brought the heavy jars of wine from the storeroom to the banquet hall of Nabal's large house.

She was glowing with perspiration, but that only enhanced her beauty. She was 17 years younger than her husband and less than half his weight. He also had other, younger wives as a testament to his wealth and station, and they were helping with the feast by serving the 50 or so guests and chief shepherds reclining at the massive tables laden with elaborate centerpieces and trays of every imaginable delicacy.

It was an especially busy time, as they were serving the noon meal on the last day of the feast. Word reached Abigail in the kitchen that 10 more men had arrived. Abigail sighed, *My husband has invited more guests?*

Then a while later, one of the chief shepherds left the banquet hall and came into the kitchen, "Abigail!" he called.

She looked up from the bread she was taking from the oven just as the shepherd saw her. He ran over and spoke excitedly in a loud whisper.

"Mistress, some men came from David to offer greetings and, in the spirit of the celebration, asked master to share from his supply with them, but he rebuffed them, saying, 'Who is this David? So many slaves have escaped from their masters these days. Why should I give my bread and meat to men from who-knows-where?'" the man repeated, appearing very alarmed.

"The men went away dejected. I fear when David hears it, he will take vengeance on us all because of our master," the shepherd continued. "David and his men were with us for many days as we sheared the sheep, and they didn't harm us but provided protection. I don't know what you can do, but Nabal was so bitter and unreasonable I fear David will retaliate."

Abigail thought hard about what the family's trusted manager had told her. The words he reported Nabal had said were certainly in character. She knew how cruel her husband could be and she had the bruises to prove it. After several days of wine, her husband's churlishness would be amplified.

"Thank you for telling me. I'll take care of it. Rejoin the feast before my husband misses you."

Her mind was racing now. Shortly she drew her steward aside and began giving instructions.

❧ 64 ❧

Azel and the other men of David – 400 of them – were on the march. The other 200 had stayed to guard the camp.

They had been told without warning that they were to gird themselves for battle and be ready to march, but they did not know why or where they were going. David was riding at the head of the column, setting a rapid pace. Azel couldn't fathom what the emergency was.

Then his friend and David's nephew, Asahel, appeared at his side.

"Why do we march?" Azel asked him.

"Nabal has rewarded our protection with insults. David rides to take vengeance. He has vowed to leave not one man alive in all Nabal's household."

Azel was surprised. *Why would the man not appreciate what they had done in protecting his shepherds and flocks, even while he celebrated the shearing season?*

Abigail goaded her donkey to go faster. She was determined to intercept the attack she was certain was coming. She had not told her husband she was going. She had left a skeleton crew in the kitchen. She hoped that Nabal and the others would be sleeping off their wine in the heat of the afternoon.

When they had gone about five miles, she saw them coming. The men were riding donkeys and were armed to the teeth. A shiver ran down her spine, though it was hot under the afternoon sun. She saw the man in the lead and knew instinctively that it was David. He was sitting straight on his donkey and was urging it forward, determination evident on his bronze face with fire dancing in his eyes.

When they were near, Abigail dismounted, knelt and bowed, her forehead all but touching the earth, in front of David, who stopped and ordered the soldiers to halt.

"Lord, you should blame me and only me. Please hear what I have to say," Abigail began. "You should pay no attention to that wicked man, Nabal. His name means 'fool' and it fits him perfectly. If I had seen your men, I would have treated them differently.

"Now, Yahweh has kept you, my master, from bloodshed. May your enemies and anyone who wishes you harm be like Nabal."

She rose and pointed behind her, where her steward and two maid servants were on their own donkeys and holding the reins of more donkeys, loaded down with food.

"Let this gift which I, your servant, have brought to you, my master, be given to the men who follow you. I have brought 200 loaves of bread, two skins of wine, five dressed sheep, five measures of roasted grain, 100 cakes of raisins and 200 cakes of pressed figs." Abigail paused only the length of time she needed to take a breath.

"Please forgive my offense, for Yahweh will certainly make your dynasty last forever, because you fight His battles. Let no wrongdoing be found in you as long as you live. Even though someone pursues you to take your life, you will be protected by the Lord God. Your enemies' lives God will hurl away like a stone from a sling.

"When Yahweh has fulfilled all his promises to you and has appointed you leader over Israel, my master will not have on his conscience the guilt of needless bloodshed. When Yahweh has brought you success, remember me, your humble servant," Abigail finished, once again bowing with her forehead low.

David was amazed at the courage and resourcefulness of this young woman. Her poise and rhetorical skill was impressive indeed. She was courageous for asking him to blame her instead of her husband, although she had called him a fool, so she was probably defending her household more than him.

He was impressed at how she had referenced his future dynasty and Saul's efforts to kill him, even including a figure of speech involving a sling. He was suddenly seized with great relief.

"Praise Yahweh, the God of Israel, who sent you to meet me today. May you be blessed for your wisdom and for preventing me from shedding blood today. If you had not come to meet me, not one man in Nabal's house would have been left alive by tomorrow morning.

"We will accept your gifts. Go home in peace, knowing that I have heard you and granted your request."

❦ 65 ❦

Abigail, her steward and the servant girls arrived back home and stabled the donkeys as the sun was going down.

The kitchen was empty except for Nabal's two younger wives who were still serving wine. They looked at her with hollow, tired eyes, but said nothing. Abigail followed one of them as she carried a carafe into the banquet hall.

The fifty or so men were roaring drunk, laughing and telling bawdy jokes and mocking one another. Nabal was in rare form, presiding over the festivities, his loud guffaws bouncing off the plastered walls. One man reached out and pinched the young wife of Nabal carrying the carafe and laughed when she jerked and moved away. Others laughed too. Nabal didn't seem to notice or care.

Broken pottery littered the floor and spilled wine stained the table cloths. This feast was costing a fortune, but Nabal could afford it. He was in no condition to hear what had happened, so Abigail left, deciding she would tell him what had happened tomorrow when the feast was done.

That night, David's band of refugees had a feast of their own. Azel brought his family's portion of mutton which Dani immediately put over the fire to roast. They enjoyed some of the best wine they had ever had, and Adriel found the date cakes like a fly drawn to honey. Eliel stopped by as well, and the family ate the delicious food together until they could eat no more.

All around them, others were luxuriating in the sumptuous feast the wife of Nabal had so generously brought and as night fell, they retired with full stomachs and smiles on their faces.

The outcome of the day could have been so much worse, Azel thought, as he drifted off in slumber.

The next morning, Abigail saw to it that her kitchen staff began the process of cleaning up the mess left by the revelers and then went to the private quarters of the huge house. She went to the entrance of Nabal's bed chamber and opened the double doors, knowing that he likely wouldn't hear her if she knocked, because he would be sleeping off his celebration.

He was sprawled diagonally across the bed, still dressed as he had been last night, with wine and dried food down the front of his expensive tunic. She looked at his flabby frame and could barely control her anger. His arrogance and insolence might have gotten them all killed yesterday, but he was oblivious.

She pulled back the drapes, letting a shaft of bright, morning sun splash across the bed, but he didn't stir.

"Nabal! Wake up," she shouted. "You need to attend to some news."

He coughed and squinted at the sunlight, then turned away from it and groaned, putting one hand on his head.

"You missed something yesterday while you were drunk," Abigail said loudly. Nabal responded by groaning and putting his hands over his ears.

"Listen, you need to hear this," she continued. "Yesterday after you sent David's men away empty-handed, David and all his men were riding here to put you and everyone in this household to the sword. Your arrogance and stupidity almost got us all killed, if it hadn't been for me. I went and met David and his men on the road and took the supplies he wanted and begged for mercy, so he relented, no thanks to you!"

Nabal then turned and looked at her with wide eyes as the import of her words dawned on his foggy mind. Suddenly he clapped a hand to his chest, raised his head and closed his eyes tightly. A gasp escaped his lips and he fell back on the bed, motionless.

Abigail looked down at her despicable husband. She watched closely and saw that his chest was rising and falling.

He is still breathing, she thought, but she felt nothing.

❧ 66 ❧

Azel was putting together supplies for another overnight foraging expedition. Dani was putting away the leftovers from their breakfast and Adriel was playing with some other children in the camp.

Something caught Azel's attention and he turned. To his surprise, he saw the woman who had met them on the road a couple of weeks ago, the wife of Nabal. She was riding a donkey and with her were five young women, apparently her maid servants. Why was she here?

Other of David's men were accompanying them on their way and out of curiosity, Azel decided to follow the growing entourage.

The men directed the woman to David's tent. He came through the tent flap and walked toward her. She immediately dismounted and started to bow down, but David stopped her.

"Welcome. Thank you for accepting my invitation. Your husband who was a trial to you is dead and now you shall be my wife."

Azel was surprised again, because he hadn't heard all this. Nabal was dead? And his wife would be the new wife of their champion? To Azel this seemed like poetic justice indeed.

Only later did Azel learn the details of how Nabal's heart had failed him when he learned of the close call he and his household had experienced and, after lying still as a stone for 10 days, he had passed away.

❧ 67 ☙

Once again, the more-than-one-thousand-member community of David was on the move. Azel led the donkey carrying Dani and Adriel. It was to be a long journey. He would follow David anywhere, but recent events were confusing to him, in spite of his loyalty.

They were on their way to Philistia, of all places, and even stranger, to Gath, the city of Goliath, the giant David had slain. What's more, they were going to seek refuge. It seemed that David had lost courage just when it seemed to Azel there was much about which to be encouraged.

As had happened over and over, the people of the region near Carmel had reported to Saul that David was hiding there. Once again Saul had come after them with three thousand men; five times the number of warriors that were with David. Admittedly that was discouraging, but what happened next could have been seen as a glimmer of hope.

As had happened at En-Gedi, David again had a perfect opportunity to kill Saul, but he had again refused.

This time, Saul was asleep in his camp and David was able to get close enough to steal into his tent and take his spear and water jug. Azel didn't miss the significance of David taking Saul's spear.

Once again, when David revealed what he had done and restored Saul's water jug to him, but not his spear, Saul had sworn he wouldn't pursue David. David's reaction, rather than be encouraged, was to become despondent and to move their large community again; this time clear across the land to the west, almost to the Great Sea.

Moving was a greater task now than it had been in the beginning. The families of David's 600 men continued growing over the years, as families do. Also, since David's marriage to Abigail, he had acquired Nabal's substantial herds and flocks. The magnificent house where Nabal had lived and died they had simply abandoned and his other wives and servants had drifted away.

David had overseen the barter of some of the animals for other supplies the community needed, but there were still significant numbers of sheep and goats that had to be moved. It was both a blessing and a curse: a blessing because there was no shortage of milk and meat on the hoof, and wool and goat hair for making woolen clothing and mohair cloth, but it was a curse because there was no way they could move fast, and if Saul found them, they would be vulnerable.

They could only hope he didn't learn where they were going now and pursue them before they obtained asylum.

❦ 68 ❦

When they arrived at Gath, David ordered his men to establish their camp outside the walls of the city. There was no way such a large company could find lodging inside the city, and he had another arrangement in mind, anyway.

When the work of establishing the camp was underway, David went to see King Achish. He took Joab and Benaiah with him.

As they entered the gate of the city, they were conscious of curious eyes watching them from every direction. Probably not everyone knew who they were and how strange it was to see them here, but some certainly did. David knew they couldn't let their guard down.

"I am David of Israel," he told the soldier standing guard at the gate of the king's palace. "I wish to see the king."

"Wait here," the man said, his eyes wide, then he went through the open gate and spoke to another soldier. That man then went toward the palace.

David, Joab and Benaiah waited in silence, not knowing how long they would have to wait or even if the king would see them or if they would have to fight their way out of the palace. The soldier standing guard eyed them warily while they waited.

The other soldier was back surprisingly soon. "The king will see you. Follow me."

They followed the man through the gate and down a long colonnade where the sun threw shadows of great pillars against the wall that had tall wooden doors at intervals its entire length. Finally, they came to a set of double doors with intricate carvings of Philistine triumphs, overlaid with gold.

The soldier pushed one of the doors open and motioned for them to follow him inside.

Once in the anteroom, the soldier turned to them and said, "You'll have to leave your weapons here."

The trio looked at one another and none of them moved to take off their swords.

"No one is allowed to take his sword into the throne room," the soldier emphasized.

At last, David unbuckled the belt to which his scabbard was attached and laid it against the wall. Benaiah and Joab reluctantly followed his example.

The soldier then waved them forward again. They followed a couple of paces behind him. They were now in an interior hallway with doors on either side. Large columns stood on either side of the hallway with heavy, rectangular stones spanning the tops of them to support the high roof. There were brightly painted clay pots on either side, out of which grew exotic plants common to the coastal area, some with brightly colored flowers. The polished-stone floor shone, reflecting the light like a peaceful lake. The three men who had been camping in the wilderness for months looked at one another, amazed at the opulence of the king's palace.

So, this is how a king lives, David thought.

Finally, they went through another set of double doors and the soldier called out, "David, the champion of Israel, to see the great king of Gath!"

David walked forward and Joab and Benaiah followed. When they were close to the throne, all three knelt on one knee and bowed their heads low.

"O King, may you live long," David said. "Your humble servants appear before you in need of sanctuary. Saul, your enemy, has sworn to kill us."

"Rise," said Achish, so the three men rose to their feet. The man sitting on the ornate, gilded throne before them was alert and vigorous, though it was obvious he was getting old.

"What brings the champion of Israel to take refuge among his enemies?"

"Saul has accused me of betraying him and desiring to be king in his place and in place of his sons. I have been unable to convince him otherwise, so he is intent on killing me."

"You are much too humble," Achish said with a hint of sarcasm. "Everyone in Israel and the surrounding countries believes you are the rightful heir to Saul's throne, ever since you slew my champion. It is the poorest kept secret, indeed."

"It is true the prophet Samuel anointed me, but I have no clear path to the throne and Samuel doesn't have the power to bring it to pass."

"Oh!" King Achish exclaimed. "You have not heard?"

"Heard what?"

"I'm surprised that I know more of what has transpired in Saul's kingdom than you. Nevertheless, it gives me no pleasure to be the one to tell you, Samuel is dead!"

David's eyes grew wide as he struggled to maintain his composure. Finally, he was able to speak.

"No, I hadn't heard. All the more reason that his prophecy cannot be realized."

He swallowed, then continued, "I have never presumed anything with regard to Saul. He has treated me with contempt, but I have ever treated him as a father."

"But here you are, a refugee from your own country. Ah, well, Saul is my enemy, and he is yours as well, so why should we not be in league?"

David was silent.

"You know, you are something of a curiosity to me," Achish said, standing and walking a few steps from his throne. "You might say I have been a student of yours, David. I have watched as you led Saul's army on successful campaigns. You have great talent; an incredible mind for strategy in such a young man."

"Thank you. Your kindness is unexpected."

"So, I am glad for this opportunity to get to know you. You are welcome to make your homes here in Gath as my guest," Achish spread his arms wide as a gesture of welcome.

"You are too kind, your majesty but, if I have found favor in your sight," David began tentatively, "your servant is not worthy to live in the royal city with your majesty. Also, our numbers are great, well over a thousand displaced souls and great flocks and herds. If it may be agreeable to your majesty, a small town, one of your satellites, could be given us to be our home, at least until our mutual enemy has died."

Achish thought a moment. "Very well, there is a small town to the south that has room for the building of new homes and would have fields suitable for flocks. It is Ziklag. Do you know it?"

"Yes, your majesty, I do, and I agree, that would be a good fit for us. Your kindness is unbounded."

David smiled inwardly. That was what he was hoping for. Ziklag was on the border of Judah and far enough from Gath that Achish wouldn't be able to watch them too closely, yet being inside Philistia, Saul would leave it alone.

❦ 69 ❦

It wasn't that unusual, but it took Azel by surprise anyway. After they had been in Philistia for a few weeks, Achish made David his "Bodyguard for Life." Azel knew that kings often set as personal guards people of other countries because they could not gain the throne by murdering the king, therefore they made ideal bodyguards to protect the king. As a result, cohorts were organized from David's 600 men to rotate duty guarding the palace of Achish in Gath.

Azel had recently returned from his time in Gath and was continuing work on a house for Dani and Adriel with Eliel's help. He struggled to lift a heavy, rectangular stone to the top of two wooden doorposts, standing on the ladder as Eliel lifted the other end from the ground. When they finally had it in place, Azel dropped down to the ground, breathing rapidly. He looked up to admire their handiwork, the lintel stone sitting securely atop the two door posts and slapped Eliel on the shoulder.

Soon Dani would have a real house again; their first real home since they had the family compound next to his brother's home in Gibeah.

They were still living in their tent while the house was under construction, as were many others. He had stacked the thick, mud-brick walls as high as the tops of the windows and would soon be able to finish the walls. Timbers for the rafters of the flat roof would be needed soon.

They had been on the run for eight years and, except for a few days in Keilah, they had not lived in a permanent dwelling, only their tent or even sleeping under the stars.

Azel knew Dani's nesting instinct would kick in as soon as the house was finished. He looked forward to the rest and luxury that would be possible when the house was finished.

He got up, having caught his breath, climbed atop a ladder and began to lay mud bricks atop the stone lintel, slopping mud between each course to hold them in place.

Azel planted a kiss on Dani's cheek and hoisted his pack onto his back. "We shouldn't be long," he assured her, knowing she would understand that "not long" meant "not many days."

David's men were going out to plunder again; something they hadn't done since arriving in Ziklag. But they needed supplies and goods they could barter.

They left at dusk, all 600 men, marching solemnly, contemplating what they were about to do. Only after they were on the road, did Azel learn where they were going. There was a Geshurite town to the south, not very far from Ziklag, so it didn't take too long for them to arrive. The Geshurites were scattered; this town was far from their point of origin to the north and across the Jordan river.

"We will spoil the town," David said to the men gathered around him. "Gather the spoil including the flocks and herds into the square, and," he hesitated only slightly, "put the entire population to the sword. No one must be allowed to tell who did this."

By now it was very late; the middle of the night. David and his men slipped into the town and began their bloody business.

Azel and a couple of his fellow members of Asahel's cohort smashed through the front door of a house and brought out a bewildered man and his family. The man made a feeble effort to resist, but Azel brought his sharp sword down upon his neck so he fell and lay silent. The women screamed and Azel's friends killed them quickly as well. Suddenly, a small girl screamed and ran out of the house trying to run around the corner of the mud-brick structure. One of Azel's fellows threw his spear which passed through the child's body and silenced her screams as she tumbled to the ground.

Azel's stomach churned and he turned away. "Come," he said to the others. "Let's be on to the next house."

The gruesome work continued until the several hundred inhabitants were all dead and the men began the work of gathering the spoil for travel back to Ziklag. Once they had gathered everything and loaded the valuables on pack animals, they torched the town.

This was just the first of many raids as David's band enriched itself. Some of these riches found their way to the elders of towns in Judah, like Lachish and Hebron. Azel thought he could see what David was doing and he marveled at his shrewdness. He was definitely playing the long game.

The road was familiar, as were the towns along it, meandering east through northern Judah. Even though he was headed to his boyhood home, Eliam was wary, watching each approaching traveler closely for signs of recognition or alarm. He wasn't worried about handling petty bandits, but he silently sized up each traveler for whether they might be inclined to relay his whereabouts to the king.

He had left Ziklag early this morning and was determined to reach his father's house in time for the evening meal. He was fit and strong and had no trouble keeping up the pace.

He had joined David's band relatively recently and his strength and skill with weapons had made him indispensable to the refugees. He had left his wife behind in the relative safety of Ziklag. She could not have made the trip, for she would likely give birth sometime in the next month. He was hurrying now, so he could accomplish his mission and hurry back to her.

The donkey he was leading was sometimes obstinate, and he had to use both enticement of food and threats of punishment to keep it going. It was laden with supplies that would be welcomed in his hometown of Giloh, north of Judah's main city of Hebron: things like fine rugs and gold and silver table service, plus pottery of colorful Philistine design.

The donkey is justified in balking at times under its burden, Eliam admitted to himself.

He passed Adullam and then Keilah, remembering that someone from that town had revealed the presence of David's refugees to King Saul and caused them to flee. He had no way of knowing who he could trust.

He made good time and, though the sun was low at his back, he saw the walls of the small village of Giloh ahead. He gave the reins an extra tug and pushed forward toward the open city gate.

Once inside the town, he first went to the marketplace and let the donkey drink his fill from the pool. He also availed himself of the jar from the well to have a long drink. Then he led the donkey down a familiar street toward the house where he had been born a little over 20 years before.

When he reached the house, he entered the walled compound through the gate and tied the donkey to a post.

"Father!" he cried.

The door at the front of the house opened and a 45-year-old man emerged. His black hair was peppered with gray, and he bore himself with an air of sophistication, but he wasn't aloof at all. He ran to embrace his son.

"Eliam, my son," Ahithophel exclaimed. "It is so good to know you are all right."

"Hello, father."

"Come in. Your mother is just setting food on the table."

After they ate their fill, Eliam related the adventures he and his wife had shared with the other outcasts following David, being sure to gloss over details that might alarm them, as the light of oil lamps flickered from the central table.

Eliam knew his parents' sympathies were with David, but his father, as an elder of Gihon, had to walk a political tightrope with the Benjamite king. He had influence with the tribal leadership in Hebron, Judah's main city. That would almost certainly be important when circumstances were right at some future time.

"Tell David we thank him sincerely for what you have brought," Ahithophel told his son as they began preparing for bed. "We will use these supplies to enhance the efficiency of our village government. Tell him also that we know he is a loyal Israelite and that your sojourn among the Philistines is a necessary, but temporary, departure."

"And find a way to let us know when our grandchild is born," Eliam's mother added eagerly.

Their time in Philistia had been a time of relative peace and security, compared to their years on the run. Azel thought how ironic it was that they were more prosperous and secure among the Philistines than in Judah.

The house he had built for the family served them well. After they had lived in it a few months, he had added an outdoor forge so he could begin training his sons in their trade. This was long overdue for Eliel, who was 18 when they arrived, and it was now time for Adriel to begin his training, for his next birthday would be his twelfth. This training had been postponed while they had been on the run.

Dani had flourished as well during the more than a year they had been there. *A woman needs a home*, Azel thought. She had become an expert weaver and was sought after for producing linen, wool and goat-hair cloth which she sold or bartered in the market in Ziklag.

One day, she came to Azel while he was working with Adriel with a look on her face that he had seen before.

"Husband, I'm happy to be able to tell you, you will be a father again."

Azel ran to her and took her in his arms. "To be a father again so late in our lives together! What a blessing! When will the child be born?"

"Likely spring," Dani said, smiling up at him.

❧

For Eliam's wife, Batya, her baby would come much sooner. She had a relatively easy labor, thankfully.

When Eliam was allowed to enter the house to see mother and child, he was proud of the daughter who lay upon her mother's breast. She was a beautiful baby even as a newborn.

They decided to give her a name similar to her mother's – Batya meant "daughter of the Lord." The name they gave their new baby was "Bat-sheva," which over time would become "Bathsheba," meaning "daughter of an oath."

<h1 style="text-align:center">❦ 70 ❦</h1>

"Where did you go raiding today?" Achish asked offhandedly, as he accepted a dish of grapes proffered by a slave girl in his throne room.

"Bethuel of Judah," David lied, without hesitation and without looking at his host. David and his loyal refugees had been the "guests" of King Achish of Gath for almost a year and four months now, and David had grown comfortable around the king, though he never completely let down his guard.

"Good, good." Achish replied. "You are burning bridges with your old masters and you can be loyal to me."

"Of course, sire."

"That is good now, because Spring is coming once again, when we will war against the kingdom of Saul and I want you by my side. You and your men will be my personal guards. I know you are eager to fight against our enemy." Achish regarded the young hero before him.

"Of course," David replied, flashing a smile toward the king. "When do we leave?"

"Two days."

"I will have my men assemble in Gath, ready to march then. Where will we go?"

"We attack the north. There is good growing land in the Jezreel Valley."

"So I have heard."

"Good, go and make your preparations."

"Until then," David said, bowing and backing away from the throne.

❦

"What are we going to do?"

"We will march with them," David answered the question from his top general, his nephew, Joab.

"How can we do that? I know Saul wants to kill us, but you are to sit on his throne one day and the Philistines will then be YOUR enemies."

"I understand the issues," David said impatiently. "For now, this is what we must do. Achish trusts us, to the point of making us his bodyguards in the battle."

"Never mind that his trust is built on lies!"

"How much of what we do is built on lies at present, just to stay alive?"

"How can we do this?" Joab shook his head.

"We do what we must do in every situation. That is our lot until God sees fit to give me the kingdom."

ᕦ 71 ᕤ

Jeriah was tired, which was to be expected at his age. The king he served was older than he, yet he continued to lead campaigns. Another spring meant yet another battle with the Philistines. Their lust for the highlands claimed by Israel had not lessened with the passing of years.

He was in Gibeah, in the bed chamber he shared with Shelomith, the last day of his leave before he must report. Abner's spies had relayed word that the Philistines would try to take the fertile Jezreel Valley far to the north, so there would be a long march. Jeriah did not relish it as he would have in years past. His responsibility for the past several years was for direct service of the king, preparing everything he would need for the march and the battle itself. In the battle, he would be the king's armor bearer and bodyguard, his last line of defense. Rarely did the fighting get so close to the king that he was personally in danger.

Shelomith came into the room and helped him roll up his bedroll, adding raisins, almonds and a little dried mutton which he would eat along the way during the march.

"Will you never leave this work?" she asked. "You have served faithfully and long enough."

"I serve the king. He will not live forever. I promise, when he dies, I will step aside."

Shelomith didn't seem too reassured by his answer. "I will pray for your safety."

"The safest place I can be is by the king's side," he answered, "but thank you."

He kissed her and went downstairs to the smith shop he and his son had built, with help from his brother, whom he had not seen for five years. There he found Misha'el, as he knew he would. The forge was his now.

"Misha'el, I'm leaving soon. We march north day after tomorrow."

Misha'el laid down his hammer and grasped his father's hand. Jeriah realized that his 25-year-old was stronger than he; the work at the forge having hardened him. He was proud of his firstborn son and knew the household was in good hands with him.

"Be safe, father. I look forward to your return."

"I look forward to it as well. I'm tired and ready to give my responsibility to others younger than me."

Misha'el smiled as Jeriah turned to leave. Shelomith was standing outside in the courtyard. She was crying.

"What's wrong?" Jeriah asked.

"I don't want you to go."

"I must go. I will return, as I always have."

"Swear it," Shelomith said.

"I cannot swear. The will of Yahweh will be done," he said, surprised at her demand. "I serve Yahweh as I serve the king. My fate, and yours as well, are in His hand."

Though his words did not seem to comfort her, he hugged and kissed her once again and left through the gate of the compound.

From the street, he looked back and saw her watching him from the open gate. He gave a little wave and she returned it with a small turn of her palm, her tears still flowing.

As he made his way to the royal complex, he wondered why she wanted him to swear that he would return. Did she have some premonition about this campaign being different from the others?

He put it out of his mind, knowing that he must soon leave for the march.

❧ 72 ❧

"You will be gone too long!" exclaimed Dani as she threw her arms around Azel's neck. "I don't want you to go."

I don't want to go either, Azel thought, but he said, "We'll be back before you know it."

"But how can you march with the Philistines after all they have done to our people?"

"We are in a difficult spot, I guess. We look to them for protection for now. Hopefully not much longer."

Just then Adriel entered and embraced his father.

"You take care of your mother," Azel said. Adriel would be a man soon, but he was hardly prepared for the responsibility, should both Azel and Eliel fail to return from the battle.

Azel's throat tightened, and he decided he needed to join the others at the marketplace.

"Until I return," he said, kissing each of them on the cheek. Then he turned again and caressed Dani's abdomen, with its growing, new life.

He left through the door he had constructed with his own hands and glanced back to see them both looking after him. They waved and he waved back then, straightening his pack and the weapons on his back, turned and strode away.

As he approached the marketplace, Eliel joined him. They nodded, but neither spoke.

Eliam had left before, but this time was different. He had often gone on foraging and raiding trips, staying away sometimes for several days.

This time, though, he wouldn't just be leaving Batya, his wife, but his baby girl as well.

Bathsheba was growing and developing fast. She was walking and getting into everything, and talking, too. It was evident she was very intelligent and was already able to bargain with her parents for whatever she wanted.

Eliam hadn't known it was possible to love someone as much as he loved Batya, but Bathsheba was in a different category altogether.

He kissed and embraced each of his girls, with tears running down Batya's face and Bathsheba uncharacteristically quiet as she watched what was happening, not fully understanding.

Eliam shouldered his bag and bedroll, having already strapped on his sword and dagger. He then picked up his spear and turned again to see his wife and daughter looking at him with shiny eyes.

"I'll be back before you know it," he said.

"Make sure you are," Batya answered.

Abigail's fingers refused to obey her as she worked to mend a small tear in one of David's tunics. She blinked and a tear began trickling down her right cheek, but she quickly wiped it away with the back of her hand and continued working with the needle.

Finally, the thread and needle cooperated and she tied it off with a fix that would have to do, because David was anxious to be gone.

Ahinoam appeared with a leather bag of food: dried mutton and fruit, such as dried figs and raisins, plus a few dates she had acquired in the marketplace. Her eyes met Abigail's and they both then looked away.

Best to be on-task and not think too much, Abigail thought. She knew Ahinoam was feeling the same.

David entered then. "Ready?" he asked.

"Here is food for your trip," Ahinoam volunteered.

"And your extra tunic is mended," Abigail said as she stood up and brought the tunic to him, folding it as she went.

"Thank you both," David said, as he shouldered the leather bag of food and took the folded tunic and stuffed it in another bag slung over his other shoulder.

"I have no idea how long I'll be away this time."

Both women looked at him with sad eyes. Abigail was afraid to say anything, lest he hear her voice break into a sob.

"Until then," Ahinoam threw her arms around him and kissed him. Abigail came close then and he kissed her as well.

"Be safe," Abigail was finally able to say.

"Pray for us," David said.

"Yes," both women said in unison.

With that, David turned and went out the front door of their house.

⚜ 73 ⚜

The five armies of the Philistines marched together on the coastal road going north and a little east, following the coast toward Tyre of Phonecia. They would not go that far however, for their destination was the fertile Vale of Jezreel. The five kings had indicated this would be their present incursion into the land claimed by the Hebrews.

Azel marched with the 600 men under David's command. Since he had been designated as King Achish's personal guard, they marched at the end of the column of the army of Gath, along with Achish's generals.

The green banners of Gath fluttered over the heads of the infantry, their ranks followed by mounted troops and, after them, heavy chariots made of iron.

It was a new experience for David's men to be marching with Philistine armor and weapons. They had never been so well-equipped, even when many of them had served in King Saul's army.

Late on the second day of the march, when the armies were passing the Canaanite city of Aphek, David's men were ordered to halt, while the rest of the units in the army of Gath continued on.

"What's happening?" Azel asked Asahel.

"I don't know. Go, see and report back."

Azel obeyed the order, urging his donkey forward to the front of the column where David rode in the royal chariot with King Achish. The generals of the army of Gath flanked them and, facing them were the other kings of the Philistines and their officers. Azel sensed the tension in the air before he heard their words.

"But David has been with me, serving loyally, for almost a year and a half," Achish said.

"What's to keep him from turning on us in battle to curry favor with Saul?" The king of Ashdod said.

"Yes, his sword could easily be turned against us!" said the king of Gaza.

"The Hebrews still sing about him: 'Saul has slain thousands, but David tens of thousands,'" argued Ekron's king. "His sympathies will likely be with them."

"All right!" Achish shouted. "You've made your point."

"Send these men back to where they came from!" Ashdod's king demanded. "Their presence is a liability we can't afford."

With that the other kings and their attending officers rode away to rejoin their respective armies.

As Azel watched, Achish turned to David. "I'm sorry, I know you are an honest man and I'm glad to have you serve with me. I have found no fault in you the whole time, but the other kings think you are not reliable, so take your men and leave in peace. We can't do anything the other kings think improper."

"What have I done?" David argued, though Azel wondered it if was just for show. "What can they see in me that would disqualify me to fight the enemies of my lord the king?"

"I know, and I would rather have you with me, but I can't go against the others. You and your men camp here tonight, then in the morning, return to Ziklag."

"As you wish," David answered, and he stepped down from the chariot.

Azel dismounted and spoke to him. "Commander, take my mount." He held out the reins to David.

"Thank you, Captain." He turned and checked to see that the Philistine column had moved away out of hearing before speaking again.

"I never cease to be amazed at the way the Lord works to solve our problems."

"That is why we are with you," Azel said, knowing he spoke for many when he said, "The Lord is with you."

❧ 74 ❧

It had to be a miracle of God, Azel thought as he walked along, light-hearted as could be. They were returning home to Ziklag without having taken part in the battle! Best of all, David's loyalty to Achish was still unquestioned by the king, even though the other rulers of the Philistines had refused to go into battle with the champion of Israel at their sides. They did not trust that David's loyalty would not turn during the battle, even if Achish believed in him.

So, they were going home!

They had risen early and marched hard from Aphek past Gath to cover the distance in a single day. It might be dark when they arrived, but they were going home to Ziklag!

Azel sped up, trotting to the head of the column to be near Asahel, his friend and commander. Eliel was already there, marching with the rank and file.

As usual, Asahel and his cohort, with their youthful strength and exuberance, were first to reach the crest of the ridge that led to Ziklag, so they were the first to pause, look down the road and see the smoke. Though they were still more than five miles away, there could be no mistake.

Ziklag was burning.

Asahel turned and shouted to the main body of David's company, "Ziklag burns! I see its smoke!"

Within seconds, David and Joab caught up and watched the smoke rising upward in the afternoon sky.

"It is not still burning," Joab corrected his brother bitterly. "This was done some time ago."

Azel considered Joab's words and realized they had been gone a week, with marching from Ziklag to Gath, where they had waited for the army to march, then the trek to the Jezreel valley and finally their return after the other kings had refused to have them present for the battle.

"Come, we must get there quickly," David said, and Azel, Eliel, Asahel and the rest of his men took off at a sprint, dropping their packs to lighten their loads.

"Do not leave your weapons, in case those who did this remain gathering the spoils," David urged them, but Azel doubted the perpetrators would have lingered. The men ran as fast as they were able, fear for what they would find driving them.

"Those with no family, stay with the stuff," Joab cried loudly, referring to the gear being discarded by the men who were speeding up the valley. Several men who had moved forward out of curiosity stopped moving to watch those running toward Ziklag, sharing their fear at what they would find, then beginning to gather up abandoned belongings.

The road was often narrow, and the 300-odd men jostled one another, their sandals slapping the flat stones as they hurried the last few miles to their homes – if they still had homes – determined to get there before sunset.

Eliel, with his friends Adino and Shammah, were at the front of the column hurrying toward Ziklag, running with others Asahel's company. As he continued toward the ascending smoke, he worried about what they would find when they arrived. Could it be that his mother and little brother would be found dead?

He couldn't bear the thought and put it out of his mind to focus on just moving as fast as his weary legs would allow. Though he was young and strong, the all-day march had wearied even him. To allow him to make good time, he had cast aside his pack with its heavy supplies, barely touched since they hadn't been allowed to enter the battle. He hoped those who stayed behind would take good care of it.

But he still carried his sword and his dagger sheathed in his belt, ready to use them if they found those who destroyed their town still there.

He sensed that his father was behind him and marveled that he was able to keep up, but then realized that, of course, he was motivated by the same fear of what they would find when they finally arrived home.

After half an hour, Asahel's band reached the point where they could see the first buildings at the entrance to the village, or at least they could see where the buildings had been. Only charred skeletons remained of roofs and many stone or mud-brick walls had been knocked down or fallen, weakened by the fire. As they approached, they slowed and listened, but there was no sound except the hissing of still warm embers. The smoke caught in their throats and their heaving lungs ached and stung. Each of the young men went to his own house, only to find it in ruins, ransacked, and everything of value gone.

But at least there were no bodies.

Asahel first noted that fact. He had feared Joab's reaction if his wife and daughter's charred bodies had been in the ash and rubble. Somewhat reassured, he quickly surveyed the houses in the compound he and Abishai shared with Joab and his wife, his anger growing as he remembered the hard work it had been to build the stone walls of the small extra room they had built together when they had first brought their families there.

Now the walls were scattered rubble on the ground. Broken pottery was everywhere among the ashes. Furniture that had not been burned had been smashed beyond repair. Anything of value had been taken. There was not even a goat to break the silence.

Then he saw it: an arrow in a beam. With great effort, he pulled it from the charred wood and examined the tip. Bronze. No one needed to tell him.

Amalekites.

It was their kind of craft. If it had been Philistine, the tip would have been iron, but this was the work of Amalek. There was no mistaking the windings on the shaft.

He turned and ran back the way he had come, passing many other men rushing to their homes. As he reached the square in the center of town, he met David and Joab.

"What is the news?" David asked him.

"All our families have been taken. There are no bodies," Asahel emphasized first, to reassure them. "But I found this." He handed the arrow to David.

"Amalekites." David said flatly. Joab cursed.

"They have taken everything of value and destroyed what they did not wish to take." Asahel added.

David sunk to the ground and sat cross-legged, holding his head in his hands.

"Will you not see your house?" Joab asked him.

"Go yourself and see your own house. Be sure your wife and child are not there," David said pointing toward Joab's home. "I will go to my house soon enough."

Joab and Asahel left him and ran back the way Asahel had just come.

Eliam ran to his house and found a scrap of wood to serve as a torch. With help from a smoldering ember, he got the torch burning and began searching the ashes. The ash was half a cubit deep in places, because scorched bricks and broken pottery was mixed in.

The torch light was pitifully poor, so he finally tossed it aside so he could use both hands to sift through the ashes with only moonlight to show him differences in materials ranging only from black to deep blue.

He felt his way along as if a blind man, feeling urgency, but fearing to move too fast lest he wound his hands on the sharp shards of pottery buried in the ashes.

He first searched the bedroom where he, Batya and one-year-old Bathsheba had slept, fearing what he would find, but his search revealed only broken bricks and pottery and a few metallic objects which survived the fire.

They must be taken, he thought, feeling first relief, then apprehension of a different kind.

❦ 75 ❦

David looked up and surveyed the square. The merchants' canopies were burned and their poles knocked down, some of which smoldered still. He wondered if Ahinoam and Abigail were alive and if they were, would they wish they were dead instead of being in the hands of the Amalekites?

Saul had been ordered to kill men, women, children and even cattle of the Amalekites, and he had made an effort, but David realized there were still clans of them deep in the Sinai that Saul had failed – or had not tried – to find.

David looked to the right as a loud voice nearby wailed in mourning. Another and another joined in chorus as the men saw the devastation and considered their loved ones' fates.

He started to think "If only…" but stopped himself. Many times before they had left their families behind and raided villages themselves. Why would he think this time would be different? Nothing could have been done.

But they could do something now.

If there are no bodies in the ashes, then all our loved ones have been taken from Ziklag alive, he thought. That meant the Amalekites were moving with captives, flocks, and a great deal of spoil; Ziklag may not have been their only conquest. They would be slowed and might even be in a celebratory mood, with all their success. With luck and God's blessing, they could recover their families and deal judgment to the Amalekites.

"Where is Abiathar?" David asked a man running by.

"Gone to his house, I suppose," shrugged the man, who didn't stop to discuss further.

David rose quickly and strode off toward Abiathar's house. When he arrived, it was fully dark and he found the priest calf-deep in ashes, his white robe dingy and smeared, holding a torch. He looked up and saw David.

"They burned the scrolls! I have only fragments!" Abiathar cried, part in pain, part in anger.

"But our families live."

"May Yahweh grant it!"

"Where is the ephod?"

"My servant brings it behind me."

"When he arrives, I wish to ask something of the Lord," David said.

"I thought you might," the young priest smiled bitterly.

Azel and Eliel arrived at their house to find a smoking ruin, as did their neighbors. Azel found wood for a torch and he and Eliel used their spears to probe and stir the ashes. They managed to find a few bronze dishes that had survived the fire, but no trace of Dani and Adriel. They shared a look both understood.

"Do you find any bodies?" came the shout from his neighbor.

"No," Azel called back. "They must have taken them."

Azel knew that didn't guarantee they were still alive, but it meant there was a chance. They would be taken into slavery, which could be a fate worse than death.

"Come to the marketplace!" one of the others shouted from down the street. "All are gathering."

When Azel, Eliel and the others arrived at the marketplace, torches defined the space, casting dancing shadows on the skeletons of nearby buildings.

The rest of the men whom Joab had ordered to gather their supplies had now joined them in the marketplace and seen the destruction. They huddled on the ground, tears mingled with gray ash and black charcoal on their sunburned faces. They spoke in hushed tones that were occasionally interrupted by a loud, pained cry. All were waiting for David.

"We followed David loyally, but he has brought us to this!" came a shout from a man Azel didn't know. Others shouted in agreement or disagreement; it was impossible to tell.

"We should stone him!" another man stood and cried loudly. Others near him attempted to restrain him. Azel could hear wailing and weeping around the circle of the 600 men. He marveled at how quickly their mood had changed.

Why would they think what happened was David's fault?

They didn't have to wait long before David appeared. Abiathar was with him, wearing the ephod. Joab and Abishai stood on either side of the priest and their chieftain.

"We must inquire of the Lord," David began, loud enough for all to hear, "to see what we must do now."

A murmur went through the tired, filthy men.

"The Lord couldn't prevent this!" shouted a tall muscular man with ash in his hair. "Why should we ask anything of Him, or you!?" A few men shouted more angry, grieving nonsense.

Ignoring them, Abiathar turned and faced David and David knelt before him.

"Lord God," David began in a strong voice. "Would You that we pursue these Amalekites who have taken our families and destroyed our homes? Will we be able to overtake them and recover those we love?"

All eyes went to the ephod. For several seconds nothing seemed to happen. Then those sitting closest gasped. The Urim stone was glowing faintly in the relative darkness.

"Rise then and come with me!" David shouted as he rose to his feet. "Yahweh has given them into our hands!"

After a moment's hesitation, 600 men roared in agreement and stood brandishing swords and spears. Then they began gathering supplies for the march.

<h1 style="text-align:center">❦ 76 ❦</h1>

At first the men moved quickly over the arid terrain. It was still a couple of hours until daybreak and the air was cool as they quick-stepped toward the Negev. They stopped when they arrived at the waters of Nahal Besor. Those who arrived first plunged into the stream and quickly drank and washed in one motion.

Refreshed, they waded to the other side, eager to continue. Over a wide area of the flat bank, men waded in, until two thirds of them had reached the other side where David motioned for them to wait on a narrow, sandy spit.

Eliel, Adino, Shammah and Eleazar, part of Asahel's cohort, scrambled up the steep bank on the far side of the brook to see the stragglers approaching the sandy northern shore where they had just been. The 200 or so remaining men stretched out over a quarter mile back toward Ziklag.

Asahel fought his impatience. "We must move quickly! These are slowing us down."

Below he could see his brother and uncle, looking across the stream toward those who were approaching, gasping and staggering, obviously exhausted.

It was true, Asahel had to admit, that they had marched from Jezreel to Gath to Ziklag, only to begin a march again without sleep or much food. Yet the lives of their women and children depended on their speed now.

The first of the weary stragglers arrived at the water's edge and simply collapsed into the stream, drinking and washing their faces, then drawing back and lying on the far bank, exhausted. More men arrived, some sinking to the sand before even reaching the water.

"Hurry and let us go!" Asahel shouted. "Our families' lives hang on our haste!"

David looked at Joab. "We must move quickly. We should let these who are weary stay with the baggage. They can recover while we travel light."

"Yes, that is best," Joab agreed.

"Let those who are too weary stay here and guard our baggage," David shouted across the stream. "Those of us who can move quickly will go rescue our loved ones."

The men on the far side of the bank appeared crestfallen, but relieved. A few moved through the water and joined those who would be going on. Others fell on their backs, breathing hard.

"When you have recovered, come to the south side of the brook and camp with the baggage." David called. "We will return when we have engaged those who raided our homes."

Asahel needed to hear no more. "Come, let's go!" he called, and he and the other members of his troop who had scrambled to the top of the ridge began moving south, following the tracks left in the sand by the Amalekites and the cast-off articles of clothing and trinkets of spoil they had carelessly discarded. Azel caught up with them just as they headed out.

"Ho there! Who is that?" Adino sped off into a gulley and leapt down. Asahel and the others followed him. Adino was on top of a swarthy man, dressed in rags and covered in dust. The man stopped struggling when he saw the drawn swords of Eliel, Shammah and Eleazar.

They pulled the man to his feet, just as Asahel came to see what was going on.

"Who are you and where are you from?" Asahel demanded.

"I am a poor Egyptian, slave of an Amalekite," the man said in a tremulous, high voice.

"Were you with the band that raided Ziklag?"

"We attacked many towns of the Negev, of both the Cherethites and of Judah. I escaped. Please do not return me to my cruel master," said the slave, appearing unsure that his present company would be less cruel.

"Can you tell us where they went?"

"Yes," the Egyptian said, brightening a little. "I can take you there, for they are returning to their homes to celebrate their great victories."

"Then you will come with me to tell your story to our chieftain," Asahel replied.

David was near the middle of the column, so Asahel's troop had to thread their way through several advancing ranks before arriving in front of the Commander and his lieutenants.

"We found this escaped slave of the Amalekite band. He says he can lead us to their home base."

"Is this so?" David sized up the bedraggled Egyptian.

"Yes, lord. I was the slave of a warrior, who commanded fifty men. I know the way well. I will gladly take you there so you may have your vengeance." The man squinted at David, failing to hide his relish at the prospect of seeing his former master brought low.

"Give this man food and drink," David commanded the men nearby. "Then he will show us where they have taken our wives and children." Then to Asahel, he said, "Good work, son of Zeruiah, and your cohort."

"Thank you." Asahel smiled at his men and directed them to hurry with him to the front of the column once again.

Adino's face glowed with pride as he hurried along with the rest of Asahel's young men as they moved quickly to the front of the procession.

"What a fortunate thing, discovering that Egyptian," Eleazar said. "Yahweh has smiled on us."

"I pray that is true and tragedy isn't just ahead," Eliel said.

The others said nothing, realizing their friend feared for the fate of his family.

"I will believe for the best," Adino said eventually. "He certainly provided an escape from fighting our own people on the side of the Philistines."

"Yes, that was an amazing turn of events," Eliel agreed. "We were spared fighting against our people and still, the king trusts our commander, David."

"Certainly, no such plan could have been devised by human minds," Shammah said.

"Certainly not," Eliel said, then they hurried on in silence to save their breath.

⇜ 77 ⇝

King Saul and his army were exhausted by their march to the North. They had undertaken a rapid, forced march to intercept the Philistines, who were invading once again.

They finally stopped on the northern slope of Mt. Gilboa, near the source of the Kishon River that watered the fertile Plain of Jezreel on its way to the Sea. Within an hour, a city of tents arose as the soldiers made camp, just as they had many times before. Another hour and the smell of roasting meat was everywhere throughout the camp. Periodic bursts of laughter punctuated the time as the army settled in.

From the door of his tent, Saul could see the Philistine encampment through the haze, far across the valley in Shunem. The Sea People were far from their land in the South, having tramped their way up the coast through the lands of Judah, Ephraim and Western Manasseh on the Coastal Highway until they had massed on the high ground of the relatively small Mt. Moreh which rose from the floor of the vast valley of Jezreel in land claimed by the tribe of Issachar. There they prepared for battle with their long-time enemy in one more attempt to gain control of the fertile valley with all its resources and strategic importance.

But Saul was not eager to go down into the valley to meet the Philistines yet again. He was tired, dejected and paralyzed with fear. For over 40 years he had led Israel in fighting the many enemies of the new, fragile kingdom. As he looked out across the wide valley at his life-long enemy, the voices in his mind plagued him, uttering condemnations of his ability as king and warrior. He sat under an awning before his tent, squinting into the distance where he knew the Philistine lords were looking back at him.

As he looked across the valley, he absent-mindedly recalled the stories told by old men when he was a boy; how Deborah and Barak descended misty Mt. Tabor, visible to Saul on the northern horizon, into the Vale of Jezreel with 10,000 men of Naphtali and Zebulon and routed the Canaanites who had oppressed them for 20 years; a much greater army with chariots of iron which mired in the soft, fertile soil on that rainy day, enabling God's people to win an important victory.

And through the shimmering heat, Saul could see, beyond the Philistine camp, the place where Gideon defeated an innumerable host of Midianites with only his 300 valiant men, armed only with torches and trumpets. They had driven the Midianites past the very spot where Saul sat until they snared them in a trap where 10,000 soldiers of Israel waited to utterly destroy them.

But these victories from the dim and unfocused past did not inspire Saul. He was in no frame of mind to take courage from them.

What he saw before him now was a mighty Philistine army, equipped with strong, modern iron weapons, like the double-edged straight swords that could be thrust as well as swung, and armor, like the heavy helmets and mail that deflected Israelite arrows, and the heavy, iron chariots which would be deadly on the level ground of the valley.

The Sea People were tall and strong; a warrior race from a distant, mysterious land, whereas, except for a small professional core, Israel's army was made up of shepherds and shopkeepers, fishers and vintners. How could they endure?

God had been with the judges and with Samuel, but God had not spoken to Saul for some time. How he longed to hear from the Lord now, but Samuel was dead and other prophets spoke only of doom. Not only that, the ephod was lost in the massacre of the priests, so it could not be consulted. Saul's own dreams were common and useless.

Saul regretted his banishing of the necromancers and witches years ago. He had haughtily denounced and even killed many of them in an effort to appease Samuel, but now he would gladly consult them.

What choice do I have?

"Find a medium for me," Saul ordered his cousin Abner abruptly. "I need a word from the Lord."

"Yes, lord. As you ask," said the General, regarding him with surprise. He excused himself from Saul's tent.

"Do you know anyone who would know of the existence of a spiritist in the area?" Abner asked Jeriah, who stood guard nearby.

. Jeriah's eyebrows raised in a question mark as he answered, "I don't know, but I'll find out." He then went to learn what he could.

Jeriah soon had the information Abner had requested and brought it to him. Abner immediately went to the king again.

"There is a witch in En-dor," he told Saul. They exchanged looks, with no need to say that the way to En-dor was a treacherous journey past the Philistine camp.

"I should disguise myself," Saul said.

Abner did not respond.

❧ 78 ❧

The Egyptian was as good as his word, leading David's 400 men to the wide valley that led to the Amalekite raiding party's town many miles to the south. David, Joab and a few scouts went to the crest of the low rocky rim from which they could see some distance.

The Amalekite raiders were, as David knew they would be, stretched out over the space of a mile, with all the men occupied with herding the sheep, goats and oxen they had taken, as well as the human captives. There were heavy wagons of valuable spoil as well, pulled by oxen and donkeys and moving slower than a man could walk. There was no evidence of guards or pickets on the perimeter. Perhaps their success and distance from their conquests had lulled them into a feeling of security.

"There would be little cover for our approach," Joab said, calling attention to the flat terrain, "but night will soon give the ability to get close and gain the advantage of surprise."

"Yes, and if they stop and make camp for the night, they will not likely expect that they are followed," David commented. "I've seen enough."

David returned to his little army and detailed a few men to scout the high places along the valley to track the movement of the Amalekites. The main body he led on a parallel route, shadowing them from the other side of the ridge. Couriers moved back and forth constantly between the scouts and David, reporting any change in movement. Other relevant information came to light as the scouts observed the company over the next couple of hours.

"They are not disciplined and are ill-prepared for an attack," one scout reported. "Their entire attention is on their spoils and their captives and moving them along."

David, Joab and others of the inner circle began to plan their attack, while their men readied their weapons.

"I saw no rearguard," David commented. "They don't expect to be pursued."

"After nightfall there will likely be feasting," Abishai said.

"And carousing," Joab added, not needing to express his concern for the safety of his wife and daughter in an armed camp full of drunken warriors.

"So we will go at the third hour after sunset," David decided. "We only have 400 men and their force may be larger. We can only succeed by surprising them. We must ring their camp about to make them think we are many more than we are."

"I say we split and rush them from east and west, parting on each side thus," Joab drew a plan in the sand as he spoke. His finger traced a line from the east toward a round stone representing the Amalekites. When his finger reached the stone he circled to the right. Then he drew another line from the west and similarly circled to the right. When he had finished, he had encircled the camp.

Joab was becoming a master strategist, always seeing clearly the way to the heart of the enemies' vulnerabilities. "When we have run past their perimeter with torches blazing, we turn in..." His voice trailed off. There was no reason to say what they would do after that.

"It is a good plan," David nodded. "Abishai, take 200 to the east. I will accompany you. Joab, you will lead from the west. Asahel will be your vanguard. Do not light your torches until you are near the camp."

"Yes, Commander. May Yahweh fight for you."

"And for you."

<h1 style="text-align:center">❧ 79 ☙</h1>

At twilight, King Saul left the encampment in the mist of evening with his two guards, Jeriah and Joash, dressed as travelers with weapons hidden under gray, mohair cloaks.

Saul wore no armor and no crown, and his head was covered with the hood of his cloak, so anyone seeing him on the road would think him no more remarkable than a shepherd or fisherman from the nearby Sea of Kinnereth, except for his height. The journey would be made in the dark and no torch could be lit because they would pass within a few yards of the Philistine camp, across the river and up a steep, rocky rise to the remote village of En-dor.

The scrubby trees on the riverbank were black against the night sky and the river reflected the bare light of the quarter-moon. The water was not deep at this time of year, so they easily waded across, replenishing their waterskins as they went. Upstream they could see the eastern edge of the Philistine army's camp. Cookfires twinkled in the distance, marking the perimeter.

Saul regretted that in his haste he had not brought food. He had been too apprehensive all day to eat, but now he was hungry.

They started up the embankment on the other side of the river, knowing that it would be uphill the rest of the way.

The trip was noteworthy because it was uneventful. Travelling this wild country at night was dangerous. Besides Philistine sentries who were bound to be about, lions lived in this country, not to mention robbers who would knock a traveler on the head for the ring on his finger. Yet not even an eagle could be seen in the sky. Perhaps the massing armies had spooked the predators, both animal and human, so they saw nothing to give the three men pause.

⚜ 80 ⚜

Abigail's leg still hurt where a big Amalekite had kicked her to prevent her from helping a young woman who had fallen on the trail. She had been powerless to help the young woman when the oaf had mercilessly beaten her with his fists. Since that moment two days ago, the woman, just a girl really, had not left her side, seldom speaking.

Her name was Sela, and she was the daughter of one of David's men whom Abigail hadn't gotten to know yet. She was probably no more than 14 years old.

They had been walking for three days and nights, pausing only for brief rests, even in the cold desert night. Several hundred women and children were tied to towropes that stretched behind oxcarts and beasts of burden.

Abigail's wrists were smeared with dried blood from the ropes rubbing her wrists raw. Her arms had nearly been dislocated more than once because of the jerking of the ox cart she was tied behind and the movements of other women restrained by the same towrope.

They were guarded by rough men with the coarse hair and unkempt beards characteristic of Amalekites. They had the look of those who stand before a bountiful table after having fasted for a week. Abigail wondered how long they would wait before they took what they wanted.

There were hundreds, perhaps thousands, of plundered goats, sheep, asses and a few oxen being driven alongside the captive women and children. Their bleating and mooing never stopped and the dust they kicked up choked Abigail's already parched throat. Wagonloads of spoil yet to be sorted and gloated over moved slowly in the procession that stretched for what must have been a mile.

But the biggest prizes stumbled along with Abigail. The women on either side of her wept as they pondered their fates. Abigail knew that some would be raped and cast aside. Others would be taken as wives of strange, rough men if they were lucky and as slaves to be worked to death if they were not as lucky.

Abigail had barely let herself think of the fact that their men had not been in Ziklag. The men of the other towns had been slaughtered no doubt, but David and his men were with the Philistines, so at least they were safe.

How long it would be before their men knew of their fate she could not guess. There was to be a battle and David and his men were to fight Saul on the side of Philistia. Perhaps, she thought wistfully, their present predicament was the judgment of Yahweh. David had always said it was wrong to lift your hand against the Lord's anointed.

Suddenly, the rough men ordered them to stop. The women collapsed where they stood, exhausted and terribly thirsty. A half hour went by and the women simply lay on the hot sand recovering, while the men worked to organize a sprawling camp. Abigail raised her head to assess the situation. It was late afternoon and it appeared they would finally stop for the night for the first time in three days. Perhaps they had travelled far enough that their captors felt they would not be pursued.

As the sun sank in the west, the wagons were driven into a circle around the captives, some having to be brought from some distance down the trail. When all were inside the circled wagons, torches were lit and tied to tall stakes in the center of the makeshift camp, casting long, dancing shadows on the ground in an eerie oval. Chests were brought from the wagons and the men drew out food and drink.

The men were talking loudly and jesting, and occasionally arguing loudly with one another in a tongue Abigail barely understood.

She watched them warily as they set out wineskins and cups on hastily erected tables. She was glad the difficult journey was over for now, but a night of feasting in the camp of these Amalekites promised new horrors. She knew all too well how men can be when wine flows freely.

<h1 style="text-align:center">❦ 81 ❧</h1>

Dani lay on the still-hot sand, exhausted. Adriel sat beside her, tears cutting furrows in the dirt that darkened his face.

"Mother, are you all right?"

Dani heard the question, but she was so weary she could only manage to open her eyes and look at her son to reassure him that she was alive.

She was four-months pregnant and the forced march into the desert was more than she could bear, yet she had found the strength somehow to keep on her feet and keep moving. She felt she had to for the sake of Adriel, who was in many ways still a boy, though he was nearly ready for his initiation as a man.

She knew she needed water. Her condition demanded it, but with her hands tied to the tow rope and none being offered, she didn't know what would become of her. Somehow their captors didn't seem the type to show mercy, especially for a pregnant woman, who would likely be seen as a burden and simply cast aside.

For that reason, she was glad she wasn't further along. Perhaps they had not noticed she was with child.

Batya and Bathsheba had crawled under the wagon to which they were tied when the caravan had been ordered to stop. Batya believed they might be protected there. Bathsheba was too young to be able to walk the distance they had come, so Batya had carried her most of the way.

Her back ached sharply as she lay Bathsheba on the sand. They were both exhausted as they lay behind a solid wagon wheel. Bathsheba was apparently too tired to cry. She was soon asleep and Batya wondered if she dared sleep herself, but she also knew her daughter badly needed water.

She peaked around the edge of the wheel to see what was going on.

Abigail had not seen Ahinoam since yesterday on the trail. She had not seen or heard of anyone being killed so she hoped she was just being kept elsewhere. There were many women she didn't know here. They were not all of Judah. Joab's wife and daughter, Bartha and Merak were nearby, though there had been little opportunity to communicate, much less plot escape.

The attack had been terrifying. Abigail and Ahinoam had been rousted out of bed in a horror of torches and burning houses. Strong men with faces painted red and black had hit them repeatedly to cow them, then herded them out of Ziklag as it burned. The next three days had been hot and dirty and the nights freezing as they descended the Negev and felt the desert's harsh extremes. The Amalekites raided another town on the way, adding to their captives and their spoil.

A very large man the others had called "Urgrel," covered with black hair, came toward the women and drew his sword. He approached the first woman and she nearly fainted, but he used the sword to cut the cord holding her wrists to the tow rope. She looked at him wide-eyed as she rubbed her bleeding wrists. He cut loose several others, then came to Abigail and Sela and cut their cords as well.

When he had released about 20 women, he gruffly ordered them to follow him in a Canaanite dialect. The women followed to the center of the camp where a great bonfire was being built. Abigail wondered where the wood came from. This country had almost no vegetation. Soon other men brought a couple of sheep and a young ox and swiftly slashed their throats. Blood gushed from the wounds and the men began butchering them immediately.

"Pour!" Urgrel ordered Abigail, Sela and others of the women to begin pouring wine from the spoil in the wagons as men came forward with wooden and pottery cups. Still others he ordered to finish the butchering and roasting of the animals over the bonfire that was just beginning to burn.

Abigail and Sela poured wine from wineskins into the cups the men thrust before them. Scores of men came and then came again to fill their cups. The more they drank the louder they became and the more they stared at Abigail, Sela and the others salaciously.

Now, the smell of roasting meat coming from the bonfire made the women look at each other sadly. They were beyond hungry, but more than that, they needed water. Watching the men with their wine was very hard. So far they had been offered nothing.

❦ 82 ❦

It was now totally dark. The only light was from the flickering torches. The men finished eating, although they continued to drink. Abigail attempted to move into the shadows, holding Sela's hand, but she didn't get far. She started and turned in the direction of a sudden sound. Sela grabbed her arm and cried out in fear. The noise was a scream of a woman nearby as a huge warrior with a pottery cup in one hand grabbed her hair roughly.

"Quiet!" he roared, pulling her to her feet. He turned, pulling her behind him. She screamed as she lost her footing and was dragged toward the bonfire. Other men began taking other women. Abigail grasped Sela's arm, pulling her down close to the ground and trying to back away into the shadows, but Urgrel's pock-marked face bent over Abigail. He smashed his fist into the side of her face and she lost her hold on Sela's arm. When she was able to get up, she saw Urgrel taking Sela away. The poor girl was too terrified to scream but her wide eyes met Abigail's for one long moment.

They took eight women to the bonfire. Those who remained watched fearfully. The women were made to stand around the fire surrounded by scores of drunken men. Suddenly, out of nowhere, some poorly performed music began: a lyre, a pipe and some kind of drum. In the rude Amalekite language, the men demanded that the women dance.

Fear and uncertainty showed on the women's faces. Their hesitancy was seen as obstinacy by the men, so Urgrel struck the one closest to him with the back of his hand. She fell sprawling and the others began moving tentatively to the music. Abigail saw that tears were running down Sela's face, but she was trying to dance. The woman the oaf had knocked down slowly got up and joined in the reluctant dance with the others as the drunken men began shouting and laughing at the women.

"Dance, Philistine whores!" one loud voice pierced the din.

"Pick up those skirts!" Urgrel growled.

"Show us something!" another called out.

Urgrel reached out as Sela went by and violently jerked her tunic, so it ripped open in front. The men laughed as she tried to pull her clothes together to stay covered. Two other men simultaneously pulled at the clothes of another woman and ripped them almost entirely off her. She screamed and fell to the ground in a fetal position. One of the men jumped on top of her, pinning her to the ground.

Abigail feared what would happen next, but suddenly firelight flared behind her. She turned and looked beyond the wagons and the flocks at the edge of the camp, seeing men running past holding torches. A couple of Amalekite men who were not in the celebration at the bonfire also saw and ran to see what was happening. Before they reached the wagons, well-shot arrows struck them down.

Then, the men running around the camp turned and began coming between the wagons toward the place where Abigail was sitting. Her heart leaped when she saw that one of the men was wearing a Philistine helmet. Was it too much to hope that David had come for them?

It would be a miracle!

❧ 83 ❧

"Great is Yahweh, God of Israel!" shouted a small band of Hebrews as they ran between wagons and through startled flocks of sheep into the camp. David ran behind his bodyguards with Abishai. To their right and left the rest of the 200 commanded by Abishai were spread thinly around half the perimeter of the camp and were now also entering its periphery.

They burst upon a knot of Amalekites who had obviously been drinking. David charged one of the men, his sword leading the way. In the torchlight, the man's eyes were wide under bushy eyebrows. He feebly raised a dagger with one hand and raised the other, palm out, as if he could stop David's pumping legs from moving him closer. David's iron sword went through the man's midsection as if through a green gourd. He gave a muffled cry and fell backward.

David slashed through his neck to be certain the man was finished and looked up to see an inebriated Amalekite about to swing an ax at Abishai, who was battling another desert-dweller. The weight of the ax was almost more than he could manage in his condition, so he was moving slowly enough for David's flashing sword to sever the man's ax hand at the wrist before the ax could reach Abishai's head. The man screamed as the ax fell and David cut the scream short with another thrust of his sword.

They were then met by another band of Amalekites in full rout. Abishai held out his spear and impaled two of them at once, their weight breaking the spear's shaft as they fell. The Hebrews nearest David collided with and tripped others, falling to the ground and desperately fighting hand-to-hand.

David's sword moved quickly to end three of the struggles for his men and they rose and looked ahead. There they saw about 10 Amalekites skirting them to the right, going for the edge of the camp, looking for a way of escape. Behind them, David's band saw their brothers in arms, apparently having already driven through from the other side.

"After them!" David ordered, and they all started after the escaping Amalekites. Two tripped one another in their haste and the first of David's men fell upon them and ended their journey forever. The other Israelites caught the running men and engaged them.

"They're getting away!" The call came from the left and David looked to see another similar group, attempting to reach the darkened perimeter and safety. A few were mounting donkeys to ride away. David looked at Abishai and they took off running in that direction. David paused to recover a dropped spear and Abishai followed suit. They both released them at the same time and caught the leaders between the shoulder blades. When they fell, three others tripped over them and could not recover before David and Abishai's swords prostrated them forever.

Benaiah passed them running at full speed, pursuing those who remained. David and Abishai followed.

Armed men in Philistine armor rushed past Abigail. Along the way they hacked and stabbed any Amalekite they encountered with their iron swords, then continued toward the bonfire at the center of the camp where most of the drunken men still goaded the women to dance, unaware of the violence a few yards away. Abigail stood up and called to the invaders running by, "Who are you?"

One of the men slowed and turned toward Abigail. "Men of Israel," he replied. Abigail thought she saw a glimmer of recognition in his eyes.

"Of David?"

"Yes."

"Yahweh be praised!" Abigail cried, and the other women nearby cheered and rose up as the men hurried on in pursuit of the Amalekite raiders.

The noise and confusion were growing all around her now and Abigail looked in all directions, trying to see someone she knew, especially hoping to see David, but knowing he would be very busy just now. At last, she looked back toward the bonfire again and saw a lopsided battle going on. The drunken Amalekites, who finally understood what was happening, were no match for the fury of David's men, as they hacked and chopped their way through the celebrating crowd. The Hebrews seemed to come from every direction, creating a chaotic, deafening and bloody confusion.

Panic seized the Amalekites and they ran about, trying to escape, but for most, there would be no escape. Everywhere they turned an Israelite sword or spear struck them down.

Abigail saw Sela on the ground and she ran toward her. Upon reaching her, she saw that she was all right but bewildered and nearly paralyzed with fear. Abigail was pulling Sela to her feet when she was jostled and heard a scream in her ear.

"Abigail!"

It was Ahinoam. They embraced tightly, relief flooding both of them as each realized the other was safe. When they looked up, they and the other women were all but alone. The Amalekites were either dead or fled with David's men pursuing them into the night. There were no prisoners.

The brute, Urgrel, lay a short distance away by the bonfire. A pool of blood was still growing under his hairy body and his eyes stared lifelessly into the night sky. Other Amalekites lay bloodied and motionless all around.

"Have you seen David?" Abigail asked.

"No, but I saw Asahel," Ahinoam assured her. "I'm sure he's here." She looked in one direction, then another in the firelight.

Abigail found a wine jug and drank deeply, then offered it to Sela. "Ahinoam, this is Sela."

"Yes, I know Sela," Ahinoam answered, then turning to Sela, she assured her, "Your father will find you soon."

Batya awoke, only then realizing she had been asleep, to see bright torches and hear shouting. Men were running past the wagon and she looked around the wheel to see men striking down her Amalekites captors.

"Eliam!" she shouted. One of the men who looked familiar turned and looked at her.

"He is here. He will find you," he said.

"Praise Yahweh!" Batya burst into tears.

❧ 84 ❧

Azel's sword flashed in the torchlight, felling Amalekite after Amalekite until none remained to pursue. He was exhausted but would not rest until he found Dani and Adriel.

Eliel and his friends Adino, Shammah and Eleazar were with him as he came upon a group of women of David's band and asked them breathlessly, "Have you seen my wife, Dani, and our son, Adriel?" The women shook their heads, but one of them arose and ran to him, throwing her arms around him.

"Thank you! Thank you for coming. Is my husband with you?"

"Yes, he is with Joab. He will find you," Azel answered, freeing himself from her embrace.

He went on through the camp finding more bedraggled women and children, many of whom he did not know, because they were from other places and nations the Amalekites had raided.

Then he heard a familiar voice.

"Father!"

It was Adriel. Azel turned to look in the direction of the voice and saw his young son standing some distance away with many other captives between. He was motioning for Azel to come to him.

Azel and Eliel hurried through the chaotic crowd, struggling to get through the mass of humanity and having to step over the many dead Amalekites in the path.

Finally, they reached Adriel and Azel saw Dani on the ground, both of them still restrained by the tow rope.

"I think she needs water," Adriel said as he and his brother, Eliel, embraced. Eliel's sword quickly freed his hands from the ropes.

"Go find water – or wine – whatever you can!" Azel told them and Eliel and Adriel left to find what they could.

Then Azel tenderly took Dani's face in his hands. Her eyes opened and then widened with recognition, and they embraced for a long moment without speaking. Azel's heart was bursting with joy and relief. The dam holding back his pain since finding them gone from Ziklag finally burst and tears ran down his face as a moan came from deep within.

He cut the ropes restraining her and, just then, Adriel returned with a jar of wine found near the bonfire. Azel held it to her lips. She drank a little, then coughed, then drank some more.

"Adriel, go again and, if possible, find food."

Adriel left to see what he could find as Eliel returned with a jug of water.

"Dani, when Adriel returns, Eliel and I must help with pursuing those still alive. Stay here, take up weapons from those fallen in case any of these Gentiles is still alive. I will return as soon as we know we have the victory over them."

Dani nodded, understanding, and they embraced again.

❧ **85** ❧

Saul was glad Jeriah had received good information on the location of the witch's house, so he was able to lead the way, even on this night with minimal moonlight.

Saul and his companions arrived to find a small mud-brick hovel behind a tangle of barren tree branches. The façade was dark and no light came from the windows.

Saul shivered at the prospect of approaching a witch's house at such a dark hour, but his desire for answers drove him to pound on the witch's rickety door. It was after midnight, but she opened to them as if she often had visitors at this hour.

"Come, come. The air is damp," she said, hardly looking at them, turning to lead them into the dark house. She was a toothless, old woman in a ragged black tunic and cloak with wiry, white hair and one eye that looked away when she talked. The three men followed her into a damp room that served as her divining chamber. The air was hot and humid and there was no breeze.

"Sit," she said abruptly, directing them to sit cross-legged on woven reed mats on the packed-earth floor. A single oil lamp sat on the floor in the middle of the room, burning fitfully, which caused their shadows to dance on the walls as they found places to sit. The old woman sat down with some difficulty across from the trio as they watched her wide-eyed.

"What would you have me do for you?" the woman asked, as she spread bony hands over her faded black cloak.

"I would that you contact the spirit of someone whose name I shall tell you," Saul replied, barely above a whisper.

The woman frowned suspiciously as she looked the men up and down. "You know that King Saul has done away with all who do such things. They are all dead. Or do you come to trap me so I will be killed as well?"

"I swear by the Living God, no punishment will befall you if you do this," Saul assured her.

"Very well. Who do you want me to call up?"

"Samuel."

After measuring the trio before her for another long moment, she raised her hands above her head and closed her eyes. A low moan escaped her wrinkled mouth. "Sam – u – el. Sam – u – el!"

She opened her eyes and screamed. "You have deceived me! YOU are Saul!"

"You have nothing to fear," Saul hurried to assure her once more, realizing his identity had been revealed to her, but uncertain as to how. "What have you seen?"

"I see a spirit ascending out of the earth."

"What is its appearance?"

"It is an old man, wearing a white robe," the woman said.

"Samuel!" Saul whispered as he bowed his face to the ground. Jeriah and the other guard said nothing, but they also looked down. Then a gust of wind blew out the lamp and it was dark.

"Why have you brought me up?" demanded a stern male voice from the darkness. Saul's heart convulsed at the sound of the voice. *Could it be? Was this indeed Samuel? The voice could be Samuel's*, he thought, *but would his voice sound the same in death?*

"I – I am distressed and greatly afraid," Saul began, his voice trembling as much as his hands. "The Philistines are marauding across the land and Yahweh will not answer me through prophets, priests or dreams, so I came to you."

"Why do you consult me now that the Lord has become your enemy?" said the voice angrily. "Yahweh is doing what He prophesied through me when I was alive. He is wresting the kingdom from your hands and giving it to your neighbor, David. You know this is happening because you did not obey the Lord concerning the Amalekites."

The voice from the darkness was not finished.

"Israel will fall to the Philistines and tomorrow you and your sons will join ME!"

The spirit voice then gave a high shrieking sound that could have been a sinister laugh. At that, Saul collapsed, trembling. Then there was silence.

The old woman lit the lamp once again, looking at Saul, who moaned softly.

"You must be hungry," the witch said matter-of-factly. "Stay. I will bring food." She arose stiffly.

"No, I will not eat!" Saul answered.

"Look, your servant has obeyed you and taken my life in my hands," the old woman said in her gravelly voice. "Now you WILL eat so you'll have strength to go on your way."

"Yes, majesty. Eat," urged Jeriah.

"All right."

And with that, the witch sauntered off to prepare food for the men.

❦ 86 ❦

Hours had gone by as David's men pursued the Amalekites. The women and children sat in small groups talking, sleeping or eating the roasted meat at the bonfire.

They had gathered water jugs and the wineskins scattered around the fire from which they had drunk deeply. The roasted meat intended for their captors was devoured by the ravenous women and children.

Some worried and prayed for their men as they pursued the fleeing raiders. A few had picked up Amalekite weapons and stood ready should any of their captors revive. Abigail stood holding a dagger, watching the rocks and scrubby trees along the horizon, silhouetted against the night sky. Ahinoam and Sela slept at her feet.

Finally, the men of Israel began drifting back into the camp, each rejoicing to have found wives and children alive, then sinking down wearily, nursing minor injuries and wiping blood from their weapons.

Suddenly a cheer went up on the far side of the camp. Abigail looked beyond the men's raised swords and shields to see David, riding a donkey, coming toward the bonfire with Abishai by his side. He looked weary and was covered in dust and dried blood. He raised his sword in salute to the cheering men, then his eyes settled on Abigail.

She ran toward him and he laid aside his sword and shield in time to catch her in a warm embrace that they held for half a minute. Then Abigail saw Ahinoam, standing nearby, tears streaming down her face, but smiling. Abigail released her hold on David's neck and held out her hand to Ahinoam, who came forward, kissed David, laid her head on his shoulder and wept.

When Azel returned to the place he had left Adriel and Dani, she was sitting up. Adriel had found meat, so she was feeling better. Then Eliel arrived and embraced his mother tenderly. He tried, but failed to prevent the tears of relief from streaming down his face.

He then turned and embraced his little brother as well and the four of them held one another for a long moment.

There was activity all around them as David's men began mopping up the camp, but then orders came, and some men were assigned as pickets around the perimeter and others were allowed to sleep.

Azel lay down beside Dani with Adriel on the other side of him and they all slept deeply and long, while Eliel stood watch over his reunited family.

<h1 style="text-align:center">◄§ 87 §►</h1>

"But where is my father?" Jonathan demanded, slapping his sword against his shield.

"He is on a vital, secret errand and will return momentarily," Abner replied, hoping that saying it would make Jonathan believe it true. In fact, he had not thought consulting a medium to be wise at this important time, but Saul was always headstrong and not easily turned aside when he had decided to do something. The best Abner could do was to look out for his interests and serve him in ways he would never know and might not appreciate.

"It is odd indeed that he did not tell me what he was doing," Jonathan huffed, but even as he said it, he knew it wasn't true. Saul often left him out of his planning, because of his relationship with David. Abner and Jonathan's younger brothers were closer to his father than he now.

Suddenly, he felt a wave of homesickness, which was unusual. He thought of Mara and his son, Mephibosheth, now a handful at five years old. As he was leaving, Mara had been unusually attentive, fussing over every detail of his pack containing his personal belongings. When he had left their home, as he had many times before, he had embraced and kissed her as always, and had bent down to hug and kiss little Mephibosheth, but as he had gone through the gate of their compound, he had looked back to see Mara with tears flowing from shining eyes and Mephibosheth clinging to her skirts with fear in his own eyes.

He hadn't understood her weeping, for his leaving for campaigns or kingdom business was routine. Now, he wished he could be back there to reassure her, but the distance and urgency of the coming battle made that impossible.

In addition to missing his wife and child, he supposed the rare homesickness was due to his father's absence and emotional distance from him even when they were near one another. The memory of the spear his father had thrown at him was still fresh, all these years later.

But Abner was right: Jonathan's father did return mid-morning, looking ashen and gaunt. He commanded that all the army of Israel prepare for battle, but there was no need; they were ready. Jonathan had seen to that.

Back in camp, Jeriah was exhausted after the all-night trek to En-Dor and back. The king had received the supernatural word he had desired, whether it was the spirit of Samuel, now long dead, or an evil spirit impersonating the prophet. The voice had certainly spoken of things that Samuel would know and would bring up to taunt the king. Jeriah couldn't be sure, but he shuddered as he remembered the apparently disembodied voice which had pronounced a curse on the king and his sons as well.

He feared the words uttered by the fearsome spirit would doom them in the battle, no matter who had spoken them.

He hadn't dared raise his eyes when the spirit was speaking, so he could not say for sure who had spoken or whether they were truly able to foretell the future.

His conscience accused him when he remembered the old women they had executed during the king's ban of the mediums and witches, but ultimately, he had following the orders of the king, both then and last night, contradictory though they were.

Though Jeriah was very tired, there would be no rest, for the army was ready to attack and he would have to take his place next to the king.

An hour later, they marched down into the Jezreel Valley, a sight to behold with their white, blue and purple banners aloft and their armor and weapons glinting in the sun. Here and there, Hebrew songs erupted as the men tramped along in measured ranks. They had a consciousness that God was on their side and that Israel would win a great battle against the uncircumcised horde today.

Abinidab rode a donkey at the head of his thousand men. Immediately behind him a proud rank of infantry marched with spears held high, their feet pounding a constant rhythm. To his right he could see the band of hundreds commanded by his younger brother, Malchishua, marching before their father's company in the main body of the army. Beyond Malchishua, he saw the banners of Jonathan's veteran soldiers, which made up the strong right flank.

As always at the heart of the host, his father rode his own donkey, wearing his golden crown and armband, with his golden clasp holding his purple robe together over his bronze breastplate. Beside the king rode Jeriah, his armor bearer and a hero in his own right. Saul's mounted guard rode ahead of the king and beside him was General Abner and the loyal, battle-hardened warriors of the hill tribes of Benjamin, Ephraim and Manassah.

Abinidab saw his father's head was down and realized he was discouraged or the evil spirit had its hold on him, as the mystics said. He often suffered with depression – some called it madness – though it seemed different today.

But there was no time to think of that now.

Abinidab looked ahead as the startling sound of a loud cheer echoed across the valley and he saw that the Philistines were moving as well. A chill went through him as he saw how wide their battle line spread across the valley floor. Their charge had begun and would be upon them sooner than he had expected. They were coming at a trot, with iron spearheads held high. The dust was rising, kicked up by thousands of feet and backlit by the sun.

A ram's horn sounded urgently from near Saul's position. "Archers at the ready!" Abinidab commanded, and his junior officers repeated the call, each to his units of 100 and 50. The rest of the army parted along the battle line, infantry before and behind, leaving in the middle a double rank of men armed with bows, who quickly aimed their arrows high and prepared to release them. But a similar order had already been given among the Philistine ranks, and silent, iron-tipped arrows fell like rain into the first ranks of Abinidab's troops. Men screamed as arrows sliced through exposed arms and legs and even penetrated leather breastplates and bronze mail. Other men fell without a sound when arrows randomly dealt lethal blows.

The line wavered and the Hebrew archers lost their concentration, but the ram's horn sounded again and Abinidab shouted, "RELEASE!"

The archers refocused and sent more than 1,000 arrows in an arc over the first protective ranks of their comrades and into the advancing fury of the Philistines. There, warriors stumbled as Hebrew arrows found their marks.

But still they came.

There was another long and loud sound of the trumpet. "Charge!" Abinidab ordered, pointing his sword toward the armies of Gaza and Gath before them. He shouted for his donkey to move, slapping its rump. A shout went up and the army surged forward.

❧ **88** ❧

On the right side of Israel's battle line, Jonathan urged his troops forward with the call, "The sword of the Lord!" His men cheered the familiar battle cry and surged toward the heathen hoard. It was the call that Gideon's men had used when they went against a much larger force just a short distance from this very field. As Jonathan looked forward, he knew they would face a larger force than their own as well.

Suddenly the first line of the Philistines stopped and coming forward at a gallop was a line of chariots, each with archers. Behind them came cavalry with iron-tipped spears, their horses appearing to blow smoke from their nostrils.

"Archers! Release!" Jonathan called, and as soon as their arrows were away, he ordered his own troops forward to meet the Philistine chariots, the Philistines' horses' hooves thundering on the valley floor.

Within seconds the two waves crashed against each other, with men and horses crying out in pain and fury. Spears smashed through armor and unhorsed riders. Horses fell and were trampled and run over by other horses pulling chariots.

Chariots capsized as they hit holes or ran over stones, throwing their passengers into heaps on the ground. Philistine archers in the remaining chariots shot their arrows into the advancing Hebrews, whose spears jolted Philistine chariot drivers in return.

Into the fray came the infantry of both armies, every man hacking at his enemy with swords of bronze or iron, fended off with shields of leather, wood, and bronze. It seemed everyone was shouting at once and the dust being kicked into the air made it difficult to breathe. Men fought with weapons until they broke or were knocked from their hands, then fought to the death with fists and broken spear shafts, caked in sweat, blood and dust.

❦ 89 ❦

From his position by King Saul's side, Jeriah could see the battle was not going well. To the left, Abinidab's ranks were holding but being pushed back by overwhelming numbers and the powerful chariots of the enemy.

Ahead of him, Malchishua's front line was suffering the brunt of the assault. The Philistines had driven deep into their ranks and the fighting was getting dangerously close to the king. Some men were already trying to run to the rear and officers were slapping them with the sides of their swords if the men were lucky and dipping their blades in Israelite blood if they were not.

On the right, Jonathan's veterans were collapsing; it was no longer possible to discern an organized battle line through the dust.

In the middle of the fray, Malchishua, Saul's younger son and commander of a thousand, had lost his donkey to uneven ground which shattered its leg, so he was now riding a Philistine horse he acquired on the field after killing its rider.

His armor bearer was dead, killed by two arrows which hit him at once. Malchishua's captain over the first company was also dead. The chain of command had broken down as the men fought to survive in the face of overwhelming odds.

Malchishua's right thigh was bruised and bleeding, the wound from a stone on the field when the donkey fell. He slashed at first one then another Philistine infantryman as he urged the horse forward, iron sword clanging against iron sword. He called out, attempting to rally his troops, but the din was so great no one heard or heeded.

As he thrusted and parried to his right, he suddenly felt a fiery pain in his left side. He looked and saw a large Philistine holding a spear. With a wicked grin under a helmet that obscured most of his face, the warrior pushed the spear further into Malchishua's side, causing him to cry out and slip to the right. Desperately he held onto the saddle, so he did not see the other Philistine, whose battle ax caught him in the back. He finally fell to the ground, and everything went black.

Abinidab and his cohort were fighting a running battle. He and what was left of his personal guard were drawing back toward Mt. Gilboa, trying to execute an orderly retreat, but their numbers were dwindling. No matter how many of the Sea People they killed, there always seemed to be more.

One by one, his faithful men went down, some to arrows or spears, some to iron swords heavy enough to sever limbs.

Abinidab had only his armor bearer and one member of his personal guard nearby as they scrambled over the rocks at the base of Mount Gilboa. They attempted to hide as they climbed to try to get back to their camp, but Philistine bowmen brought down a hail of arrows that could find them behind any rock. Abinidab was hit in the calf of his left leg and fell hard.

His armor bearer rushed to his aid but was himself hit in the back and fell on top of Abinidab. Before he could recover and escape, Philistine warriors found Abinidab and their swords quickly ended his life.

Jonathan's donkey reached the battle line and he threw a short spear at an advancing horseman, unseating him neatly. He grasped another spear and threw it at a Philistine chariot but did not see the result because an arrow struck his left hand, passing through his palm. He involuntarily cried out and bent over on his donkey's back. Only then did he see that his armor bearer was dead having fallen off his donkey, an iron-tipped arrow having pierced his bronze breastplate.

Jonathan looked for someone to help him with his wounded hand, but his men were outnumbered and could do nothing but fight for their lives. Jonathan dismounted to deal with the arrow, crouching behind the donkey with the crush of men and horses in hand-to-hand combat all around. Jonathan took his sword and, aiming close to the back of his left hand, brought it down with all his strength, cutting the arrow's shaft. Crying out in great pain, he recovered and then pulled the half arrow through and out of his hand. Just then his donkey shuddered and fell to the ground, having been hit by a spear. She would not be able to bear him to safety.

Grasping his sword with his good right hand and painfully gripping his shield in his wounded left, Jonathan stood and raised his sword against the Philistine nearest him. He brought down the weapon with all his strength and divided the man's helmet and skull with one blow. The man fell like a tree brought down by a woodsman's ax.

Without stopping he swung his sword to one side and caught another of the Sea People on the side of his head. The man fell and didn't rise again.

Immediately Jonathan was faced by another Philistine. The large warrior deflected Jonathan's sword blow with his shield and thrust his spear, catching Jonathan in the left shoulder because he couldn't lift his shield high enough with his wounded hand.

A throaty cry escaped Jonathan's lips. He tried to strike the Philistine once again, but he dodged to Jonathan's left, out of the arc of his falling sword. The Philistine jerked the spear out of Jonathan's shoulder, immediately thrusting it again, this time hitting him near the breastbone.

Jonathan could not lift his sword again after that, and he collapsed to the ground in a seated position. The Philistine drew back for one final blow. The spear tore through Jonathan's mid-section. He fell back, eyes staring into the dust-obscured sky.

He would not move again.

❧ 90 ❦

"Lord King, we must move back!" Abner called to his cousin from his donkey.

Saul didn't answer. He turned from Abner and looked again at the desperate struggle ahead. Just in front of him his personal guards stood grimly waiting to defend their king as the battle grew closer.

"Yes lord," pleaded Jeriah. "Please withdraw."

As Saul watched his loyal men, two fell with arrows through their neck and chest. Saul couldn't help but look up and see the arrows raining down on their position and one of them found him, slicing through his right shoulder. He tumbled off his donkey, falling on his left wrist, snapping it. Saul writhed in agony on the ground as his alarmed armor bearer jumped to his side.

"Get him away from here!" Abner shouted to Jeriah, who obeyed without a word. Quickly, but carefully, Jeriah lifted the king onto his own donkey, took the reins and turned the animal around, moving toward the rear and safety.

Other men used the sight of the wounded king as their excuse to run, and there were not enough officers threatening them to turn them back to the battle.

Jeriah drove the donkey as fast as it would go, but they were finally stopped a couple of miles up the side of Mt. Gilboa when the donkey slipped on the rocky soil and fell. Once again, Saul was injured, shattering his shinbone on a stone in the fall.

"Please," Saul begged Jeriah pitifully from where he lay on the ground, "Do not let me be taken alive by these uncircumcised dogs! Run me through!" Saul held out his sword to his armor bearer, pommel first.

"I cannot!" Jeriah recoiled in horror, refusing to take the sword. "I cannot lift my hand against the Lord's anointed. I will not, though you order me to do so!"

Saul looked back at Jeriah with a fatalistic frown. "You were always a better man than I."

Then, with difficulty, he raised himself to his knees. "So be it," he said, and he dropped the sword's handle to the ground in front of him, putting its point to his abdomen. Then, his eyes meeting Jeriah's, he fell forward, driving the sword through his body to its hilt, its point slicing through his abdomen and protruding from his back.

The first king of Israel was dead in that instant, lying on his face.

Horrified at seeing the king he had served for most of his life die in front of him, Jeriah suddenly remembered the words of the apparition at En-Dor.

He turned the king over to try to do something for him, but Saul's lifeless eyes stared at nothing.

Could I have stopped him? Jeriah asked himself. It had happened so fast!

Jeriah was seized by the conviction that he had failed in his responsibility to protect the king. Instinctively, he knew he must do the honorable thing: without considering any other course of action, he took his own sword, placed the handle on the ground and the point at his abdomen, and fell on it just as Saul had.

Pain flamed through his torso, the sword's point breaking a rib in his back and tearing through muscle and skin to emerge behind him. He lay face down, unable to move as hot, sticky blood pooled on the stony soil beneath him.

In the fog of pain, he wondered if he would now meet Yahweh, to stand judged for how he had lived his life.

His last fleeting thoughts were of Shelomith, his beloved, and their children, Misha'el and Zaina, who would now care for her. She would rage and cry when he did not return. And she would clothe herself in black as a widow.

She must have foreseen this day.

His final thought was, *Yahweh receive my spirit.*

And then, Jeriah died at the side of the monarch he had served so long and so well.

❦ 91 ❦

Close upon the heels of the Philistine rear guard as it swept over the bloody battlefield, human vultures passed through. One such man was an Amalekite, many miles from the home of his people in the Negev, an outcast of more than one land. He was one of many drifters who accompanied the armies with no personal stake in the outcome of the battle, except how they might enrich themselves with discarded wealth on the battlefield. These wretches were shameless when it came to stealing from the bodies of the dead.

It was dangerous, for many of the bodies on any battlefield were of men only dying, not yet dead, and if roused were more likely than not to be violent. The victorious army might be a danger as well, since they would naturally regard all spoil as their own. He made a pretense of selling pork to the Philistine army, so he was tolerated.

Amalek picked his way through the bodies on the slope of Mt. Gilboa, where the battlefield was eerily quiet. The retreating Israelites had left plenty of plunder for him.

Then he saw it: the purple robe and the glint of gold. He hurried toward the one wearing the expensive robe and crown. He had to step over many bodies which surrounded him. I was obvious they had tried to protect him but couldn't.

He looked down at the man in the gold crown and royal robe. Could it be?

It must be him.

As he removed the crown and golden arm band from the lifeless body, he had an idea.

❧ 92 ❧

"Bring King Achish," Bishroth, a Philistine officer ordered his lieutenant as he dismounted and looked down at the blood-soaked body of Israel's king. The lieutenant turned his horse and rode away at a gallop.

Bishroth, a tall, light-haired commander whose strength had earned him successive promotions, turned the body over so the late king's eyes gazed unblinking into the afternoon sky. He grasped the sword which had ended his life and pulled it free, casting it aside as if it was irrelevant.

"You and you," Bishroth said, gesturing to two blood-stained soldiers passing by, pursuing the fleeing Hebrew army. "Guard this man's body with your lives."

The two soldiers looked down and their eyes widened as they saw the clasp on King Saul's bloody purple cloak.

Captain Bishroth saw the royal chariot from half a mile away, coming up the gentle slope. He waved his heavy iron sword and began walking up toward the place where King Saul's body was being guarded by two of his infantrymen. Other Philistine soldiers loitered nearby, waiting to see what would be done with the body of Israel's king.

Soon the chariot arrived and Achish, King of Gath, stepped down, his green cape flowing behind him. He was as fresh as if he had not been in the battle at all.

"It is him," Achish said without apparent emotion, as he looked down at Saul's corpse. "Your sword," Achish demanded from Bishroth, who held out his double-edged, iron sword grip first. Achish took it, raised it high and brought it down with all his strength on Saul's neck, severing forever head from body.

"Put him in my chariot," Achish ordered the two men who had been guarding the body. "Saul's sons are also dead on the field." Then, so all could hear, "The kingdom of Israel is no more! Dagon has won a great victory for his people today!"

A cheer went up from all those who were standing by. Once the body and decapitated head were loaded in the chariot, Achish once again boarded it and went back down the slope toward the valley floor. Bishroth mounted his horse and followed.

A place in the heart of the battlefield had been cleared of corpses and the wounded so that the commanding officers and kings of the Philistine cities could conduct their post-mortem. The bodies of Jonathan, Abinidab, and Malchishua lay in an oxcart, their blood mingling and dripping to the trampled field below. The kings of Gaza and Ekron and the generals of their armies stood beside the oxcart with grim smiles on their faces. They looked up when the chariot of Achish arrived with Saul's remains.

"Our victory over Saul and Israel is total," Achish announced loudly with ill-concealed pleasure. "Glory be to Dagon," the other kings and their officers cheered when they saw the blood-soaked body in the chariot.

Achish directed a couple of foot soldiers nearby to move Saul's body to the oxcart. When they had done it, Achish turned to Bishroth.

"The army is pursuing the Hebrews south from Gilboa and east to Beth-Shan. I want to take these bodies there to be displayed deep in the heart of Israel. You and your guard will accompany the bodies there," Achish said.

"It would be my honor, my lord," Bishroth answered, bowing slightly. To the oxcart driver, a fat, sweaty oaf with a scraggly beard, he said, "Begin your journey. We will catch up with you within the hour."

❧ 93 ☙

Incredibly, not one of the women and children taken from Ziklag by the Amalekites was seriously injured or killed. Nor were there any casualties among David's men. They had achieved complete surprise and had killed most of the Amalekite band, except for a few young men who escaped in the night.

After setting up their own camp outside the Amalekite camp with its many corpses, Joab selected men to guard the perimeter. David told all to rest as long as they could, even though it was almost dawn. After a late start, everyone knew it would take the rest of the next day before they were ready to move.

Though the women were now free and able to help on the journey, there was a great deal of spoil to deal with, and the going would be slow. There were large numbers of sheep, goats, oxen and donkeys, plus a few horses. There were also many carts of spoil taken by the Amalekites on their raids.

"We will continue moving through the tomorrow night, much as the Amalekites did," David informed his men, "to put as much distance as possible between us and the Amalekite homeland in the desert.

"We will also deploy scouts and pickets surrounding the main body and moving parallel to it, out perhaps 200 cubits, ensuring that we cannot be surprised as we were able to do to them."

David's men smiled grimly. As usual, their commander had planned wisely.

The next day, the 400 men with their recovered wives and children, plus all the spoil captured from the Amalekites, arrived once again at the Brook Besor, where the 200 men who had been too weary to accompany the 400 waited with their baggage. There were more tearful reunions as the wives and children of the 200 greeted husbands and fathers.

David had his guard sound assembly and the entire company, well over 1,000 people, gathered to hear what was to be said.

❦ 94 ❧

Although it was less than twenty miles, the journey down to the Canaanite town of Beth-Shan in the Jordan River Valley seemed to take forever, with the marching Philistine troops and their mounted officers impatiently shadowing the plodding oxcart and its ghastly cargo. They moved on the well-traveled road alongside the Harod River which flowed into the Jordan through the Jezreel Valley.

It was lush, green country, with productive farmland and abundant game, which was one of the main reasons Captain Bishroth's people had been trying for years to gain control of it. Now they finally had broken the resistance of Israel and they could control the entire coast, with its trading highway from Egypt to Aram and the rich valleys as well.

Bishroth looked forward to spending some time in the Canaanite city of Beth-Shan. The oasis city just west of the Jordan River was known for its wealth and free-flowing wine. There would be feasting for days, and plenty of opportunities for honoring the gods who had brought them victory by visiting the temple of Ashtoreth and its prostitutes. It would be a luxurious change from the grueling, gritty work of war.

At last, they saw the city of Beth Shan, with its stone walls which had withstood the invasion of the Hebrews four hundred years ago.

Achish and a large contingent of the army had already arrived with the news that the bodies were coming, so Beth-Shan's governor and the priest of the temple of Ashtoreth greeted the party a mile from the city gate, at the head of a collection of musicians playing lyres and flutes and drums, and shrine prostitutes clicking finger cymbals, dancing and scattering rose petals on the ground before the cart and its escort. Bishroth's heart raced as he saw the dancing young women, their painted lips smiling and lithe bodies dressed in thin, close-fitting linen tunics, revealing as much as they concealed.

Soon they were met by another delegation of priests from the temple of Ashtoreth who sang the praises of their goddess in enabling the Philistines to win the great battle over their mutual neighbor and rival. As they continued with music, dancing and ritual, they were finally met by the Philistine king himself in his royal chariot.

From there, he led the procession through the city gates as the citizens cheered and threw things at the lifeless bodies of their enemies.

Once the parade arrived at the city square, Bishroth saw that a large platform stood before the great temple of the goddess. A look from Achish told him that the bodies were to be placed there. He pointed at his men who had been marching and fighting for a week and directed them to carry the bodies up the broad stairs to the platform. As they laboriously carried the dead weight including armor, Achish and other dignitaries solemnly mounted the platform and stood in a half circle. Bishroth's men laid the four bodies in a row before the dignitaries. The citizens gathered round the platform raucously cheering until Achish raised his hand and silenced them.

After speeches by the governor, various dignitaries and the King of Gath, a burly soldier from the king's personal guard mounted the platform carrying a battle ax. He set about the task which had been planned by the king as the climax of the ceremony.

The crowd cheered at the sight and the soldier raised a muscular arm and waved the ax at them, which only drove them to cheer louder. He dipped his head and the red horse-hair plume on his helmet waved in the sun. He stopped at the stiff body of Malchishua and brought down the ax on his neck. The head rolled away, but with little blood. He then beheaded Abinidab as the crowd cheered and danced wildly. Finally, the large warrior severed the head of Jonathan.

"Gather the heads to be placed in the temple of Dagon," Achish commanded, and soldiers standing nearby obeyed, using Saul's purple cloak like a duffel bag. They left, carrying their grisly burden, toward the temple of Dagon nearby. As the crowd cheered and danced with abandon, the armor was stripped from the headless bodies and carried away with great pomp by the priests to the temple of Ashtoreth, where they would be lain before the image of the goddess.

When the priests had completed their ritual, Bishroth's men then put the bodies back on the cart and took them out the main gate of the town and hung them from the wall on either side of the gate at intervals of about 20 cubits where they would have maximum impact as the elements, decay and scavengers destroyed them.

No one could question the total victory of the Philistines.

Word of the desecration of the bodies of Israel's royals spread quickly in Israel. The effect was almost universal panic and desperate grief throughout the country.

The one exception was Jabesh-Gilead, across the Jordan River from Beth-Shan. The old men of the town had not forgotten how Saul had rallied Israel to their aid when they were besieged almost 40 years before.

"We must do something," Achim Ben-Hasem said urgently. He was an old stone cutter and elder of the town who remembered well how Saul had rescued them.

"What can we do? The Philistines are at Beth-Shan," said a young fisherman's apprentice.

"Perhaps not anymore. And they won't be expecting us to come," Achim replied. "We shall go by night. We will cut them down and bring them back before they know we were there."

"I agree," put in Joseph, the judge of Jabesh-Gilead and its environs east of the Jordan. He too remembered what Saul had done years earlier. That would be the final word.

❦ 95 ❦

A messenger, covered in blood and dust arrived in Gibeath-Saul and breathlessly announced the tragic news that the king and his three sons were dead upon the field. This immediately sent the whole town into a panic, everyone fearing the Philistines would soon be at their gates.

Ish-bosheth, Saul's only remaining son by his wife, ran to his father's house and burst in to see his mother, Ahinoam, sitting in the middle of the floor, staring at nothing, her eyes red and swollen.

She had no one at home with her anymore, except Rizpah, her husband's concubine, and her two children.

"Mother, we must leave immediately!" Ish-bosheth said, attempting to shake his mother out of her apparent trance.

"To go where?" she cried, the loss of her husband and three sons all at once having immobilized her.

"Beyond Jordan. Uncle Abner says Mahanaim."

"He is going there? Has he returned?"

"It was the word of the messenger to us; that we should flee to Mahanaim and meet him there."

It took tremendous concentration, but Ish-bosheth did not break down himself, seeing his mother so grief stricken.

"Mother, our servants are gathered with the carts to take us away. We must be going."

Ahinoam simply moaned and rocked back and forth.

In desperation, he turned to his father's concubine Rizpah, who, though grieving her own loss, appeared at least able to act. Her children were there, not fully comprehending what was happening.

"Help me pack her things," he said. "We must be going."

❧

CRASH! A clay water jar shattered as Mara ran by, gathering up things to take on the unexpected journey. She had knocked it off its stand in her haste.

"It doesn't matter!" she said to no one in particular. "I wasn't going to take it anyway."

Her leather bag was nearly full, but she had so much she wanted to take. She was out of space in the bag and out of time. The messenger had said the Philistines were marching toward them and would soon arrive.

The messenger had also said her husband, Jonathan, the prince and heir to the throne, had fallen on the battlefield. He would not be coming home.

She wiped a tear, but steeled herself for what she must do.

"Dorit! We must hurry!" Mara called to her nanny. "Bring Mephibosheth! We must be going!"

The wide-eyed girl appeared in the doorway from a bedroom, carrying the five-year-old boy and a bag of her own. Reassured that Dorit was following with her son, Mara turned to leave by the front door, when she heard another CRASH, followed by screams from both the girl and Mephibosheth.

Mara spun around and saw her son under the girl, who had apparently fallen on top of him. The boy was continuing to scream in pain.

"What's wrong?" Mara demanded.

"I don't know," Dorit said, starting to cry. "I'm sorry."

"Mephi, what is wrong?"

"My feet! My feet!" the boy screamed in obvious agony.

"Can you walk?"

"No, mama! No!"

"Pick him up, Dorit. We must go," Mara directed the servant girl.

Mara took Dorit's bag and shouldered both it and her own as the nanny picked up the screaming boy and they all headed out of the house to a waiting cart, with Jonathan's servant, Ziba, now a young man of 19, to drive it.

"Hurry, we must be going!" Ziba said, then he stopped, seeing that Mephibosheth had been seriously hurt.

As Dorit lowered the frightened, crying child into the cart, Mara was horrified to see that both his bare feet were turned inward at the ankles at impossible angles, but there was no time and nothing to be done.

"Let us go!" Mara said and she and Dorit boarded the cart as Ziba slapped the donkey's rump to get them going.

All around them people were fleeing: some in carts, some on donkeys, some on foot. Soon Gibeah would be deserted, ripe for the picking by the marauding Philistines.

"Oh my God!" Mara half prayed; half sobbed. "Why is this happening?!" She tried to comfort Mephibosheth, who was still sobbing.

Shelomith hurriedly prepared to leave, assisted by her son, Misha'el. She had no news about her husband, but she feared the worst.

She also knew that the messenger's description of the disastrous battle and the death of the king and his sons was causing the whole population of Gibeah to flee, and she did not want to be there when the Philistines arrived.

"Do you have everything, mother?" Misha'el asked.

"I don't know. I guess." She hadn't realized until now how much Misha'el looked like Jeriah.

"We are to go to Zaina's and Ithiel's house in Mizpah and live with Ithiel's family for a while," Misha'el reminded her. "I have donkeys ready."

"Then I guess we'd better go."

Shelomith took a slow look around at the house that had been their home for so long. She had no idea if the Philistines would leave it standing. Briefly she thought of Dani, her sister-in-law, whom she had not seen in five years. She wondered where she was now.

Then she turned and followed her strong son through the door to escape the calamity unfolding around them.

❧

How fitting that it's raining.

Michal's thoughts were as gloomy as the dark clouds outside her window. A messenger had brought news to her village that caused her to weep until no more tears would come.

In her life, she had known sunny, mountaintop days, but also dark valleys. Today was the darkest, with the confusion of emotions roiling in her heart like the storm clouds above.

Her father was dead. She felt the normal and socially respectable grief about that, but other emotions conflicted with the normal ones.

His madness would not torment her anymore. That gave her grim satisfaction, followed immediately by guilt.

She had loved her father, as every daughter should, but his capriciousness and vindictiveness were a trial to her and others as well.

She had been so happy in her privilege, growing up in the royal family, marrying a dashing hero when she was so young, but before she could give him a son, her father had taken it all away. He had forced her to be the wife of one of his patrons whom she had not even known.

Now, eight years later, she had to admit that Paltiel had been a wonderful husband, doting on her and giving her everything she wanted.

She had initially been hateful toward him, because of the circumstances which led to her forced marriage, but over the years he had won her heart. She regretted she had not been able to give him children.

Not only was her father, the king, dead, but her three oldest brothers were dead as well. She wouldn't bother to flee with the remnant of her family, across the Jordan out of reach of the Philistines. What would be the point? She was virtually invisible in the household of Paltiel.

Michal hated politics, but she couldn't help wondering what would become of the kingdom in which she had been a life-long princess.

❧ 96 ❧

What reward will I receive? the Amalekite wondered as he made his way as quickly as his legs could move toward the Philistine city where he believed he would find David.

Now that Saul and his sons were dead, all eyes would turn to David. *Surely that is how it must play out.* Though he was not a Hebrew and was exiled from his people, he believed he understood enough of the politics of this land to read the writing on the wall and he saw an opportunity for himself.

What reward will he give me? He again considered the many possibilities as David assumed the throne and the riches which would come with it.

In his pouch, slung over his shoulder, he carried the crown and arm band of the late king. Surely this would endear him to the rival and now future king and he would bestow riches, land, wives, or cattle or all of them. He only needed to enhance his story to ensure his own future.

When he arrived at Ziklag, he found it a charred ruin. He could not stop to consider why; he must see David.

"I have news of the battle. Where is your master, David?" the Amalekite asked the first person he encountered. The man, whose clothes and muscular arms were smeared with black ash, motioned for him to follow.

They did not go inside the town, but instead to an encampment outside it, which was a hive of activity, with men, women and children coming and going, apparently in an effort to recover from the tragedy of the town's destruction. As they went, men and women stopped what they were doing, mouths agape, looking at him.

He wasn't sure why his presence provoked such a response, but he wouldn't be distracted now, when he was on the verge of receiving acclaim and rewards.

They arrived at a large tent near the center of the camp, probably a temporary meeting place, he supposed, because a number of men were gathered around a table having some sort of conference. His escort announced, "Commander, this man says he has news of the battle."

"Why are you here?!" the man David looked at him with strong piercing eyes. He was shorter than expected, but his presence was still imposing. His face displayed anger the Amalekite did not understand. Others stood around them with similarly menacing faces, but he reasoned that their mood would change when he shared his good news, so he hastened to begin his tale.

"Israel was in retreat," Amalek began. "Many fell and are dead, including Saul and his sons."

His audience appeared to pay closer attention now. This was the opportunity to which he had looked forward.

"It happened that I was on Mount Gilboa when I saw King Saul, leaning on his spear, wounded, and Philistine chariots and riders were approaching fast. The king saw me and called out, 'Young man!' I answered, 'What would you like me to do?' and his answer was, 'Who are you?' and I said, 'I am an Amalekite.' Then he held out his sword to me and said, 'Come kill me, I am dying, but I don't want to be alive when the Philistines get here.'

David and all the men with him leaned in slightly and he knew this was his moment.

"So, I took his sword and killed him, because I knew he couldn't survive. I then took his crown and arm band," he said, taking them from his pouch and laying them on the table in front of David, "and brought them here to you." *Where they belong,* he didn't say.

The Amalekite stifled a smile as he looked at the men around the table, expecting them to erupt in rejoicing. Instead they all turned and looked at David expectantly.

David's face fell as he looked down at the crown and he took hold of his tunic and ripped it open, then began to weep. The other men soon followed, tearing their own garments and crying out in grief.

What is happening? the Amalekite wondered desperately. *Were not Saul and David bitter enemies? Were not Saul and his sons obstacles between David and the throne?*

"Who are you and where are you from?" David demanded.

"I am an alien, an Amalekite," he answered, trembling.

"How is it you did not fear to raise your hand against the Lord's anointed? His blood is on your head! Your own mouth testifies against you!" Then turning to the man who brought him into the tent, he said, "Strike him down!"

Benaiah wasted no time drawing his sword and running the man through, then pulling the sword out, hacked at his neck for good measure as he fell. Others joined in and soon the despicable Amalekite who dared to kill the king of Israel was himself dead.

Benaiah turned and received an approving nod from David, who then announced, "We mourn for Saul and his sons! The glory of Israel lies slain on the heights! How have the mighty fallen?!" he said, his voice breaking. "I will put my feelings to paper in a lament. Now go to your tents. We mourn for the house of Saul!"

Azel was dazed as he left the tent after seeing the Amalekite killed.

Saul and his sons dead? What did this mean for them? Could they come out of hiding? What did it mean for David? Would he seize the throne?

But one thing he knew for certain: he knew that his brother, Jeriah, who served at the king's side for so long, would not have allowed the king to be killed unless he himself was dead.

Azel then sat down on the ground and wept, not because David had ordered them to mourn for Saul and his sons, but because his brother was dead.

It must be so.

Now, he was the only surviving member of the family of his childhood. A flood of memories came to him, of their times together on the hills around Mizpah, of hours in the forge learning the coppersmith's trade from their father, Eldad, and the tender care of their mother, Hadassah. He recalled battles fought while he and Jeriah were together in the same army, until their diverging loyalties caused them to clash, with Azel as an outcast and his brother on the chase.

He suddenly needed to find Dani. She would understand.

⚜ **97** ⚜

It was a humid, stifling night and the sky was obscured by motionless clouds. As Canaanite guards patrolled the walls of Beth-Shan just west of the Jordan River, they hurried past the section of the wall where the headless corpses were hung, facing the road from the west.

After a week, the stench was becoming unbearable. The stagnant, warm air of the rift valley made the smell that much worse.

The lonely guard was bored and sleepy and wondered if anyone would know if he simply sat for a while in the tower at the southeast corner of the town, rather than walking past the bodies for the twentieth time tonight.

The visiting Philistines, several hundred of them, had come as conquering heroes and had left their mark with drunken celebrating and carousing all through the town. They had finally gone, taking their uproarious celebrations with them.

The prominent citizens of Beth-Shan, including the guard's superiors, were sleeping soundly, recovering from the final day of celebration. As he pondered his own duty while others feasted, he removed his heavy helmet and smoothed his black, sweat-soaked hair.

Then he thought he heard something at the base of the wall. He went to the battlement and looked over. It was his last act, as a silent dagger slit his throat and he fell back on the parapet.

Achim stood over the Canaanite guard with the bloody dagger in his hand after topping the ladder leaning against the wall. The fisherman's apprentice quickly followed up the ladder. Together they moved quickly to the outer edge of the wall and severed the ropes suspending the body of Prince Jonathan, gently lowering it to the waiting arms of their comrades from Jabesh-Gilead.

Farther down the wall, six others were performing the same work for the other three bodies. Two other Canaanite guards lay dead as well.

Close to the base of the wall, four Gileadites received each of the bodies in blankets and bore them quickly and lovingly away through the trees and brush. Achim and the others climbed down the ladder they had lain against the wall for this purpose. Stealthily they bore it away through the trees.

Safely away from the city, the men stopped to properly shroud the stiff, headless bodies and tie them to the backs of donkeys. Together the men mounted their donkeys and rode toward the ford across the Jordan River, bearing their precious cargo, intent on giving them the proper burial they deserved on the other side of the Jordan in Jabesh-Gilead, the city of Saul's grandmother.

❦ 98 ❦

Abner had barely escaped the battle with his life. It was a miracle he was not wounded when so many had fallen.

From a distance, he had seen his cousin, the king, die by his own hand. Then his faithful armor bearer died by his side in the same way. There had been no reason to stay after that.

He had fled the battlefield with just a couple of his aides. With them, under cover of night, he had passed Beth Shan and forded the Jordan River.

His mind reeled, knowing the monarchy he had helped found and the administration he had developed and directed for forty years was gone in an afternoon. Not only was the king dead, but his three sons were lost as well.

What a disaster!

In the few days since he arrived in Mahanaim, he had been able to find a place for him and his wife and children to live, though they were yet to join him. The compound also included homes for Saul's widow and concubine and her family, as well as Jonathan's family. He had sent a messenger to warn them all —the extended family of the king – to escape and join him across the Jordan.

He hoped they had escaped Gibeah before the Philistines came, as they almost certainly would.

He hadn't even considered returning there. He knew the Philistines would overrun it and finish the job of destroying every trace of the reign of his cousin, Saul.

No, he had to flee, for he was certain the Philistines knew his name and the role he had played in Saul's administration. He would find refuge across the natural barrier of the Jordan, where the Philistines had never gone, too far away for them to notice or care.

But all was not lost, however hopeless it might appear right now. He still had one more piece in the game.

THE END

The Story Continues.

Coming... *The Eternal Kingdom*

The third novel in the "Age of the Kingdom" series begins where *Exile of the King* left off.

At first it appears the way is clear for David to be crowned king, so the tribe of Judah does just that, but then he must face civil war. One act of treachery after another reveals shifting loyalties.

David receives a prophecy that his kingdom will be without end, but the full realization of the promise is just beyond his grasp. Can the nation be healed and reunited? Can the cycle of attacks from enemies be ended and peace realized?

For updates, go to **www.ageofthekingdomseries.com** and sign up for the email list.

About the Author:

Gary L. Ivey wrote *Quest for a King* and *Exile of the King*, the first two books of the "Age of the Kingdom" series, from his home in Hawaii. He is a husband, father and grandfather.

He has written two other novels in the "Backlash" series: *Backlash* and *Backlash 2: Justice Denied*.

He has also written a number of screenplays which have been honored at a variety of film festivals.

He has been a music minister, a pastor, a Christian magazine editor, media producer and a TV ministry director.

He is Vice President of a marketing and web development firm based in Georgia, which he co-owns with his wife of 50 years.

www.ageofthekingdomseries.com   www.garyivey.com
www.backlashbook.com   www.studioiv.productions

Go to **www.garyivey.com** for blog posts about his projects, freedom and the free market, and random thoughts and to order from the online store.

Follow Gary L. Ivey
Facebook: **@GaryIveyAuthor**
Instagram: **@garyivey**
X (Twitter):   **@gary_ivey**

www.ingramcontent.com/pod-product-compliance
Lightning Source LLC
Chambersburg PA
CBHW031253120726
47906CB00003B/730